DAVID YOUNG

STASI WINTER

ZAFFRE

First published in Great Britain in 2020 by

ZAFFRE
80–81 Wimpole St, London W1G 9RE
www.zaffrebooks.co.uk

ISBN: 978–1–78576–546–9

Also available as an ebook

1 3 5 7 9 10 8 6 4 2

Typeset by IDSUK (Data Connection) Ltd
Printed and bound in Great Britain by Clays Ltd, Elcograf S.p.A.

Zaffre is an imprint of Bonnier Books UK
www.bonnierbooks.co.uk

For Stephanie

For details about the real-life weather conditions in the
winter of 1978/79 please see the author's note
at the end of this book.

Prologue

The Ostsee north of Rostock, East Germany
January 1979

The figures moved like ghosts blown in by the Siberian wind –
ethereal, colourless, camouflaged so well that she couldn't be sure
they were there. The bitter north-east wind had transformed the
Ostsee into a sea of jagged white and grey, blocks of ice broken
by the waves and icebreakers, then refrozen as the thermometer
plunged still further, like some collapsed ancient monument
whose giant stones lay scattered in random patterns. Only those
blocks were in fact made of seawater – frozen so hard you could
almost believe it really had petrified.

This was the Republic's 'catastrophe winter'.

A hundred-year winter.

A killer winter.

Major Karin Müller carefully moved forward over the frozen sea, her finger resting on the Makarov's trigger guard.
There was no crunch of ice – the layer of new snow softened
the fall of her boots, as though she was tiptoeing around in fur-
covered slippers. As snowflakes hit her face, she expected them

to melt. They didn't – it was too cold. Instead, they collected on her eyelids and nose, so that every so often she had to wipe them off with her gloved left hand.

She couldn't be sure who was who. Two of the ghosts were her quarry – but one was her deputy, *Hauptmann* Werner Tilsner. Together, Müller and Tilsner made up the major part of the Republic's Serious Crimes Department. But what exactly was *he* up to? Allegedly he had gone on ahead to get closer to the *Republikflüchtlinge* – the escapers – to cut them off. Yet when the mist and snow temporarily cleared, it was as if he'd become one of them, camouflaged in matching white.

Then – as the visibility suddenly improved again – she saw the girl's telltale shock of red hair. 'Wildcat' was her code name, given to her as part of a deal some four years earlier. A deal brokered by her handler in the Ministry for State Security, Klaus Jäger. A deal that Müller herself had wanted no part of. But who was she to defy the Stasi?

She raised the gun. Brought the shock of red hair into her sights.

'Irma Behrendt!' she cried. 'Stop there and raise your hands! Otherwise I won't hesitate to shoot!'

Tilsner seemed to be nearer to the girl, yet he was continuing to move, rather than helping Müller to arrest her.

Her focus returned to the girl. Irma had ignored her warning; she'd tucked her hair back under what looked like a bed sheet covering her head, and had broken into a run.

'This is your last warning, Irma! Don't do this to yourself, to your family! Stop or I'll shoot!'

The girl continued running.

Müller's finger wrapped more tightly around the freezing cold metal of the trigger.

And began to squeeze.

1

I am still the same girl – the same Irma Behrendt – who made that fateful telephone call almost four years ago. That's what I tell myself. But that phone call still haunts me, now as a twenty-year-old woman, just as it did then as a sixteen-year-old girl, only recently released from the hell that is the Republic's reform school system. Having to force my finger to turn the dial, and then knowing – as soon as I talked to him, the local officer in Bergen from the Ministry for State Security – that there was no turning back. I had made my choice.

You probably wonder why I did it. I know I do. But I wanted, above everything, to keep my mother out of jail this time. I naively thought that by co-operating, by giving them information, by spying on her, that I would be helping. That's what I told myself anyway. That's how I still justify it.

I was barely sixteen. Can you really judge me? Would you have done anything different? You can't say, because you've never been in the position that I'd been put into.

When I followed her and the man she'd met up Wilhelm-Pieck-Straße, past the piles of snow, hunching into my anorak to try to keep out the wind, I knew that I was going to do it. I couldn't face being sent back to *Jugendwerkhof Prora Ost*. My friend had been abused then killed by them. I'd been treated as little more than a slave. Yet – to my shame – I still co-operated when the Stasi officer Jäger asked me to.

So I watched them as they walked out along the *Seebrücke*, the wooden pier that was such a landmark in our little seaside town until the authorities demolished most of it earlier this year. Of course, he wasn't necessarily a dissident. He could have been a secret lover. But my job wasn't to assess the situation, it was simply to report on it. I watched them for a few moments through the telescope – the one the children use in summer to look at boats out on the sea. But there were no boats that day. Just a woman with angular features and red hair – an older version of me, really – standing talking to a man on a pier. Easter had been and gone, not that observance of religious holidays was encouraged in the Republic, but winter still hadn't released its grip on Rügen. Behind them, I could see a lamppost sugar-coated with layer upon layer of sea ice. It was certainly a romantic setting. But in my heart, I knew this rendezvous had nothing to do with romance.

I slowly walked over to the yellow phone box, pulled back the hood of my anorak, and dialled the Bergen-auf-Rügen number that Jäger had given me. When the operator answered, I asked for the person whose name he'd written down – *Hauptmann* Gerd Steiger – and identified myself by my new code name, Wildcat.

What did I think would happen? Jäger had convinced me that reporting on my mother's activities was the best way of keeping her out of jail. That if the Stasi had her under close surveillance through a family member, they could protect her from herself. Protect her from falling into her old ways. Nip anything in the bud before it became too serious.

So I made that phone call.

I gave a description of the man she'd met.

The next day – at the campsite where my grandmother is the manager – they arrested my mother. She was sent back to Hoheneck women's prison. She's been there ever since.

They tricked me, and I'm sure I'm not the first.

I felt so alone then. So awful. I'd condemned my own mother to a life back in jail, so soon after her release.

Yet still they wanted me to spy for them. On relations, on friends and on enemies. I continued to give them information, but I made sure it was useless. Frau Kästner buying some fish was constructed into an elaborate, detailed report. Herr Schlender getting a delivery of coal was made out to be some highly suspicious activity. My old boyfriend Laurenz's love of the cinema was reported on in intricate detail, even though the films we went to see together were 'approved' and on general release in the Republic.

But then I met Dieter.

He was based at the other end of Prora to the *Jugendwerkhof* – the hated reform school I was determined never to be sent back to. He'd refused to do his regular National Service with the People's Army. So he'd been sent to Rügen – to Prora – to join a construction brigade, working on roads, bridges, and the harbour at Sassnitz.

Dieter's helped the scales fall from my eyes. He's taught me what's right and what's wrong.

Now he has a plan.

A plan to change everything.

And he wants me to be a part of it, alongside him.

2

The meeting hadn't been one Karin Müller had been looking forward to, and now it was over before it had really begun. She and her ex-boyfriend, Emil, were supposed to have been discussing access arrangements for their two-and-a-half-year-old twins, Jannika and Johannes. But this very moment, Emil had stormed off without them getting any closer to resolving their differences. The two children – oblivious to the frostiness between their parents – were happily playing with toys in the sandpit. Johannes was wielding a garish plastic representation of the *Soyuz* craft which had launched East Germany's first cosmonaut into space some four months earlier. He propelled it like a javelin towards his unwitting sister, hitting her square on the side of the head.

'Johannes!' cried Müller, as her daughter started bawling. 'If you don't play nicely, we're going straight home.' She rushed to her daughter, picked her up, and after checking there was no real damage, kissed the side of the girl's head better. 'Now, say

STASI WINTER | 10

sorry, Johannes, and give your sister a kiss too.' The boy reluctantly complied, transforming Jannika's tears into a shy grin, confirming Müller's suspicions that the tears had mostly been play-acting. The spat would soon be forgotten, unlike the rift between Müller and her ex. She knew the only reason he'd got together with her was because he'd been detailed by his Stasi bosses to keep tabs on her. The result, a few months later and not without a little drama, had been the twins – children that doctors had said Müller would never be able to have because of a sexual attack on her years earlier at her police college. Despite the baggage around their birth, whenever she saw them Müller was filled with joy and unconditional love.

The chilly atmosphere between Müller and Emil reflected the way the temperature had suddenly dropped here in Berlin: a relatively mild Christmas cut short by Siberian temperatures. The leaden skies overhead were the embodiment of what the Republic's weather forecasters had been predicting. Snow was imminent – and the fall could be heavy, especially from Berlin northwards to the Ostsee coast.

Despite the weather, Müller relished the chance to spend the Christmas and New Year period with the twins and her maternal grandmother, Helga. She was the twins' great-grandmother, but still a sprightly woman in her sixties who'd been their full-time carer until Müller's decision to quit her career as a detective in the Republic's People's Police more than a year previously. It wasn't something she regretted, but as Helga had pointed out, their savings were now pretty much used up. Müller was in that grey area of employment that officially didn't exist in the Republic: not working, but not unemployed. No one was unemployed here. No one was homeless. That was the official line, and one that Müller respected. She'd seen with her own eyes, and from her own experience, that it only told half the truth. Nevertheless, the industrial strife, strikes and general discontent that had seemed ever present in the West – judging by the Western TV news she watched with the illegally aligned aerial in the Strausberger Platz apartment – were indeed absent. Or at least, absent in public. She had no doubt that behind closed doors, in the privacy of the family, grumblings went on. The lack of ability to travel to the western part of Germany, to the BRD – especially for families that had been split up when the Anti-Fascist Protection Barrier had been erected – that was a source of constant grievance. But everyone – from the cradle to the grave – was given constant reminders of its necessity. How else could the counter-revolutionaries, the fascists, and – yes – even the Nazis, be kept at bay? Yet she knew that was again a half-truth. Nazis still existed this side of the Wall. Her last case before she handed her resignation to the police had been evidence enough of that.

And those Nazis – at least in the present day – hadn't even been law-breakers. They were supposed to be upholders of the law, defenders of the Republic. Yet their past deeds had come back to haunt them, and Müller had decided she could no longer work with them. In the case of one of them, she hadn't been entirely surprised. A Stasi colonel with an all too smooth mien that seemed to have been cultivated by aping one of the well-known presenters of the BRD's nightly news programme. But the other? That had been a shock, and had prompted her resignation decision. None other than her own deputy in the short-lived Serious Crimes Department of the People's Police, *Hauptmann* Werner Tilsner. Tilsner, who she'd long suspected was an unofficial informant for the Ministry for State Security, the *MfS*, aka the Stasi. That much had been true. But the last case had revealed he had been something far worse. A member of the Hitler Youth who had stood alongside the boy who would later become that Stasi colonel, gun poised, as a 1,000-strong group of slave labourers were massacred. An utterly senseless, disgusting crime perpetrated just hours before the Nazis surrendered.

She hadn't spoken to him since.

She didn't intend to ever again.

Müller's musings about her past career were made possible by the fact the twins had begun playing sweetly together. Johannes – clearly taking his mother's chastisement to heart – was allowing Jannika to play with the rocket, and she in turn had offered him her doll. Müller allowed a smile to broaden across her face, and as a first snowflake landed on her nose, it transformed into a small laugh. A laugh that died in her throat when she saw a man approaching from the direction Emil had so recently departed towards.

His silhouette, his confident gait, were horribly familiar.

So too, as he drew closer, was the sandy, shoulder-length hair, and smarmy expression.

The spitting image of that West German newsreader she'd just been thinking about.

Klaus Jäger.

Oberst Klaus Jäger of the Ministry for State Security. His appearance sent a sudden chill through her bones. The bitter cold which in the company of the twins she'd been able to ignore, now set her teeth chattering, her back and shoulders shivering.

'It's been a long time, Karin.' The use of her first name, the faux friendliness, wasn't going to disarm her. She knew what he was.

'*Oberst* Jäger,' she nodded. 'What brings you here? I wish I could believe it was something good, but in my experience that tends not to be the case.' She was no longer in the police – why should she kowtow to him? But what she said was only partly true. Her last dealing with the Stasi colonel had brought her unbridled and surprising happiness. He'd arranged travel warrants and visas for a visit to her father. A father she'd never seen before, conceived as she was as the result of a brief relationship between a victorious Red Army soldier and a teenage German girl at the very end of the Second World War. But that had been the exception and had only come about – Müller knew full well – because she had a hold on him: her knowledge of Jäger's part in the slave labourer massacre, and a threat to expose them to the Western press.

She noticed he was carrying a shopping bag. He arranged his winter overcoat, sat down next to her on the bench, and delved into it.

'I've bought some Christmas presents – for the children.'

Müller tried to hide the shock from her face. Surely there had to be something more to his visit than playing an avuncular

Weihnachtsmann? But she couldn't think of anything she'd done that would arouse the interest of the Stasi. The only change to her life since quitting the *Kriminalpolizei* had been a gradual erosion of her and Helga's funds. Her grandmother had saved a little money from her pension by living with her in Berlin rather than in her own flat in Leipzig. But Müller had reached the point where she needed an income again – she'd recently applied for a job teaching at the People's Police university in Potsdam. It seemed the logical option if she wasn't going to return to the force – and she was determined that would not happen.

'That's kind of you. They'll be thrilled – although they've probably received too many already.'

'They're only this young once, Karin. Enjoy it while you can. Mine are already heading towards becoming bratty teenagers. Always answering their father back.' He raised a sandy-coloured eyebrow wryly.

The presents, she could see, were neatly wrapped – one for each twin, with name tags on the wrapping.

'Something for you too,' he said, his face colouring as though he was embarrassed. Müller couldn't believe that. Stasi colonel Klaus Jäger did not do embarrassment. 'It's a little thank you for keeping your side of the bargain.'

Now it was Müller who found her face reddening.

'Open it,' he prompted in a half-whisper.

Müller wasn't sure whether it would be better to save the moment for later. She didn't want either joy or disappointment to register on her face – she didn't want Jäger to have anything on her. Thanks to what she'd found out about his past, their relationship had performed a *volte face*, with her – for once – holding the trump cards. That was how she wanted to keep it. Curiosity got the better of her, however, and she started to tear at the paper with her gloved hands. The noise alerted the twins. They rushed over and Jäger handed each of them their own carefully wrapped gift.

'Who's this man, Mutti?' demanded Jannika. Johannes, meanwhile, had already torn into his package: a soft Sandmänn-chen doll, dressed as a cosmonaut, presumably in honour of the Republic's own real-life space hero, Sigmund Jähn.

'I'm a friend,' said Jäger.

Müller wasn't prepared to let that assertion pass without being corrected. 'He's someone I used to work with, darling.'

'Where?' asked Jannika.

'Never you mind, Miss Nosey-Parker,' said Müller, tweaking her daughter's nose. But one thing she was sure of, Jäger was no friend of hers – Christmas presents or not. 'Why don't you open the present he's brought you? Johannes is already playing with his.' Her son had wrapped the Sandmännchen's legs round his rocket and was attempting to launch him onto another planet – the sandpit. The toy doll predictably fell off midflight.

Müller turned her attention to her own gift. From the shape and obviously liquid contents she guessed it was some sort of perfume. It was. Chanel No. 5. The exact brand Jäger had instructed her to buy from the Kaufhaus des Westens in West Berlin on her cross-border mission nearly four years earlier. In fact, Müller wouldn't put it past him to be recycling the same bottle. It looked identical.

'I know what you're thinking, Karin, but even I wouldn't stoop that low. I purchased it myself this side of the Anti-Fascist Protection Barrier – in an Intershop.'

Müller sprayed a little on the back of her wrist. She half-wondered if it would immediately turn to ice, given the bitter cold. But even with her rudimentary knowledge of physics, she knew the alcohol within the mixture would prevent that – never mind her own skin temperature. She briefly inhaled the scent and its telltale melange of flowers, citrus fruits and soap.

'Thank you,' she said. She meant it, but it didn't mean she wouldn't hesitate to use her knowledge about Jäger's past to her own advantage should she need to. She knew that. He knew that. It didn't need to be spelled out.

There seemed little more to say. Jäger hitched up his trouser legs, and started to get up.

As he did so, he mentioned one more thing. Müller sensed this was his real message.

'I heard you'd applied for a job at the People's Police college,' he said in a flat tone.

It wasn't a surprise that the Stasi knew her every movement. An agent would probably vet all applications. In any case, there had been plenty of evidence of surveillance of her – covert and ostentatiously overt. The Barkas camper van parked outside the Strausberger Platz apartment block for months on end with its twitching curtains and all too obvious cameras. The listening device she'd discovered stitched into the apartment wall after Johannes had unwittingly thrown a toy at just the right spot in a fit of temper.

But Jäger's next utterance still had the power to make her blood run cold. On the surface it was so benign. Underneath, there flowed rivers of meaning.

They were his parting words, delivered with his trademark supercilious smirk.

'I wish you the best of luck with it.'

3

People's Police HQ, Keibelstraße, East Berlin

Müller felt a fluttering inside her chest as she entered her old place of work near Alexanderplatz. She knew the austere brick-built building had the ability to evoke even stronger feelings amongst many who entered its walls. It wasn't simply an administrative headquarters for the police. Its reputation as a fearsome remand centre almost rivalled that of the Stasi prisons at Hohenschönhausen and Bautzen. But Müller's own sense of nervousness was irrational. She no longer worked here. Unless she broke the law, the agency within had no power over her. Her former boss, *Oberst* Reiniger, had simply called her in to discuss her application to put her old policing skills to work, teaching at the People's Police university.

Before she went up to his offices, she diverted to the ground floor women's toilets to check her make-up. The face that looked back at her would – in most people's eyes – still be judged an attractive one. The prominent cheekbones she now knew were probably inherited from her father's Russian side of the family. But it was a face that looked older, more careworn, than when she and Tilsner had started out in the Mitte Murder Commission, in that temporary office under Marx-Engels-Platz S-Bahn station. The dark circles round her eyes were more obvious these days. She used a dab of concealer to blend them in with the lighter skin tone on the rest of her face. As she did, she noticed her finger tremble slightly. Why? Was it Jäger's *Weihnachtsmann* visit to bring those presents that had unnerved her? Probably not so much the visit, as his mentioning her job application. She needed the money. She didn't want her old adversary putting any spokes in the wheel. As she looked at the image of her face, framed by dirty blond hair, she told herself she had nothing to fear. She could harm Jäger more than he could harm her, thanks to her intimate knowledge of his past history. With a couple of deep breaths, she almost literally pulled herself together – shaking her shoulders and stretching to try to ease the tension – and set off to see Reiniger.

'Ah, Karin, so pleased you could make it.' Her portly former boss was dressed in full uniform, as was his custom. Tilsner and Müller always felt it was to show off the three gold stars and entwined silver braid on his shoulder epaulettes, should anyone not realise he was a full colonel. Plenty of other officers of the same rank would be in plain clothes. 'Coffee?' he asked from his desk, sitting under the ubiquitous photograph of Erich Honecker, complete with his trademark horn-rimmed spectacles.

'That would be lovely, Comrade *Oberst*.' As a civilian, Müller had no need to use the 'Comrade, this . . . Comrade, that' style of honorifics that lent official meetings in the Republic such a stilted air. She did it all the same, out of force of habit.

Reiniger turned to his secretary. 'Truda – could you fetch us two coffees, please? I'm sure you remember how Karin takes hers.'

'Of course, Comrade *Oberst*.' The matronly woman shuffled off to do her boss's bidding. Müller briefly thought how incongruous it was that the People's Police had gone out of its way to promote her a few years earlier – making her the first ever female head of a murder squad, the youngest of either gender too – yet the role of secretary was without exception filled by females. Equality in the Republic only went so far. Women were expected to work, just like their male counterparts. They fulfilled what in the West might be considered 'manly' jobs: she'd even seen a recent documentary about female crane operators in Rostock's docks. But once they got home, they were still expected to do the housework and cooking while their menfolk put their feet up or went out drinking in the nearest bar.

'So,' said Reiniger, shuffling a few papers on his desk. 'You made a formal request for me to provide a reference about your work with the *Kriminalpolizei* in connection with this application for a job at the police college.'

'That's right, Comrade *Oberst*.'

'Hmm.' Reiniger leant his arms on his desk, clasping his hands together. 'And you're applying as a civilian, rather than as a serving police officer.'

'Yes, of course.' She wasn't sure what Reiniger's point was.

'There is unfortunately, Karin, a slight problem.'

Müller gave no response other than a frown.

'You see, you still *are* a serving police officer.'

Müller creased her face in confusion. 'With respect, Comrade *Oberst*, I'm not. I resigned more than a year ago.'

Reiniger turned down the corners of his mouth, and shrugged his shoulders.

'Well, yes . . . and no. It's true that you handed me a letter of resignation.'

'Exactly.'

'It's also true that that is indeed the first step towards your leaving the People's Police.' Reiniger had leant back in his chair, and was rocking to and fro, his clasped hands around his ample stomach.

'The first step?' Müller couldn't understand what her former boss was driving at.

'Yes. It needs to be followed by your superior officer accepting that resignation. And . . . ' Reiniger seemed to have paused for effect. Müller knew what he was about to say, but prompted him nonetheless.

'And what?'

'And I didn't. I couldn't be sure that you were in the right frame of mind to make that decision. You had just completed a particularly stressful case – found out some uncomfortable truths about those you were working with, and – in particular – some of their superiors. It was understandable that you were disillusioned with your job.'

Müller glanced at the portrait of Comrade Honecker above Reiniger's head. The Republic he presided over had plenty of faults – she'd gradually had her eyes opened to those, and that last case had been the biggest eye-opener. But she still believed in Socialism – she still believed in the greater good for the greater number. To achieve that, you needed systems, you needed some form of control, of policing. For her, the Stasi's methods were often too underhand and deceptive to say the least. But – by and large – the People's Police was an institution she looked up to and had been proud to be a part of. Until that last case tipped her over the edge. Nonetheless, she wanted to give something back – which was why she'd applied for the teaching job.

'I wasn't just disillusioned. I made a decision to leave, and I expect you to respect that.'

'Well, you know I respect you, Karin. You wouldn't have risen so far if I didn't.' Müller was well aware that wasn't the full story. Jäger had had a hand in choosing her for some of her cases, possibly even in deciding on her promotions. He'd already admitted that had been a deliberate tactic by the Stasi – to over-promote someone green and malleable. 'But I genuinely believe your decision was made in the heat of the moment, and that you were not in the right state of mind to make it. I therefore chose not to accept your resignation, as is my right, and instead placed you on extended leave. Paid leave.'

Müller knitted her brow. '*Paid* leave? I haven't been paid.'

'You have. You just haven't been receiving it. It's been accruing pending your return to work. However, should you choose not to return to work here, and instead continue with this application to teach at the college, I would have to rescind my original decision and backdate the acceptance of your resignation. The money that has been accrued would simply go back into People's Police funds. Do you want to know how much you stand to gain . . . or to lose? It's your choice.'

Müller drew in a long breath, then exhaled equally slowly. 'This sounds horribly like blackmail, Comrade *Oberst*.'

'Then, of course, there's the question of that very lovely apartment I secured for you on Strausberger Platz. As you know, that is reserved for People's Police officers of the rank of major and above. You, your children, and your grandmother have been living there for the past year or so *because* of my decision. Should I have to rescind it, you would have to find new accommodation immediately.'

She liked Reiniger overall. He'd generally been supportive of her, like a kindly uncle – though Tilsner had found him pompous and bumbling. His deviousness here, though, seemed to come straight out of the Ministry for State Security handbook.

When Müller didn't say anything for a few moments, Reiniger continued. 'You haven't said whether you want to know the amount involved, but I'm going to tell you anyway. It's a little over thirty thousand marks.'

Thirty thousand marks? It seemed scarcely believable. Though if she did the maths, it made sense. It was simply her former monthly salary, multiplied by the number of months she'd been away from the job. She should be racing round the other side of the desk and hugging Reiniger. But the corollary would be almost too much to bear.

'So you're saying for me to get this money, I would have to come back to my old job?'

'Exactly.' Reiniger's face was plastered with a satisfied smile. 'The same role.'

'Yes. As head of the Serious Crimes Department.'

'Who would I be assigned to work with? Could I choose my own team?' Even by asking the questions, Müller knew that Reiniger would realise he was on the point of winning this little battle.

'No. You will be working with *Kriminaltechniker* Jonas Schmidt again, of course.'

'And who would be my police captain?'

'*Hauptmann* Werner Tilsner. Who else?'

'I already told you more than a year ago, Comrade *Oberst*. I absolutely refuse to work with former Nazis.'

Reiniger sighed. 'For God's sake, Karin! That was more than thirty years ago. He was just a boy during the war. Virtually all boys of his age were members of the Hitler Youth.'

'But . . .'

'No buts, Karin. Those are my terms. I need a decision by the end of today. If you agree, you have an assignment beginning tomorrow – all three of you. You can have a few hours to think it over. You need the money, we both know that, otherwise you wouldn't be applying for a teaching job. But you know the old adage, and it still holds true for you. Those who can, do. Those who can't, teach. As for Nazis, why not talk to your grandmother about your own family history? You might get a few surprises.'

'What do you mean by that?' Müller could feel her anger stirring. It felt like a personal attack. But Reiniger was already rising from his desk, then ushering her out of the office, just as

DAVID YOUNG | 25

Truda returned with the coffees. Hers, it seemed, would remain undrunk.

'Do as I say, Comrade *Major*.' The sudden use of her rank and the *Genossin* honorific, accompanied by a more serious tone, felt like a threat. 'Talk to your grandmother and give me your decision by 5 p.m. today. Bear in mind, that should you decide to continue with the teaching application, you may not be successful however glowing my reference. A little friendly warning – others may be taking an interest in your future. But I think you know that already.'

Müller knew what her decision would be, even before she had the suggested chat with Helga. They needed the money, and the larger apartment. If they had to move, there was no guarantee Helga would be able to live with them – which would immediately present childcare problems even if she succeeded with the teaching application. She would never fully trust or respect Tilsner again, but what Reiniger said about almost *all* boys of a certain age being part of the Hitler Youth had the ring of truth.

When she finally did confront Helga, her grandmother had a revelation of her own.

'I was never a Party member, but your grandfather was. I told you he died fighting for the Wehrmacht on the Eastern front in the Soviet Union. That was true. But like a lot of his fellow soldiers, he was a Nazi Party member. It didn't mean he believed in everything they did. He absolutely didn't. More than once he told me – in private of course – that he thought Hitler was a fantasist who'd lead us all to ruination. Which he did in the end.

But at one time, everyone got caught up in things. You had to live through it to understand it. Members of the Hitler Youth? They share some of the guilt of course. But they were just boys. Boys whose minds had been perverted.'

Müller didn't necessarily accept all that. In the case of Tilsner, it wasn't just his membership of the Hitler Youth which was the problem – it was what he'd actually taken part in as a member of that organisation. But she realised she would be letting her grandmother and the twins down if she didn't take a pragmatic approach. That meant returning to work, and collecting all that money she hadn't earned. It might buy them a new washing machine, or one of the new fridge-freezers she'd seen advertised. Once it was safely deposited, once this new case – whatever it was they were being assigned to – was out of the way, then she could reconsider her position and insist on her resignation if that was what she still wanted.

4

East German nightly television news
29 December 1978

Good evening, ladies and gentlemen.

A battle has begun in the north of the Republic against plunging temperatures, ice and snow, in what's being called the DDR's 'catastrophe winter' – the worst conditions since the severe winter of 1962/63.

The island of Rügen has been completely cut off from the rest of the country and most homes there are without power.

Brave troops from the People's Army – including paratroops stationed in Prora on the Ostsee coast – are helping to deliver supplies of food.

These pictures taken from an army helicopter show troops on skis trying to reach a passenger train stuck in snow drifts of up to six metres high between Bergen auf Rügen and Binz. To give you some idea of what that means, it's as high as a two-storey house.

The weather changed dramatically and catastrophically on the evening of 28 December when – after a relatively mild Christmas period – the mercury in thermometers plunged by up to fifteen degrees Celsius.

The government of the workers' and peasants' state has been meeting in emergency session. The head of the State Council, Comrade Erich Honecker, has announced a state of emergency, saying that all resources possible will be directed towards rescue and relief efforts.

The situation is also severe in other parts of Europe, including the northern BRD, Denmark and Scotland.

A government spokesman has urged citizens throughout the Ostsee coast region and Bezirk Rostock to stay indoors wherever possible.

A middle-aged female citizen who ignored this advice and ventured out alone in unsuitable clothing has unfortunately been found dead through exposure to the cold near Binz.

More on this story as we get it including a special report by our correspondent in Bezirk Rostock.

Meanwhile in other news . . .

Miners in the Upper Lausitz region have been congratulated for breaking their targets for the sixth month in a row . . .

5

The helicopter banked violently as Müller, Tilsner and Schmidt set off from the People's Army base near Greifswald. Müller found herself clutching her stomach, fighting the waves of nausea – and the traumatic memories of the last time she'd been in a similar aircraft, near her home town of Oberhof in Thuringia. The blanket of snow beneath them – with the odd farmhouse roof breaking up the pristine whiteness – was similar too. That time, she and Tilsner had been on a life and death chase to find her own abducted baby. Now, death was again the order of the day. The death of the woman found under the snowdrift in Rügen – apparently overcome by the cold snap while out shopping for supplies. Yet Müller knew if the explanation really was that mundane, there would be no way that Reiniger would have despatched the three of them – the small team that formed the rather grandly titled Serious Crimes Department. Their mission was to intervene over the heads of regional murder squads when the People's Police deemed it necessary: an attempt to avoid embarrassing and sensitive unexplained deaths being handed to the Stasi's own Special Commissions. In Müller's experience so far, anywhere they were sent, the Ministry for State Security would not be far behind.

She and Tilsner had hardly spoken since the three of them had begun the trip. On the car journey between Berlin and Greifswald, it had been left to Jonas Schmidt – their forensic scientist – to try to lighten the mood. His overlong explanations of the weather phenomena which had resulted in Arctic conditions being transplanted into the Republic had had more of a soporific effect on Müller. Tilsner had switched off and concentrated on making sure they didn't slide off the slushy motorways.

Now, though, it looked like it was Schmidt who needed some support. His pasty face had turned whiter than usual. Müller could tell he wasn't enjoying the ride. She edged closer to him along the bench seat, and cupped her hands over his ear to try to make herself heard above the roar of the engine and whooshing of the rotor blades above their heads.

'You don't look like this is your ideal form of transport, Jonas!' she shouted.

Schmidt shrugged, and brought his mouth up to the side of her head. As he shouted back, she could feel the flecks of spittle on her cheek, and smell the pungent flavour of whatever variety of sausage he'd been consuming on the car journey.

'Perhaps it's because I'm a scientist, Comrade *Major*! I know too much about how these things work – how much can go wrong!'

Müller was more of a fatalist. They were committed to the trip now. She didn't want to crash, but preferred not to think about it. 'Just relax and enjoy the view, Jonas. In the West, people would pay thousands of Deutschmarks for a tourist trip like this. We're getting it for free.' She tried to sound more enthusiastic than she felt. In reality, she shared many of his misgivings.

Tilsner was avoiding her gaze. They hadn't thrashed out their differences, but now wasn't the time. Müller had resolved to treat him in a professional manner until the end of this case, then let events take their own course.

As the helicopter banked again, through the flurries of snow, Müller could make out the Strelasund far below – the sea channel between the mainland of the Republic and the island of Rügen, their destination. Yet rather than open water, it looked to be completely frozen over. Ice and snow as far as the eye could see – like a giant cake perfectly coated with square kilometre after square kilometre of white icing. She wasn't unaccustomed to winter conditions like these. Having grown up in a winter sports resort – the East German answer to St Moritz – snow and ice were in her blood, and as a schoolgirl she'd been an expert ski jumper, thwarted from progressing further by the lack of national and international competitions for women. But the amount of snow and ice covering the sea and countryside here was unnatural. Instead of her usual sense of excitement at the winter conditions, they seemed to represent something more malevolent. As though a white blanket of evil had been thrown over the world.

After a few minutes, the whine of the engine changed and they began to descend. As they did, Müller spotted the unmistakable shape of Prora – the giant monolith built by Hitler as a holiday camp for Nazi workers. A huge structure – set a few metres back from the forested coast – extending into the distance. So big, she knew, it could be seen by cosmonauts in outer space, such as the real-life version of Johannes's spaceman toy.

Tilsner had seen it too. 'I wish I could say I'm delighted to be back on Rügen. But I'm not. The weather was foul last time we were here – but that out there looks like hell on earth.'

As the helicopter came in to land, Müller could see the rotor blades churning up huge flurries from drifts and piles of snow that the troops had cleared from the landing area. Soldiers still seemed to be busily clearing a path – the vortex from the aircraft almost blowing them off their feet. She could see others on skis pulling sleds loaded with supplies.

Finally, the craft settled and the whine of the blades changed into more of a gentle chugging. The cargo door was opened, and a blast of icy air – complete with isolated snowflakes – enveloped them.

Their new assignment was about to begin.

6

I want to tell you about how I met Dieter and how I fell out of love with Laurenz – I don't want you thinking badly of me, though I know I've done some wicked things in my life. Hopefully, though, you can see how I didn't have a choice.

Laurenz and I had been to see a film in the cinema in Binz. Sometimes the Binz cinema got some of the newer releases – this one had just had its premiere. *Anton der Zauberer* – 'Anton the Magician' – was its title. I remember we laughed a lot. The tensions in our relationship from the summer seemed to be forgotten, for that evening at least. Laurenz had been my boy-friend since all the trouble in the *Jugendwerkhof* and the Harz mountains. I had a lot to thank him for. He'd let me believe in my attractiveness for the first time. Before everything that had happened, I'd always been in Beate's shadow – the ugly duckling tagging along with the beautiful princess. But more than three years had passed since Beate's shocking death. I was more confi-dent now, and Laurenz's world view didn't seem to extend much beyond the borders of Rügen. I knew I wanted, needed, something more. Beate, Mathias and I had had that albeit very brief taste of the West, the glimpse of Hamburg's Reeperbahn, before it had been so cruelly snatched away. Of course, I couldn't get back there – I'd made one attempt, and was likely to be watched by the Ministry for State Security for the rest of my life. My best hope was to wait until I was a pensioner.

But I didn't want to wait. I wanted to travel – now. Even if it was only to other socialist countries. Even if I couldn't cross to the West, I still wanted to spread my wings. But all my entreaties to Laurenz that we should go travelling that summer were rebuffed by him.

'You can't afford to give up your job at the campsite,' he said.

'Why not?' I argued. 'My grandmother would always take me back.'

'But what about me? Apprenticeships at the docks in Sassnitz are hard to come by. Even if you're prepared to throw in your job, I'm not.'

It seemed such a blinkered, unadventurous world view to me. I'd never told Laurenz about my previous attempt to escape – hiding away on the cargo ship to Hamburg through the Nord-Ostsee-Kanal. All the things that happened in the weeks and months after that – they weren't a part of my life I wanted to share, they weren't something I was proud of.

So we're coming out of the cinema, and I feel despite all those arguments in the summer, Laurenz and I are closer together. That maybe we do have a future together, after all. We're holding hands, then he spins me round for a kiss.

Suddenly, I hear the wolf whistles, and feel the blood rush to my face. Laurenz, too, is embarrassed and tries to hurry me along. I'm more curious. The source is a group of young men standing on the corner, laughing and smoking.

'You're just jealous,' I yell at them.

'Shush, Irma!' Laurenz tries to pull me along. 'Ignore them.'

But I've locked eyes with the ringleader, the one who I think was doing the whistling. He's smirking at me. I feel myself redden even more. Partly from the humiliation – but partly from an instant attraction. I wrench my arm away from Laurenz's, and stride over towards the group.

'Was there something you wanted to say to me?' I shout, my face close to his. Anger is coursing through my body. But so is excitement. His friends back away in mock terror. He stands his ground. His olive skin is drawn tight across his cheekbones, accentuating his Mediterranean looks, set off with dark hair. There's an air of mystery about him – and of menace too. But I don't feel frightened. Instead, I'm excited.

He says nothing.

'Maybe you need a girlfriend of your own,' I say, 'but I doubt you could find one.' He laughs at that and blows me a kiss.

Laurenz is hanging back, not wanting a confrontation. I realise in that moment that he's too timid for me. Too passive.

Despite this, I turn and stride back towards him, grab him for another kiss, but as I do I'm looking over his shoulder. Looking into the eyes of the boy who whistled at me, my heart beating rapidly in my chest. I realise then that I don't want Laurenz any more. I want the mystery man on the corner.

Back in Sellin, I try to find out from my girlfriends who the men in Binz were. Laurenz himself had given me some clue.

'Sorry about that,' he'd said at the time.

'Why?'

'They're troublemakers. I'd heard about them in Sassnitz. Some of them have been helping with the construction of the new harbour wall there.'

I couldn't get the image of that one guy out of my head. 'How does that make them troublemakers?'

'They've all refused to do their national service with the People's Army. Or at least refused to serve with regular units that might – in the worst case scenario if America launches an attack – be called up to fight. So all they're allowed to do is construction and repair work – on roads, railways, and the harbour. That sort of thing. It's best to keep out of their way, Irma.'

But I didn't want to keep out of their way. Gradually, with titbits of information from my girlfriends, people who knew people in Binz, I found out what the ringleader was called. Dieter Schwarz, a construction soldier barracked at Prora West – the opposite end of the complex to where the *Jugendwerkhof* was.

I just knew that I wanted to meet him again.

As soon as possible.

7

Müller followed Tilsner out of the helicopter, jumping down beside him, wind-blown snow whirled up by the slowing rotor blades softening her landing. She could feel the pores on her face closing up as the icy air slapped her cheeks. Pulling her faux fur hat over her ears, she ducked into a crouch behind him – wondering at that moment how she'd ever fancied her deputy. Either he'd put on too many layers to guard against the cold, or he'd been following Jonas Schmidt's example in scoffing too many sausages. Her view was the latter. He'd let himself go to seed now that his ex-wife Koletta had cut him free.

A welcoming party of other People's Police officers was waiting. She recognised *Oberst* Drescher from the island's headquarters at Bergen auf Rügen. The officer had the same surname as her former student detective turned rival murder squad head, Elke – but as far as she knew they weren't related. Their last meeting had seen the colonel sending Müller back to Berlin in disgrace, and as he shook her hand, he failed to disguise his distaste.

'Comrade *Major* Müller,' he said. 'Welcome again to our island. I'm afraid you're unlikely to find it as comfortable as last time.' Then he turned to her deputy. '*Hauptmann* Tilsner. Still part of the same team, then?' There was a knowing tone in his voice now, as though he might have been made aware of Tilsner's other role – supplying information to the Ministry for State Security, the Stasi. 'Anyway, let's not dawdle out here in the cold.' He pointed to a waiting army truck or personnel carrier, equipped with caterpillar treads to drive through the snow and ice, its engine roaring almost as loudly as the helicopter behind them. Müller wiped the snow away from her face to take a closer look. There was a man in a heavy overcoat and hat standing beside it. 'That's *Hauptmann* Günther Hummel, head of our murder squad here. Though the information he's gleaned so far points to this death being natural. So, I'm slightly surprised the Hauptstadt has deemed it necessary to send you two—'

'Three,' corrected Müller, nodding towards Schmidt, as she tried to make her mouth work in the bitter cold air. Both she and Drescher were enveloped in cloudlets of condensing breath. 'I think you met our forensic scientist, Comrade *Kriminaltechniker* Schmidt last time we were here.'

'Quite,' said Drescher with a thin smile. 'Anyway, I had business in Prora so I thought I would welcome you. But for now, I'll leave you in Comrade Hummel's capable hands.'

Müller found herself thawing out slightly once they were inside the truck and underway. It rode high on the carriageway, at what she felt was an alarming speed, considering the number of

Trabant and Wartburg cars that had been abandoned in drifts at the roadside.

'Everything's almost ground to a halt,' explained Hummel, who unlike his superior seemed genuinely pleased to see Müller and her team. He gave off the air of an excited overgrown school-boy, delighted to be the centre of attention for once. 'These things are the only way to get around. Most of them are tied up deliver-ing supplies. As you can see, normal vehicles are just getting stuck in the snow.'

'Aren't you annoyed that we've come to trample on your patch?' asked Tilsner.

Hummel shrugged his rounded shoulders. 'Why should I be? Although I have to admit, I think it's a wasted visit. Everything points to natural causes. But I can let the pathologist explain all that.'

'And do we know who it is who's dead?' asked Müller.

'No. That's the only strange thing. No identity papers, no money, nothing.'

'Yet she'd been to the shops buying provisions?' It didn't make sense to Müller. Neither, in truth, did Reiniger's decision to send them here. Unless it had been a ruse to lure her back to work.

'That's what we assume from the shopping bag she was carrying.'

'Perhaps she'd bought the stuff on credit,' offered Schmidt.

Hummel shrugged. 'Possibly. But then there still should have been a record of the transaction. Yet there is no receipt, nothing. And none of the shopkeepers remember seeing her.'

'What was she wearing?' asked Tilsner. There was a slightly bored note in his voice, as though he wasn't interested in the answer. He seemed more intent on thawing out his hands. He'd removed them from his damp gloves, and was rubbing them together vigorously, a bit like a Pioneer might with two sticks to try to spark a campfire to life.

'Well, that's an interesting question. You'll see the photos at the mortuary. Let's just say she wasn't really dressed for the weather. No wonder she froze to death.'

They lapsed into silence. Müller didn't feel like engaging Tilsner in conversation, instead turning her attention to the catastrophic scenes outside the vehicle's windows. As the previous night's television news reports had described, the drifts at the side of the road were at times almost as high as houses. Every now and then, under the banks of white she could make out the shape of an abandoned car. Presumably the occupants had got out of them safely – as far as she knew, the body they were travelling to see was the only fatality. She couldn't believe there wouldn't be others. But it didn't answer the question why they'd been sent from Berlin or, indeed, why she'd been specially brought back to head the inquiry. Someone obviously knew more. They just hadn't shared that information yet. Why? Müller shivered. Not from the cold – it was warm enough huddled in the back of this People's Army personnel carrier. It was more like an unseen and unwanted hand had caressed the back of her neck.

The hand of an organisation that liked to keep things secret.

The hand – she was sure – of the Stasi.

'I don't know why you're taking such an interest in this one,' said the senior pathologist, as the woman's body was wheeled from the cooler of the mortuary. 'I've already given my opinion – she died from, in effect, natural causes. In other words, exposure to the cold. I detected swelling to the nose, ears and hands as well as capillary damage – the classic signs of frost erythema.'

Müller was trying to hold her breath to keep out the chemical smells she associated with death. Yet she knew she had to ask questions of the man, who'd introduced himself as Dr Wilhelm Siegel. With his black horn-rimmed spectacles and puffy face, he looked like the myriad of apparatchiks in the Republic. He acted like one too. As though there was no room for discussion or disagreement.

'Thank you, Dr Siegel. And we haven't, as yet, managed to identify the body.'

'You'd have to ask your lot about that. The People's Police in Bergen, I mean. Anyway, this is her.'

He drew away a sheet that had been covering the dead woman's face.

Müller had to stifle a gasp. She looked round the room for Tilsner. His face told the same story. Yes, there was discolouration to some of her extremities. But she was still instantly recognisable to Müller – and clearly to her deputy too. It was Monika Richter, who the Berlin detectives had last encountered when she was the deputy director of *Jugendwerkhof Prora Ost* – the hated reform school where the teenage children had been housed in the graveyard girl case from nearly four years ago. Surely someone here would have recognised her? The local Stasi at the very least. Yet the authorities seemed to be sticking to their story that she was as yet unidentified. Why? Müller mouthed a silent 'shush' to Tilsner, out of sight of the others. If the authorities wanted to pretend they didn't know who the woman was, then Müller would go along with that for the time being and see where it led them. What she did know was that if the pathologist was wrong – and if this *wasn't* an accidental, natural death – then there would have been a long queue of people wanting to do the hateful woman harm. What Irma Behrendt had told Müller was enough evidence of that.

'Well, if your conclusion is she simply died of the cold, that it was misadventure in effect, Dr Siegel, I don't think I need to waste any more of your time. And I can't quite understand why we've been brought all the way from Berlin, especially in such dangerous conditions.'

'Quite,' said the doctor, a smug look of satisfaction on his face.

'Nevertheless,' said Müller, 'until I get clearance from my superiors, I don't want the body released for burial or cremation.'

The pathologist shrugged. 'As you wish. Given we don't know who she is, there isn't exactly a queue of relatives rushing to lay her to rest anyway.' He peered quizzically at Jonas Schmidt, who'd moved forward and seemed to be conducting his own examination of the woman's face, hands and feet. 'Who are you?' the doctor asked.

Müller replied on behalf of her forensic scientist. 'Comrade Schmidt is our team's *Kriminaltechniker*, Dr Siegel. Anything interesting to report, Jonas?'

'No, no,' said Schmidt, shaking his head, but still doing a careful visual examination of the body. 'Dr Siegel's findings look perfectly correct to me.'

Siegel frowned. 'And why wouldn't they? I'm not accustomed to having my work checked by police scientists.'

Tilsner laughed. 'Don't worry about, Jonas, Herr Doktor. That's just his way. He means nothing by it.'

Müller wasn't so sure. Perhaps Schmidt *had* spotted something out of place or irregular about Siegel's conclusions. If he had, now wasn't the time to discuss it.

'*Hauptmann* Tilsner's correct. We won't take up any more of your time, Dr Siegel,' said Müller. 'Thank you for showing us the body.'

Once they'd closed the doors to the mortuary room, and were making their way through the hospital back to the car park – where the army personnel carrier should be waiting for them – Müller turned to her two colleagues. She was going to tell them not to discuss any concerns until they were in private. But before she could open her mouth, she saw another member of the medical staff running towards them.

'*Major* Müller?' the woman asked. Müller looked at her nametag. The woman – girl, really – looked impossibly young to be qualified, but her name tag identified her as a doctor by the name of Renate Tritten.

'Yes.'

'I'm Dr Siegel's assistant. I wondered if I could have a quick word with you in private?'

'Anything you have to say you can say in front of my team. They're perfectly trustworthy.' As she said the words, Müller laughed inwardly. Her previous investigation had given the lie to that – in both their cases.

'That's not what I meant, really.' The young woman glanced around. 'Could you come in this room for a moment?'

Müller frowned momentarily, but nodded her assent. The junior pathologist unlocked the door. It was a tiny storeroom – little more than a cupboard. There wasn't room for all four of them even if that had been what Müller wanted.

'I'll only be a few minutes,' she said to Schmidt and Tilsner. 'It's too tight a squeeze for us all.'

'I'm sorry,' said Dr Tritten. 'But yes, it won't take a moment.'

Tilsner shrugged, while Schmidt muttered an 'of course, of course', as the two women disappeared inside, Tritten shutting the door behind her.

'Sorry,' said the young woman again. In Müller's book, she was apologising rather too much. 'I couldn't really say this in the mortuary room. But Dr Siegel's findings aren't consistent with marks on the body. And I suspect the reason you've been sent here is because of me. It's just I didn't know who to turn to. I read about one of your cases a couple of years ago. So I rang your office. But I was told you were on leave.'

'I was. Not any more.' Reiniger must have been sufficiently impressed by what this young doctor had to say that he'd decided a delegation of Berlin detectives needed to be sent, and for some reason he deemed it necessary to bring her back into the fold. Perhaps her previous dealings with the deputy director of the *Jugendwerkhof* had been enough to ensure that. 'No doubt you're about to tell me why, Dr Tritten.'

'I found an injection mark on the victim's body.'

'And?'

'Doctor Siegel glossed over my findings. Said they were irrelevant to the cause of death, which he insisted was hypothermia.'

'So you're saying it wasn't the cold that caused this woman's death?' Müller wasn't about to reveal that she knew who the victim was – at least, not until she felt she could fully trust the junior pathologist.

The woman scrunched up her face. 'Well, no, I'm not necessarily disagreeing with that. Clearly there is evidence of hypothermia. But the point is the victim had recently been injected – and in a very strange place on her body.'

Müller frowned. The confined nature of their surroundings, with barely room to move, lent a more sinister air to the doctor's revelations. 'Where?'

'She had a silver ring on the index finger of her right hand. It was fairly wide – three millimetres or so. I found the injection mark under that.'

'So what are you trying to imply?'

'I'm not trying to imply anything. I'm just saying the woman had – in the hours before her death – been injected with a substance.'

'To what end?'

'To render her temporarily paralysed.'

'So how did she come to be out shopping in the snow?'

The young doctor drew in a long breath. 'I don't think she was. I don't think she can have been. I believe her death from the cold was – in effect – staged.'

Müller felt her frustrations getting the better of her. The doctor seemed to be contradicting herself. 'Yet you don't disagree with the findings of hypothermia of Dr Siegel?'

'No. I agree with them entirely. But it's *why* she perished in the cold that is the point. It's my belief that a drug was administered, she was then dumped – helpless – in this Arctic weather, possibly even buried alive under snow – although that may have been just a natural weather phenomenon. Certainly asphyxia was present. And she'd been drugged – she was unable to save herself.'

'Even if she'd wanted to?'

'Oh, she would have wanted to all right. If my suspicions about the drug used are correct, she would have been conscious as she slowly froze to death.'

Müller paused as she let the implications sink in. 'So you're saying that she was—'

'Murdered, *Major* Müller? Yes, that's exactly what I'm saying.'

8

It doesn't take me long to find out more about Dieter. What's more problematical is trying to catch his eye again and make him notice me.

With autumn already here, and winter approaching, the camping season is pretty much over. Most of the work now involves cleaning and tidying up, gardening, that sort of thing. My grandmother's getting on a bit and not as active, so a lot of that's left to me. But I still have more time on my hands than in the summer.

Sabine looks at me as though I'm mad when I suggest going for a walk at Sassnitz harbour.

'Why? It's blowing a gale. We'll get soaked from the spray, and it's freezing. Plus it takes ages on the bus. Can't we just hang out at the café? At least it's warm in there.'

I tell her not to be so miserable.

What I don't say is the real reason I want to go for a 'walk' in Sassnitz. I know that Dieter and his company are doing work reinforcing and rebuilding the harbour wall. It's high time

Sabine and I indulged in a bit of flirting. She's a good choice as she's pretty enough to turn heads, but not so pretty as to completely overshadow me. As I think that, I feel a pang of sadness, remembering the girl who *was* pretty enough to overshadow me – and regularly did. Beate. Mathias only had eyes for her. I can't say I'm sad he's gone – in the end, he proved himself utterly shallow and a traitor. Even before that he was obsessed with Beate and tried to get in the way of our friendship at any opportunity. But Beate herself was a good friend. I can still hear her voice in my head. Her excitement when she was invited to that fancy dress party at the barracks on the top of the Brocken. And I feel a terrible shame that I did nothing to stop her going, even though I had an awful foreboding about how things would turn out.

Sabine cheers up once we get to Sassnitz, and the choking diesel fumes of the bus station are replaced by the fresh salty tang of the sea. As we walk along the start of the harbour wall and breathe in, I can taste the tiny droplets of seawater from the spray – I feel it clearing my airways, like I'm breathing life itself. When I'm away from Rügen, it's what I miss. The fresh air. The smell of the sea. Even at *Prora Ost*, although we knew we were locked up, by levering myself up and gazing out on the Ostsee, I could imagine that feeling of freedom that the sea can inspire. I know that, not many kilometres away, lies real freedom. Denmark, Sweden. But I've tried to get there once, and failed. And the pain of failure was almost worse than never having tried at all. As I skip along hand in hand with Sabine, I know I can't face that level of fear and disappointment again.

We count the waves as they hit the harbour wall, each one shaking it with a thunderous slap. It seems amazing that something so apparently solid can appear to shake beneath our feet. After the sixth wave, we know from the saying about the seventh that the really big one is next. It doesn't always work, of course, but this time it does. It crashes over the wall; we brace ourselves into the spray and wind. But even so I find myself winded. I stagger slightly then fight to regain my balance, my hair and my anorak soaking wet. It's good that there's another, higher wall behind us, otherwise I fear we'll be swept over into the harbour.

Sabine shouts in my ear. 'We ought to move to the other side, the sheltered side! It seems to be getting rougher!'

I'd wanted to show some bravado in front of Dieter and his colleagues, working away at the end by the lighthouse, just before the open sea. But it feels too dangerous. I nod, and at the next set of steps, we climb up and over to the wider, more sheltered pathway on the leeward side of the sea and wind.

When we get nearer the end of the wall, towards the harbour mouth, a People's Army soldier steps in front of our path.

'Papers,' he orders.

You need a special resident's permit at some coastal towns, although not here on Rügen, so I don't really understand what he wants.

I dig my regular ID card from my bag and thrust it under his nose. He's an earnest-seeming specimen, who looks as though he'd be more at home in a university science lab.

He peers down his bespectacled nose. Then gets out a handkerchief and wipes the spray from his glasses. 'That's not what

I mean. You need special permission to go to the end of the harbour while the building work is being carried out. Do you have that?'

Sabine smiles at him. 'Do we really need that? Can't you just let us through? We're only going for a walk.'

He suddenly becomes alert, as though sensing some sort of trap set by his superiors to test his assiduousness. Standing erect, he brings his feet together with a snap. 'No. It is forbidden to go any further without special permission. Please go back the way you came.'

I roll my eyes. There's no real reason we shouldn't go further. It's not as though the wall is crumbling into the sea. It's just being repaired and improved before the winter. But I can see this one is determined to play everything by the rules.

'Fine,' I say. 'We'll sit here then. You can't stop us doing that.'

For a moment he looks as though he might try to. He turns and walks a few metres away and leaves us to sit on a bench. Once he realises we're not planning to go any further, I climb up on the bench, and look over towards Dieter. We're close enough that I can make him out, with his Mediterranean olive skin, and dark hair which has separated into damp rats' tails, and is plastered to his head. But can he see us?

I put two fingers to my mouth, and whistle towards them. Dieter turns, but so does the guard. I wave but I'm not sure he's seen me, knows who I am, or really cares. After all, the only other time he's seen me was when he and his group were teasing Laurenz and me for kissing in public.

The guard's hovering. 'I thought I ordered you to go back the way you came.'

'No,' I say. 'You just said we couldn't go any further without a permit.'

'Well, I'm telling you now. Start walking back to the other end of the harbour wall and don't cause any more trouble.'

I'm tempted to refuse just to wind him up, but I can see him admiring Sabine from behind his glasses. Maybe that's the way to deal with him. I get closer to her and whisper in her ear.

'He's taken a shine to you. Ask him what time the construction gang usually knock off and where they go after that.'

Sabine looks at me dubiously, but friendship trumps her caution.

She poses the question.

The guard sighs. 'Look, I'll tell you, but then I want you to do as I say, and go back to the other end of the harbour wall. Otherwise one of my superiors will take it out on me for not doing my job properly.'

Sabine smiles coquettishly. 'OK, deal.'

He looks at his army-issue watch. 'They usually knock off when it starts to get dark. So about 1730 or so. Some of them hang around the bar on the port afterwards – the others just go on the army transport back to Prora.'

'Thanks,' smiles Sabine. 'See you around.'

I'm not sure if I'm imagining it or not, but as we walk towards the port office as agreed, Sabine's face seems to have coloured slightly and she looks to have an extra spring in her step.

We wait in the bar at the other end of the harbour until half-five comes around. The barmaid's eyeing us suspiciously – wondering why we've both been nursing two small Vita Colas for more than an hour. She looks like she's about to say something and come over, when there's shouting at the door, and a group of the construction soldiers come in. At the back of the group, I see Dieter, and my heart starts banging in my chest. I try to stay calm, but I can feel myself going red.

They're talking loudly to each other, laughing and joking. It looks like they're going to ignore us, so as Dieter goes past, I deliberately flick a beer mat to the floor, then lean in front of him to reach it, so he can't help but stumble into me.

'Whoops,' he says. 'Careful.'

'Sorry,' I say, sitting up again and smiling. At least I have a reason now for looking embarrassed. 'Oh, it's you again,' I continue, acting surprised.

'Ha!' he says. 'Little Miss Cinema-goer.' Then he looks around ostentatiously. 'Isn't your boyfriend chaperoning you today?'

I shrug. 'I don't have a boyfriend.'

He snorts. 'What, so you were just snogging a total stranger the other night?' I know I've caught my fish now. If he wasn't interested, he wouldn't have remembered.

'No, he *was* my boyfriend. He's not any more.' As I say this, I can feel Sabine is about to interrupt, because this is news to her – and would be to Laurenz, too, if I'd actually told him. Out of Dieter's vision, I give her a sharp kick under the table.

He pulls a sarcastic face, as though to say '*how fascinating*'. Feigning disinterest, he goes to join his friends at the bar.

'What's all that about?' hisses Sabine.

'Shush,' I say. 'Have you got a pen?'

She looks at me with disapproval, as though I'm a naughty schoolkid. But she digs in her handbag and pulls a ballpoint out all the same.

I grab it, write my name and the campsite's phone number on the beer mat, jump up and walk towards the bar. One of Dieter's friends nudges him as I approach. I can feel myself blushing like mad now, and sweat pooling in my armpits. I hope the Republic's finest deodorant is doing its job for once.

Dieter turns. I hand him the beer mat.

'We're from Sellin, the other side of Binz. If you're ever out that way, give me a call.'

I turn away and rush back towards Sabine before he can reply, and without saying anything grab my anorak and beckon her with my eyes. I want to go. I've done what I set out to do. If he's torn the mat up, or is laughing about it with his mates, I don't want to know.

Just seeing him again, being close to him, talking to him . . . it's like it's lit a fire inside me.

Sabine's looking at me as though I've got dog shit on my shoes, but I've got to run away. Put some distance between me and him and leave things to fate.

9

Binz, Island of Rügen, East Germany
Later on 30 December 1978

The anger Müller felt when she received the summons to meet him almost gave her a blood pressure headache. She put her hand to her temple, feeling the pounding underneath. *How dare they mess me around like this?*

She'd wanted to discuss the case with Tilsner and Schmidt, filling them in on what the young assistant pathologist had told her. Instead, she'd had to hitch another lift with an army personnel carrier from the hospital in Bergen. It was on its way back to Prora, suspending operations for the day as night had now fallen, even though it was not yet 5 p.m. But Jäger had 'suggested' she meet him in a bar off the esplanade in Binz. The army driver dropped her in the centre of the town. With much of the power cut off, the streets had a ghostly, deserted feel. Müller had an idea what it would look like in daylight: the same white clapboard and veranda *Bäderarchitektur* which had been prevalent in the next town along the coast, Sellin, where they'd stayed nearly four years earlier on the case that had originally brought them to Rügen. But the buildings were in shadow. Dim, flickering candlelight was evident in a few windows – or brighter lights in premises with access to emergency generators.

Stumbling through the drifting snow, it was hard going – reminiscent of climbing slopes in Oberhof after a skiing fall to try to locate a missing ski. Here, she was simply walking through a town. But it was a town transformed by the weather. Usually on a case, she might take the precaution of checking if she was being followed. Here she didn't bother. Why did she need to know if the Stasi were following her? She was on her way to meet one of their senior officers.

She finally reached the seafront, and tramped through the almost virgin snow in the direction of the bar. To her right, even in the darkness, she could see the Ostsee was completely frozen – it wasn't just the channel between Rügen and the mainland that had become a giant ice sheet. The wind howling in off the ice blew snow off the trees into her face so she had difficulty seeing where she was going. The cold penetrated her to the core.

At last, she saw what she thought was the bar, a weak light illuminating a single figure sitting at a table inside. The silhouette was unmistakably that of the Stasi colonel. Usually, Jäger went out of his way to meet in places where their conversations couldn't be overheard. Here, he evidently thought the weather was providing enough of a secrecy blanket on its own. Just one set of footprints led up to the door – and they had already almost been covered over by the drifting snow. Instead of a thriving bar in a coastal town, it was more like an isolated ski bar up a mountain. At that moment, Müller felt incredibly alone. She longed for Jannika and

Johannes, and half-wished she hadn't fallen for Reiniger's black-mail. She would much rather be at the apartment in Strausberger Platz. But that was the problem, as Reiniger had taken great joy in spelling out. If she didn't do this job, there would no longer be an apartment in Strausberger Platz. And it wasn't fair to turf Helga and the twins from their home – whatever Müller's own feelings.

'I've never known weather like it, Karin, have you? To think we were out and about in that play area just a few days ago.'

Müller nodded. She knew the Stasi colonel wasn't here to chat about the weather. And she wasn't in the mood for small talk.

In the bar it was at least warm thanks to a fire crackling and spitting out smoke in the corner. The smell of burning lignite suffused the air. It was almost choking, but a welcome change from the bitter freshness outside. Müller took off her coat and gloves, sat down, and rubbed her hands together to try to get some warmth into the ends of her fingers. Her feet felt numb with cold, and when she spoke, she struggled to get her lips to move. 'Why did you want to see me so quickly, Comrade *Oberst*? I've hardly had chance to get started on this case.'

'All in good time, Karin. And please call me Klaus. Surely we've known each other long enough to drop the formalities?' What Jäger said was true, but she didn't want him to get the mistaken impression that he was suddenly her friend, or that she trusted him. He wasn't, and she didn't. 'What can I get you to drink?' He gestured with his eyes to the bottle and two small glasses on the table. 'I recommend the schnapps to warm you up.'

Müller nodded again, even though Jäger had already started pouring into the second glass, as though his question was redundant. As always, she was having to do as he suggested – she wasn't even permitted to order her own drink.

'All right,' he said. 'I can see that you want to get down to business.'

'If we could, yes. I'm tired, and I'm not sure how I'm going to get back to Bergen. Or indeed where we're staying tonight.'

'Don't worry about that. I'd already checked with Reiniger and Drescher. That's why I suggested we meet here, but yes, I should have made that clear. You and the other two have been booked into a union rest home here in Binz. It's just round the corner. It makes sense as this is the nearest town to where the woman's body was found. And by now, you no doubt know who she is.'

Müller frowned. So Jäger knew too. She wondered *how* much he knew.

'That's another reason for basing ourselves here. It's near the *Jugendwerkhof* too. That's one of the reasons why Reiniger insisted you should take charge of this case – your intimate knowledge of the reform school because of the previous case involving Irma. How is she, by the way?'

The question was unexpected, and Müller realised immediately it was meant to unsettle her. She played a straight bat – she had nothing to hide.

'I've never spoken to her since the end of the other case. Did you expect otherwise?'

Jäger curled his lips downwards. 'Well, she might be a useful contact for you. She keeps her ear to the ground. She's provided some very useful information.'

'She works for *you*?' Müller couldn't keep the shock from her voice. Or the note of disgust.

'Of course. I told you at the time there would have to be certain compromises if we were to prevent her being sent back to *Jugendwerkhof Prora Ost*.'

'Compromise? You call that a compromise?'

Jäger slapped his hand down hard on the table, shaking the schnapps glasses and bottle. Then he seemed to swallow back his anger. Perhaps he's remembered, thought Müller with a hint of satisfaction. *Remembered that from now on – ever since I discovered what I know about his past – he's the one who has to tread with care.*

After gathering himself, he seemed to enunciate each word carefully, as though he'd already rehearsed what he wanted to say. 'Giving service to the Republic is not something to be sneered at, Karin. I'm sure that wasn't your intention. We all need to do our duty.'

Müller waited for Jäger to say more. As she did, his words echoed around her head. The reason for basing *ourselves* here. She hadn't misheard him, she was sure. It appeared that Jäger himself was going to be intimately involved in this inquiry. It was feeling horribly like a reprise of four years earlier.

'So from what you saw and learnt at the mortuary, you can see this isn't a straightforward case of a middle-aged woman freezing to death.'

'No,' replied Müller. 'I didn't expect it would be.'

'What did you make of our young Dr Tritten? Do you think she can be trusted?'

Müller had assumed Jäger knew about Tritten's theory. He wouldn't be here otherwise, and if she had used an open phone line in ringing Keibelstraße to try to alert Müller – and she had no choice but to use one – then the Stasi would have almost certainly listened in.

'I don't know enough about her to say whether she can be trusted or not. And I'm not sure quite what you're driving at. If you're asking me whether she seemed to be telling the truth about her findings, and how they conflicted with those of Dr Siegel . . . well, yes, I think she was being honest.' Müller was aware Jäger might – in asking his question – have been fishing for information. But she suspected he probably already knew more than her.

This time it was Jäger's turn to nod, thoughtfully. It set his shoulder-length, sandy hair bouncing on his head. Müller had to stifle a laugh. The Stasi colonel needed a haircut. He might still look like that famous West German newsreader – but the newsreader himself was now looking distinctly old-fashioned. Müller wasn't a fan of the punk music that so often these days was blaring out on the Western TV programmes she wasn't supposed to watch. But she was aware times had changed. The Republic – and its servants like Jäger – would have to change with them, or risk getting left behind.

When the Stasi colonel continued, Müller realised he *did* know more than she did. 'Yet,' he said, wringing his hands, 'she was dishonest in excising a section of Frau Richter's brain and sending it to her friend in the toxicology lab.'

'That's true,' said Müller, hoping that by implying that Jäger was telling her nothing she didn't already know, he might go on to tell her yet more. 'But I'm not entirely sure the poison concerned would have had the effects she claims.'

'Succinylcholine? I can assure you it does.'

'From personal experience?' She could feel Jäger bristling, and wondered if she'd overstepped the mark.

'Let's just say it's not unknown to my department, as you can imagine, and can be useful in certain circumstances.'

'But do you think the levels of the metabolites detected by her friend in the lab were sufficient to render Richter so paralysed that she couldn't save herself?' Again, Müller was winging it. Pretending she knew more than she did to winkle more information out of Jäger. But she was on fairly safe ground. From previous autopsies and conversations with pathologists, she knew it was the metabolites of the primary agent of death – the chemicals that poisons were broken down into by the body's natural reactions – that the toxicology lab would have been searching for.

'The level of succinic acid? Yes, it was sufficient, I can assure you.' Jäger was looking at her slightly quizzically, as though he'd just realised he'd given away information that she wasn't party to. It wasn't important, thought Müller, but it was nice to beat him at his own game. She allowed herself a little smirk, and made sure he saw it.

'Not a very pleasant way to go.'

'On the contrary,' Jäger demurred. 'It is – allegedly, according to those who've been saved at the last minute – one of the more peaceful ways to die. By that I mean hypothermia itself, of course. Those who are saved at the last moment often talk of feeling utter peace . . . no panic at all. Just slipping away into a deep sleep.' He laughed. 'I'm not recommending it, though, I assure you.'

'But slipping into a hypothermic state while paralysed? Wanting to struggle to save yourself, but being unable to? That would be mental torture, surely, whatever the physical feelings?'

'Hmm,' said Jäger, stroking his chin. She hoped she hadn't given him any sadistic ideas to incorporate into the Stasi manual.

'So why, Comrade *Oberst*—' she gave him the honorific deliberately, just to defy the fact that he'd asked her not to '—why are we pretending we don't know who the woman is? And why are we pretending she died a natural death?'

Jäger sighed. 'I would have thought that is obvious, Karin. And it's why I asked you to meet me. Citizens here have enough to worry about with the weather at the moment. Power still hasn't been restored. The island is cut off by road and rail. It's a serious, a dangerous situation. We don't want more panic by suggesting a murderer is on the loose. So I don't want any leaks. From you, Tilsner or Schmidt – or anyone else connected with the inquiry. You need to make that crystal clear to them. To our good Dr Tritten too. Siegel is an old hand – I have no worries on that score.'

'So he knew all along?'

'Of course he knew, Karin. He's not an idiot. That's why I asked whether Tritten can be trusted. Lean on her and make sure she understands she has to keep her mouth shut, as should her contact in the toxicology lab. No leaks. From anyone. Otherwise there will be consequences.'

'So do you mind telling me what's going on?'

Jäger's face creased into a severe frown. 'What do you mean?'

'Who's responsible?'

'I have no idea at all, Karin. That's why you, Tilsner and Schmidt are here. To find out. And to find out without creating a huge hullabaloo. Make sure that happens – both parts of it. Without fail.'

10

Müller was relieved that Jäger – at least in terms of her accommodation arrangements – was true to his word. Her lodgings, in effect a hotel even though it wasn't described as such, were around the corner from the bar. Her room looked out over the esplanade just as the bar had, although here it was merely a paved footpath – not a road. Perhaps a promenade was a better description, and beyond – she already knew – the frozen sea.

She kicked off her boots as soon as she was in the room, and flopped on the bed. But she knew she couldn't relax. Soon, she would need to meet with Tilsner and Schmidt. Hopefully their debrief could be combined with an evening meal in a quiet, non-overlooked part of the restaurant. But she also needed to contact her family in the Hauptstadt. Jannika and Johannes for the past eighteen months had been used to her being part of their lives every day. It was what she wanted, and she was devastated to have had to give it up.

Lying on the bed, she used the room telephone to dial Berlin. Such a thing – a private telephone handset for each room – would be unheard of in many parts of the Republic. Guests in most union holiday homes, or in smaller pensions still in private hands, would normally have to use communal telephones in the reception area to speak to their loved ones. She was in a privileged position, and she knew why. Rügen was a favourite holiday ground of the great and good of the Party. That would be true here in Binz. Even more so on the islet of Vilm, in the lee of the main island, which was reputed to be the holiday destination of the biggest of the Republic's bigwigs – Honecker and his ilk.

When she rang the apartment, someone picked up but said nothing for a moment. All she could hear was breathing. Then the voice of Helga in the background. 'Jannika, what are you doing? You shouldn't pick up the telephone.'

'Hello, *Schatzi*. It's Mutti.'

'Mutti! Mutti! Oma, it's Mutti!' shouted Jannika, so loudly that Müller had to move the plastic handset away from her ear. Although Helga was strictly speaking the twins' great-grandmother, they still called her 'Oma' – granny. It was less complicated that way.

'Are you being a good girl for Oma?'

'Yes, Mutti. I'm a good girl.' Müller knew that wasn't true, but in general Jannika fitted the stereotype and was certainly better behaved than her brother, though both had wilful streaks when they wanted.

'What about your brother?'

'He's naughty. Oma smack him.' Müller heard Helga in the background ordering Jannika to stop telling fibs.

'Can I talk to him?' asked Müller.

'No. Johannes sent to bed. Very bad boy. Talk to Oma?'

'Yes please, Jannika.'

'Oma. Speak to Mutti. Now!'

Müller could imagine her daughter standing on the chair at the side of the telephone table, imperiously ordering Helga and Johannes around.

'Bye, *Schatzi*. Love you,' she said down the phone line. But Jannika had already gone, bored with the telephone game. All her mother could hear was static.

The line crackled again, and Helga was speaking.

'That daughter of yours likes making up stories. She'll probably write novels when she grows up. Johannes has actually been very well behaved for once and, no, I haven't had to spank him.'

Müller laughed. 'They've been OK, then?'

'As good as gold. Mind you, I think it helps that they've got all their Christmas presents to play with. The novelty still hasn't worn off.'

Imagining her son and daughter playing with their toys sent a sudden feeling of loss surging through Müller. She stifled a sob. 'I miss them, Helga, and you.'

'I know you do, Karin. But I'm sure your decision was correct. After all, that police university was out in Potsdam. It would have been a terribly long journey each day. You'd have hardly seen anything of them. At least with your regular job you'll be in Berlin a lot of the time and your office is there.'

'What about Johannes, can I have a quick word with him?'

'I'll see if I can drag him away from his Sandmännchen cosmonaut. All his friends are jealous of it.'

Müller laughed to herself. Her son's favourite Christmas toy had been given to him by a ruthless Stasi colonel. What did that signify? At the very least, that Jäger had even managed to infiltrate her family with his shady dealings.

Müller, Tilsner and Schmidt hunted out a quiet corner of the restaurant with high-backed bench seats so that – with luck – they could discuss the case over supper without being overheard. With the power cuts on Rügen, both men's faces were transformed into ghoul-like masks by the flickering candles – the only source of light.

'I've just had a meeting with you-know-who,' she said to Tilsner.

'Reiniger?'

Müller shook her head. 'No, worse than that. Jäger.'

'A meeting with Jäger? So he's here on Rügen?'

'Exactly.'

Tilsner exhaled slowly, stretching the buttons on his shirt so his vest underneath showed through – its whiteness almost glowing in the prevailing semi-darkness. Müller couldn't help noticing again how his stomach seemed bigger. The toned detective succumbing at last to middle-aged spread. 'Why? Every time he's closely involved in a case it's the sort of inquiry we'd be better steering clear of. I'm sure this is no different. What did he have to say? And more to the point, what about your secret rendezvous with the pretty doctor?'

He was never going to change, so Müller let his 'pretty doctor' comment pass. 'Jonas will be interested in what they both had to say.' She turned to their forensic scientist, who'd been sitting quietly demolishing the contents of the bread basket.

'That was meant to be shared between all of us, Jonas,' admonished Tilsner.

'Ah.' The *Kriminaltechniker*'s embarrassment was obvious even in the dim light. 'Sorry, Comrades. I thought that was just for me. This freezing weather is enough to make anyone famished.'

'Never mind that, Jonas,' said Müller. 'Have you ever heard of succinylcholine?'

'Yes of course, Comrade *Major*. Its correct chemical name is suxamethonium chloride, but I know what it is. It's used by anaesthetists in certain circumstances. Also by psychiatrists with mentally ill patients who need electroconvulsive therapy.'

'So what are its properties?' Müller knew the answer from both the junior pathologist and from Jäger himself. But it would do no harm to get corroboration from Schmidt.

'It causes temporary paralysis. It's what's known as a neuro-muscular blocker. It works by blocking the action of acetylcholine on skeletal muscles. Acetylcholine itself acts as a neurotransmitter – in other words, a chemical message sent by nerve cells telling other cells in the body to act. So by blocking that transmitter, the succinylcholine – to use your preferred term – causes temporary paralysis.'

'And when you examined the body,' continued Müller, 'did you find any evidence of it?'

With his hands in the air in mock surrender, Schmidt pulled a wounded face. 'Be fair, please, Comrade *Major*. I simply did a superficial visual check. I could see some of the signs of hypothermia, and so – on the surface – it seemed as though Dr Siegel's conclusions were correct. But detecting the use of succinylcholine is much more difficult. Even toxicologists might not necessarily spot it.'

Müller lowered her voice, and the two others moved their heads closer to hear. 'What seems to have happened is that Dr Tritten went behind Siegel's back and arranged tests with a friend in the toxicology lab. Basically, without permission, she took a biopsy of Richter's brain—'

'—which detected elevated levels of succinic acid,' whispered Schmidt.

'Exactly, Jonas. She told you that?'

'No, it's just self-evident from what you said about the use of succinylcholine. That's what it breaks down to – its metabolite.'

Tilsner sighed. 'OK,' he said, his voice lowered to match theirs. 'That's enough of all the science. What did that mean in practice for the fragrant Frau Richter?'

'She was injected with succinylcholine, then a ring placed on her finger over the injection site,' said Müller.

'Why didn't her body show signs of a struggle?' asked Tilsner.

'Whoever did it could have used wide, soft restraints,' said Schmidt. 'Webbing, that sort of thing. You wouldn't necessarily get bruising.'

'So why,' asked Tilsner, 'are the authorities – and the pathologist even – insisting this was a natural death?'

Müller rested her elbows on the table and steepled her hands together. 'It's similar to that case a couple of years back in Halle-Neustadt. The missing babies.' She looked at Tilsner knowingly. He was aware she didn't mention that previous case lightly, given the horrific personal memories it held for her. 'The Stasi were determined there should be no adverse publicity. It's the same here.'

'Is that why Jäger's arrived?'

'I would think so.'

Tilsner stretched, then settled himself. 'Richter was a nasty piece of work. But in effect what you seem to be saying is she was rendered utterly incapable with this drug, then left out in the snow to slowly freeze to death – unable to do anything to save herself.'

Müller nodded.

'Would she have been conscious?'

There was a pause. Müller wasn't sure of the answer. Instead, Schmidt provided it. 'Without any doubt, Comrade *Hauptmann*. She would have been aware of exactly what was happening, and unable to even lift so much as a finger to try to prevent it. For her, it would be like suffering the worst forms of torture – but the pain would be almost entirely mental. Until her brain shut down from the cold, she would be sent out of her mind.'

11

Rügen, East Germany
Early December 1978

I couldn't quite believe it when my ruse with the beer mat worked.

At first, it didn't look like it would. I waited each evening by the campsite phone, willing it to ring, at the same time making excuses to Laurenz and Sabine why I couldn't go out. I felt bad about Laurenz – but I realised I didn't love him any more. As for summoning up the courage to tell him that, well, that was another story. Perhaps I was hedging my bets, but I wanted to see if Dieter would respond first before making any precipitous decisions.

When he did ring, he was quite cool about it. He pretended he couldn't remember whose number it was or why he had it written on a beer mat in his pocket. I saw through that straight away. He knew I liked going to the cinema, so invited me to see a film. I agreed, but to make sure I didn't bump into Laurenz, I suggested we meet in Bergen rather than Binz, or even Sellin itself.

That was the start of a low-level relationship. We only saw each other about once a week, and didn't get beyond a bit of kissing and cuddling. I wasn't sure how keen he was about me – and I didn't want to show how madly I was in love with him for fear of frightening him off.

I finally summoned up the courage to tell Laurenz about everything.

I said I wanted to meet at the café halfway along Wilhelm-Pieck-Straße in Sellin – the one I kept watch on a few years back when my mother met her 'contact'. It seemed appropriate somehow for something that was equally furtive, underhand and disloyal. In any case, winter was closing in, and I knew it had an open fire, albeit a smoky one because of the shitty brown coal we produce in this country – the reason why our atmosphere is so badly polluted.

Almost before I opened my mouth, it seemed as though Laurenz knew what I was going to say. In fact, in the way boys do to try to make sure their pride isn't hurt, he attempted to twist things round and make out it was he dumping me, rather than vice versa. So he was the one who spoke first after we'd been served our coffees.

'I've been meaning to have a talk with you, Irma,' he began. 'We don't seem to be having as much fun as before – I'm not sure we're really suited.'

I felt affronted. How dare he steal my lines? 'That's why I wanted to m—'

'—so I've decided we ought to end it.'

There it was. He'd said the words for me. I felt cheated even though it was what I wanted. 'Are you sure?' I found myself asking, despite the fact that *I* was the one who was sure.

He leant across the table and took my hand even though I wanted to grab it and hide it behind my back. I didn't want any physical contact with him any more. I'd found Dieter. All I could think about when I was mooning around the campsite, when I was in bed alone at night, was Dieter, his olive skin, rake-thin figure, and black hair.

'I'm sorry, Irma,' he said, stroking my hand. 'You'll find someone else. You're a good sort.'

I already have, I wanted to shout. *I already have and he's far more handsome and far more exciting than you are, Laurenz.* But the words died in my mouth before I could form them. I'd let him have his moment of triumph. In the grand scheme of things it didn't matter. What really mattered was that I was free now – free to be with whoever I wanted.

And the person I wanted was Dieter.

Dieter meets me in the bar at the entrance to Sassnitz old harbour – the one where the harbour wall they're repairing is. There are two of the other construction soldiers there – his friends. I think I recognise them from that night outside the cinema in Binz, when they were teasing Laurenz and me for kissing.

I've started to get a clearer idea of what construction soldiers are now. They're not really soldiers at all. They're young men who've refused to join fighting units of the People's Army – in the West I know they're called conscientious objectors. Those who – on principle – will not kill another man. Pacifists, I guess you could say – but in no way passive. I can see the light of rebellion in their eyes. I recognise it from looking at myself in the mirror when I was incarcerated in the *Jugendwerkhof*. When the need to escape this hateful country burned fiercely inside me too. I don't know whether these young men want to take their chances in trying to cross the border – what I do know is they must be brave to make a stand against the Republic's authorities. I feel a real thrill course through me that Dieter is one of them. He looks like a revolutionary, someone who won't kowtow. My personal Che Guevara, and just as good-looking.

Dieter's decided we're going for a walk – all four of us – back along the harbour wall towards where they've been working each day. Their shift's ended, so the guard has given up – there's no one to stop us walking right to the end, where the lighthouse is. As we walk along, Dieter takes my hand. It feels exciting, dangerous, and as the waves crash against the sea wall, I playfully try to drag him towards them. We lag behind the other two, and when he's sure they're not looking, he spins me round and grabs a quick kiss. I sense him looking over my shoulder at the others, as though he doesn't want to be seen doing anything soppy with a girl – as though he doesn't want his ultra-cool image undermined.

We get to the end of the harbour wall, and the taller of the other two – Holger, his name is – reaches into his pocket and pulls out a large rusting key. He jiggles it in the lock of the lighthouse door until finally, with the effort etched on his face, it turns and the door creaks open, the screech of metal audible even over the noise of the wind and waves.

Inside the lighthouse has a dank, eerie feel. Now darkness has fallen, every few seconds the boys' faces are weakly illuminated by the automatically rotating light high above us.

'Aren't we going to switch this room's light on?' I whisper to Dieter.

'It's too dangerous. As you can probably guess, we're not really supposed to be here. But it's a good place to talk without any danger of being overheard.' He takes a small candle from his jacket pocket, and then tries to light the end with a match. But the atmosphere in here is too damp – the matches just skid off the striking surface, no matter how quickly or sharply he flicks the matchsticks. Perhaps some sea spray has got into his pockets.

The shorter of the other two tugs back his anorak hood to reveal a shock of blond hair, then pulls a disposable lighter from his pocket. You rarely see them in the Republic – a relative in the West must have sent him it. Either that, or he bought it from an Intershop. 'Here,' he says, proffering it to Dieter. 'Try this.'

With the lighter, Dieter succeeds in lighting the candle. He tips it so the wax falls onto a table in the centre of the room, then turns it upright and presses the bottom end into the molten wax, holding it in place until it's set. The blond guy – Joachim – pulls a chair from a stack in the corner and sets it up for me by the table. Then he does the same for the others. Dieter sits next to me, then Holger pulls some cigarette papers from his pocket, and starts rolling a cigarette. At the same time, Joachim is heating the corner of a block of dark resin above the candle flame.

Once he's satisfied, he starts crumbling it into Holger's half-open cigarette – spreading it out over the tobacco. I feel slightly disappointed. With all the subterfuge, the walk to the end of the harbour, I thought they were about to discuss something exciting. Instead, it just seems to be a jaunt to get stoned on dope.

Once Joachim's finished, Holger rolls up the home-made spliff and lights it with the candle. After a few sucks, he passes it to Joachim who takes his turn, then gives it to Dieter. He takes a long drag, lets his head fall back as he savours the smoke, then offers it to me. I shake my head. They don't seem bothered that I don't want to take part. What they don't know is the reason why. Since all the trouble a few years ago, I don't want my tongue loosened. I'm not proud of the way I've agreed to work with the Stasi – and I don't want to reveal what I do in an unguarded moment, even though – in reality – all the information I provide is deliberately useless. If Dieter found out, I can tell he would dump me straight away and the other two would have nothing to do with me either. They're refuseniks – the nearest thing this Republic has to out-and-out rebels. Co-operating with the Stasi is the last thing they'd agree to do. It's the last thing I'd have agreed to do, if they'd left me with any choice. They didn't.

By the time I catch the bus back to Sellin via Bergen, I feel slightly cheated. Why did Dieter take me with him, if all he was going to do was get off his face? Maybe I've been a bit too gung-ho in getting rid of Laurenz. That's what my grandmother always says about me – that I'm always thinking the cherries in the neighbour's garden taste sweeter.

My heart sinks as I see a round-faced, bespectacled man walking down the aisle towards me. I look out of the window, hoping he hasn't seen me. But he has. Not only that but he sits in the seat next to me, widening his legs so that his right thigh is pressed hard up against mine. I try to shuffle to the side, but I'm squashed against the window – I can't.

'Hello, Irma. Fancy meeting you here.' There's a smarmy note in his voice. We both know this is no coincidental meeting. I wonder if he was following me at the harbour. I wonder if he followed me all the way from Sellin earlier in the day without me spotting. I need to be more careful.

'*Hauptmann* Steiger.' I nod slightly, but don't turn to meet his eyes.

Suddenly, his mouth is up against my ear. 'You know the drill, Wildcat.' The use of my code name is dripping with sarcasm. 'Don't ever call me *Hauptmann* in public. To you, I'm just Herr Steiger, an old family friend.'

I nod again slightly, to acknowledge the whispered admonishment.

He leans back in the bus seat and starts to talk aloud again.

'I thought I saw you with a new boyfriend, Irma. Is that correct?' There's a syrupy, insincere note to his apparently friendly tone.

'Yes, that's right.'

'He lives in an apartment block in Binz, doesn't he? Well, not Binz, exactly. A little to the west.' We both know what he's driving at. The 'apartment block' he's referring to is the construction soldiers' barracks at the far end of Prora. 'I wouldn't have thought a girl from a good family like yours would be wanting to mix with someone like that.' *Good family! Ha!* Thanks to my mother we're a targeted family – always have been, always will be. 'Do you understand what I'm saying, Irma?' Then he drops his voice to a whisper again and leans in close, squeezing my thigh far too close to my groin and far too fiercely, like he wants to hurt me. Like he wants me to remember my place, my shame. 'On second thoughts,' he hisses, 'having someone like you watch over those sorts and get inside their heads might be useful. Make sure you ring me soon with a full report. And I'd get some stronger deodorant if I were you, or perhaps start sucking mints. You stink of marijuana, Wildcat.'

With that he gives one final jab of his finger into my thigh, then gets up to leave. The driver has just started the engine and is about to pull away. 'I seem to be on the wrong bus, Irma,' he says, out loud again. 'But I look forward to bumping into you again, soon. Give my regards to your mother.'

When he mentions her and turns away, marching up the bus as though he has important business elsewhere, I feel my eyes prickling. But I fight back the tears. They may have broken my mother, sent her to the worst women's prison possible in Hoheneck, so far south that Oma and I can only visit very rarely. But Steiger and his kind will not break me.

I will never allow that to happen.

12

It wasn't how Müller had expected to be spending New Year's Eve. Instead of going out for a walk in Berlin with Helga and the twins, she and Tilsner were off for a spot of skiing. But this wasn't the winter sport she was used to in Oberhof. The People's Army *Fallschirmjäger* – the paratroop unit, also based at Prora – had visited their hotel to kit the two detectives out with cross-country ski equipment to facilitate the house-to-house inquiries they planned. In order not to raise suspicions, the two detectives would be using their old *Volkspolizei* IDs. To all intents and purposes, they were two uniform police officers looking into how a middle-aged woman came to be stranded out in the driving snow after a shopping trip – leading to her demise. Their uniforms would be a pair of winter suits provided by the army.

Tilsner couldn't help guffawing with laughter when he saw Müller's.

'You look like the abominable snowman. It's much too big for you.'

'Equality only goes so far in this Republic. They didn't have any women's sizes – this was the smallest suit available.'

Some strategically placed shoelaces managed to make the suit just about useable. They kept the suit legs from dragging on the ground, and the arms from overwhelming her gloves. Using her ski poles to propel her, Müller set off in a skating motion down the road towards where Richter's body had been discovered at the western edge of the town, behind the pedestrian promenade. She didn't need Tilsner to remind her that the last time they'd been on skis together, they'd both nearly been killed on the slopes of the Brocken – the Republic's second-highest mountain. Tilsner had saved her – but in doing so had been severely wounded. Nearly four years later, there were no visible signs of his former injuries – but he'd been in hospital for months. At one point, it was touch and go whether he'd survive.

The idea of house-to-house inquiries, searching for witnesses to what had happened, soon became almost redundant. Frau Richter had perished on a forested track a few hundred metres outside Binz's town boundary – it seemed as though she'd been heading back to *Jugendwerkhof Prora Ost*. But there were few – if any – residential homes in the vicinity.

Both detectives found the going tough, their skis sinking into the soft snow rather than gliding on top. So much of it was wind-blown, they seemed to be travelling from drift to drift, making painfully slow progress.

Müller was soon out of breath. 'How much further?' she panted, as Tilsner brushed snow away from his cellophane-covered map.

'By my reckoning, only a hundred metres or so. Just along here.'

The surroundings were deathly quiet. Usually, Müller thought, there ought at least to be some traffic on the nearby road between Binz and Sassnitz – it was only a hundred metres or so to their left. But apart from the occasional roar and clatter of an army personnel carrier, the road was empty and impass-able. The drifts alongside had occasional humps which Müller could only imagine concealed abandoned cars. There was a rail line too – she could see the signals, poking from the snow like trees whose branches had been stripped, their white painted uprights near invisible, the red of the painted metal signal flags on top making them stand out.

They set off again, willing themselves to ski those last few metres.

'Must have been just about here,' said Tilsner.

Müller swivelled her head around, first pushing the sides of her hood behind her ears. Immediately, she could feel the sting of the snow-laden wind lashing her skin.

To one side, almost buried by snow, she could see some red-and-white striped police tape flapping in the wind. Tilsner followed her eyeline and had seen it too.

'I don't think that's really doing its job in sealing off the area properly!' he shouted.

Müller surveyed the snow-covered ground. 'It's probably not needed. There are no footprints. No one's ventured here recently. And I don't blame them.' Over to the left, she spot-ted a low single-storey building. It looked as though it might be a house – although it could equally well be some sort of store associated with Prora. She knew Hitler's half-finished holiday complex – which housed both the *Jugendwerkhof* at one end and the People's Army barracks at the other – couldn't be far away. She shivered – multiple layers of clothing, gloves, thick socks and ski boots failing to keep out the cold. But she also breathed in deeply. The bitterly cold air, mixed with the faint redolence of pine from the prevailing trees, had her thinking of her child-hood home.

The snow.

The low forested mountains of Thuringia.

And the fairy-tale-like bed and breakfast house where she'd always felt like an outsider. Not unlike the building in front of them. She'd discovered three years earlier that those feelings of not belonging weren't in her imagination. She'd been adopted – and perhaps her adoptive mother Rosamund had never been able to love her as unconditionally as her own naturally conceived children: Müller's adoptive sister, Sara, and brother, Roland.

Tilsner rapped on the door. There was no sign of life inside the house – if it was indeed a house – so Müller was surprised when the door was opened a crack. Half of an elderly woman's face appeared.

'Aha! You've finally arrived. I've been waiting for you. I'm half-starved!' the woman shouted out round the door frame, almost as though she herself was deaf, and unable to modulate her voice.

Tilsner raised his voice to match the level of hers. 'We're not your personal food delivery service, I can assure you, citizen.'

He brandished his *Vopo* ID. 'Police. Open up. We need to ask you some questions.'

'All right,' the woman grumbled, opening the door fully. 'You can come in if you insist. Make sure you clean the snow off your shoes first. I don't want to have to clear up after you.'

Inside the house felt no warmer to Müller than outside. She started to take her anorak top off, then thought better of it. She wasn't sure the old crone was going to be much help anyway. There was no point freezing to death while asking her their questions.

'Haven't you got a fire burning, Frau . . . ?'

'Winter.'

'It certainly is,' responded Tilsner. 'That's why you need a fire.'

'No, my surname's Winter. What they say about the *Volkspolizei* is clearly true.'

Müller thought briefly about admonishing the woman for her rudeness, but Tilsner seemed to laugh it off.

'It is true, yes, Frau Winter. We're all as thick as two short planks.' Then the laughter in his voice died. 'But don't get clever with me. It might be cold in your house, and you may be too tight to light a fire, but I can assure you if I arrest you and take you to the remand centre at Bergen it will be far, far colder. So I suggest you forget your jokes about the police and answer our questions. All of them.'

The woman sat down heavily into the only chair in what seemed to pass as a living room, pulled a rug over herself, and adopted an even sourer expression. 'If it's about that woman found dead out there, I've already told the local police all I know.'

'What makes you think we're not local?' asked Tilsner.

'Your accents, love. Berlin, I should think. Am I right?'

Müller nodded.

'I'm sure you have your fires blazing away there, don't you? Central heating in every room too, probably. All the best stuff is reserved for Berlin. We're just an afterthought.'

There was nowhere else for Müller and Tilsner to sit. It appeared that Frau Winter was determined to be less than co-operative, and her house stank. A mixture of damp and something sweeter. Müller mentally recoiled as she suddenly recognised the smell – cat urine. The room was cold, too. The woman was either too mean or too poor to light a fire. Müller was keen to get the questioning over and move on to the next house.

'So, Frau Winter,' she said, 'you know the woman's body was discovered within a few metres of your house. Did you see anything suspicious in the days beforehand? Did you see the deceased before her death?'

The woman glowered at Müller, and for a moment the detective thought her question would remain unanswered.

'Come on!' shouted Tilsner, banging his fist down on a side table, rattling its sad collection of old ornaments, and sending up a cloud of dust. 'We haven't got all day.'

'I don't recall seeing her alive. Mind you, you haven't shown me a photograph of what she looks like. But there was something odd, yes.'

'What?' prompted Müller.

'Some soldiers with a sled.'

It wasn't *that* unusual in these conditions. She knew the army had been helping to deliver supplies – mostly by personnel carrier, but presumably someone had to distribute the food and fuel to other smaller, locations. Perhaps they used sleds – she'd seen some when they arrived on the helicopter at the barracks. They certainly couldn't use cars.

'And why do you think that might be connected with the woman's death?' asked Müller.

The woman frowned, then wiped her wispy white hair away from her leathery forehead. 'Well, I don't know that it was. You're just asking me if I could remember anything unusual.'

'Why was it unusual?' asked Tilsner. 'Everyone knows the army has been helping to deliver food supplies.'

Frau Winter shot him a withering look. 'I'm getting to it. Give me a chance. The reason I noticed them was I'd been waiting for an emergency delivery of food myself. I still am. I saw them through the net curtains, so I went round to unlock the door. As you saw earlier, the lock's a bit stiff. It took me a while to open it.' She paused and coughed to clear her throat. It turned into a hacking fit, until she seemed to be struggling for breath. Müller suddenly felt sorry for her, and leant over to try to pat her on the back – but Frau Winter shrank away.

'You really should light a fire, Frau Winter,' she said. 'You don't sound very well.'

The woman composed herself. 'I'll be all right. But I can't light a fire – I've run out of coal and wood, as well as food.'

'You were saying about the soldiers,' Tilsner reminded her.

'Yes. I was waiting for them to knock on the door, but they didn't. So I poked my head outside. That was when the worst of the snow was coming down. Visibility was very low, and I had to fight to stay on my feet because of the wind.'

'Could you still see them?' asked Müller.

'Just about, although they were skiing or sledding away from me, back towards Prora. I called after them thinking they'd missed my delivery by mistake.'

'Did they stop?'

The woman responded to Müller's question with a headshake. 'Either they couldn't hear me, or they didn't want to hear me.'

Tilsner sighed. 'Thank you, Frau Winter. But you said this was in some way unusual. In what way was it unusual?'

'Well, I can't be certain. As I say, visibility was bad. But I was really angry they hadn't delivered me anything – as they disappeared from view I was concentrating on the contents of the sled.'

'And?' prompted Müller.

'That's it. There didn't seem to *be* any contents any more. Just an empty tarpaulin.'

Tilsner scratched his chin. 'But when you'd first seen them through the window, when you rushed to unlock your door thinking they were here to bring you food, or fuel, or both – at that point there *was* something on the sled?'

The woman drew in a long breath which rattled in her rheumy throat. 'Hmm. I'm fairly sure there was. Otherwise why would I have assumed they were bringing emergency supplies? They were very near where the woman's body was found later – under that drift. And yes . . . yes, I'm sure there was something under the tarpaulin.'

'You're *sure*?' checked Müller. 'You're *certain*?'

'Well . . . I think so.' She waved her spectacles in the air. 'My eyes aren't that good, and as I say, visibility was awful.'

'And you say they were going *back* to Prora?' continued Müller. 'Does that mean you saw them arrive from that direction too?'

'Ah, no.' The woman shook her head sadly. 'I just assumed with them being army that that was where they were from.'

'How do you know they were soldiers?' Müller was losing patience. If the woman had seen what she claimed, it might be significant. But as a witness, the detective had little faith in her.

'Well, I think so. They were wearing winter army suits like you two.'

Tilsner rolled his eyes. 'Yes, but we're not soldiers, are we, Frau Winter? We're police.'

The woman shrugged. 'If you say so. Anyway, that's the only thing I saw that might be of any use. And as you *are* from the authorities, could you please make sure I'm not forgotten when they make the next delivery?'

With a small, exasperated shake of her head, Müller indicated to Tilsner it was time to go. She felt some pity for the woman. Remembering she had a packet of chocolate balls in her pocket – stored because she was worried they might get snowed in somewhere and need energy – Müller pulled it out and offered it to the woman.

Her face turned into a grimace. 'Oh no, I can't stand milk chocolate, dear. I only like the dark stuff.'

Outside, they skied to the fluttering police tape again.

'Do you think she was telling the truth?' asked Tilsner, his breath condensing in front of his face.

Müller shrugged. 'I'm sure she wasn't deliberately lying. She might have seen something. It could even have been Richter's body on the sled and they could have been the killers. Equally, it could have been soldiers with an empty sled. She might have assumed there was something on there to start with because that's what she wanted to think, hoping they were bringing her food.'

'What next?'

Putting her ski gloves back on, Müller pushed herself off with one ski and began to skate past Tilsner. 'There must be some other houses or flats nearby. We need to find more reliable witnesses.' She slid to a stop. 'And maybe we need a rethink. Perhaps we're going about this the wrong way.'

After another fifty metres or so, another house emerged from the mist and light snowfall. This was a two-storey, red brick affair. At first, Müller thought it might be some sort of railway building. But as they drew closer, from the woodshed and garage it became clear someone lived there.

They skied to the front gate and then stepped out of their bindings and propped their skis against the white picket fence that surrounded the property.

'This looks a bit more promising,' said Tilsner. 'Someone who knows how to look after their property. Perhaps they might have their wits about them, unlike grumpy guts Frau Winter.'

Müller didn't bother to reply, and strode up the freshly cleared path and knocked on the front door.

The man who opened the door listened to what Müller had to say about the woman's body, and her request to ask him a few questions, but he didn't move aside.

'I don't think I can help you,' he said.

'I'm sorry?' replied Müller. She wasn't used to people refusing to co-operate with the police.

'I'm not being unhelpful. It's just that I haven't seen anything, and in any case, like you I work for the authorities. They should have let you know.'

'What do you mean by that?' asked Tilsner, the menace in his voice undisguised.

'The People's Police – or indeed the Ministry for State Security – should have let you know that I live here with my family and that we shouldn't be disturbed.'

'Why the hell shouldn't we disturb you?' said Tilsner. 'If you like I can break your door down.'

'I don't think that will be necessary,' said the man, reaching into his jacket pocket. He produced an ID and thrust it at Müller.

Even before she'd read his name, she knew he was right. They wouldn't get anywhere here. The emblem on the identity card showed her all she needed to know. An arm holding up a rifle, with a bayonet on its end and the East German flag fluttering from it.

She read his name and rank. *Hauptmann* Gerd Steiger of the *Ministerium für Staatssicherheit*, based in Bergen auf Rügen.

A Stasi captain.

'I understand *Oberst* Jäger has arrived from Berlin to take charge of this case. If you want to interview me, you'll have to get his permission first. I'm on a day off and I'm rather busy. If you don't mind . . . ' Steiger started to shut the door in their faces. Müller was tempted to stick her foot in the frame, but thought better of it and turned on her heels.

At the hotel, Tilsner insisted he wanted a coffee to warm his insides before they decided what to do next. He lowered his voice. 'Maybe we should get in touch with Jäger. I don't want Stasi upstarts like that Steiger bloke telling us what we can and cannot do.'

Müller shrugged. Coffee seemed like an excellent idea. Contacting Jäger? She wasn't so sure.

After a quick trip to her room to fix her make-up, she met Tilsner in the restaurant a few minutes later – in the same semi-private booth they'd eaten in the previous evening.

As well as the coffees, Tilsner had ordered shots of schnapps. He offered Müller hers. She shook her head, so Tilsner proceeded to down both in one gulp then smacked his lips. 'See,' he said. 'I didn't bang my glass down on the table.'

Müller knew what he was referring to, but didn't appreciate his feeble attempt at a joke. Banging your schnapps glass down after emptying the contents down one's throat was supposed to be the fascist way of drinking it. She'd decided – reluctantly – to forget his wartime indiscretions for the moment. Perhaps Reiniger was right after all. He'd been a teenage boy – he couldn't be held responsible. But she didn't want reminding of it.

'What do you suggest next, boss?'

'We don't seem to have any witnesses, unless we count Frau Winter. And with the weather, to be honest I don't think we will make progress in that direction. We need to concentrate on Richter. Did she have any enemies?'

Tilsner snorted. 'Having met the revolting woman, I can assure you she'll have had more enemies than we've had hot coffees. For a start, anyone who attended that *Jugendwerkhof*. But I don't think that'll be the end of the list.'

'I still think that's our best way of making progress.'

'But as soon as we start asking questions like that, doesn't it become obvious we don't believe her death was an accident? What about asking that girl you saved from the reform school?'

'Irma Behrendt?' The return to Rügen had in itself been an uncomfortable reminder to Müller of the graveyard girl case from four years earlier. She and Irma had at one stage been incarcerated together by the *Jugendwerkhof's* former director, Franz Neumann, after she and Tilsner had tracked him to his lair on the foothills of the Brocken mountain. Neumann was an abuser who Müller had her own private reasons to hate. So she felt some sort of misplaced loyalty towards Irma, who would now be a young woman. Müller also knew the girl had been a favourite of her ex-husband Gottfried, during his ill-fated stint teaching at the reform school.

Tilsner nodded.

'Why should she know anything?'

'She may not. But you pretty much saved her life, didn't you? Or at least she thinks so. In fact, I probably had more to do with it.'

'By radioing for Jäger's help?'

Tilsner shot her a sarcastic grin.

'OK, I suppose it's not a bad idea. She may have friends who stayed on at the reform school after she left. Although I have to tell you, Jäger intimated that he'd managed to turn her.'

'To work for his lot?'

'That's the impression I got. Part of the deal to allow her to stay with her grandmother rather being sent back to *Jugendwerkhof Prora Ost*.'

Tilsner rubbed his hands together. 'Well then, that's to our advantage. If she's working for them, she's used to reporting on people. Perhaps even following them. She may have her ears to the ground.'

'But she lives in Sellin. I presume Richter lived in the *Jugendwerkhof* itself. They're kilometres away from each other.'

'It's an island. There's not many places to go. You'd be surprised how many people know each other, how many marriages are intermingled, that sort of thing. And she must have roots somewhere else, before she came to work at the reform school. I'll get on to the People's Police here and ask them.'

'Remember, she hasn't been identified yet,' said Müller.

'They must have reported her missing from the reform school by now, surely?'

Müller nodded. 'OK. Touch base again with Bergen People's Police, and I'll try to track down our Miss Behrendt, though I don't know how co-operative she'll be. And I'm not sure how the hell I'll get to Sellin in this weather. After that, we need to think how we'll ask questions at the *Jugendwerkhof* without raising suspicions. Perhaps at the *Fallschirmjäger* base in Prora too.'

13

Knowing the logistics of getting from Binz to Sellin were likely to prove difficult, Müller checked with the People's Army emergency co-ordinator that it was actually possible. It was, by hitching a lift on a personnel carrier to the supply depot at Bergen, in the centre of the island, and another to the coast. But there was no point turning up at the campsite run by Irma's grandmother unannounced – much though Müller favoured the element of surprise. The campsite would be closed for the winter. There was no guarantee either Irma – or her grandmother – would be in residence.

When she rang the phone number, she half expected no one would pick up. But after a few seconds an elderly woman's voice came on the line.

'People's Camping Ground Sellin. I'm afraid we're closed.'

'Is that Frau Behrendt?' asked Müller.

'I'm Irma's grandmother, if that's what you mean. My surname is actually Baumgartner. Or were you wanting my daughter?' There was a catch in the woman's voice. 'If so, I'm afraid she's unavailable.' Müller was aware of that – Jäger had informed her the woman was back in jail. He hadn't said why, but given her past history as related by her daughter Irma, Müller could guess.

'It's actually Irma I want to speak to. Is she there?'

'She is, yes.' The woman sounded wary. Had she recognised Müller's voice? After all, she and Schmidt had spent an hour or so interviewing her about her missing daughter nearly four years previously. 'Can I ask who's calling?' Clearly, time – and the fact that she wasn't seeing the detective in person – had rendered Frau Baumgartner forgetful. Müller chided herself – she'd known Irma's grandmother didn't share her granddaughter's surname. Time had erased that from her memory too: a memory that Müller normally prided herself on being near photographic.

'It's *Major* Karin Müller of the *Kriminalpolizei*.' She heard the woman give a slight gasp. 'Don't worry, Irma's not in any trouble. It's simply that I've been sent to Rügen on a case, and Irma and I . . . well, as you know, we went through a lot together in the Harz mountains that time, as she's probably told you.'

Frau Baumgartner still sounded wary. No doubt having a daughter incarcerated did that to you, thought Müller. 'She mentioned it, I think,' said the woman.

'Well, I thought it would be nice to meet her as I'm here, and catch up on her news.'

Perhaps Müller sounded friendly. The woman seemed to thaw. 'Of course. I'll get her for you. I think she's clearing the snow off the roof of the toilet block. We're a bit worried it might collapse. There's been so much of it. It'll be a couple of minutes while I fetch her for you.'

Müller was ringing from her hotel room. She spent the time looking at her reflection in the bedroom mirror. Was that a crow's foot in the corner of her eye? She smoothed it out and told herself it wasn't. In this weather, anyone's skin would dry out. There had been the white hair she'd found the other week. A single mother, in her early thirties. Still attractive, perhaps. But with Emil out of the picture – thank God! – it was time she found someone else to share her life with. Someone who could be a good father to the twins and, more to the point, someone who would stop her being an old maid married to her work.

The line crackled as someone picked up the handset.

'Frau Müller,' a young woman's voice said. 'What a lovely surprise. And a major now too, my grandmother tells me. I'm honoured, *Major* Müller.'

There was a hint of sarcasm in Irma's voice, but she sounded genuinely pleased to have received the call.

'It's good to hear your voice, Irma. You sound much more grown-up now.'

'I suppose I am, *Major* Müller. But still the same girl at heart.'

'Still a bit of a rebel?' Müller wanted to take back the words as soon as she'd uttered them. But Irma seemed unfazed.

'Oh no. I'm a good citizen.' She gave a tinkling laugh. 'A right virtuous little lamb.'

'That's good to hear, Irma. But you were put through a lot when all that happened, I felt for you.' Müller paused, but Irma said nothing. Instead, Müller got round to the point of the call. 'Your grandmother may have mentioned that I'm visiting Rügen on a case. As you're one of the few islanders I know, I wondered if I could buy you a coffee and pick your brains for a bit of local knowledge.'

It sounded a little lame, and Müller could hear the hesitation – perhaps even wariness – in Irma's reply.

'Well . . . that would be nice, of course. But I don't know if anything's open in this weather. And I'm pretty much trapped in Sellin.'

'Don't worry, I can come to you. Isn't there a café open where people can warm themselves?'

'Most of them are seasonal,' said Irma. Then, and it sounded to Müller as though it was slightly reluctantly, she came up with a suggestion. 'There's a café halfway along Wilhelm-Pieck-Straße – the street that leads to the coast and what remains of the Seebrücke. Would that suit you?'

'Perfect.' Müller looked at her watch. With having to go via Bergen and using army transport, she'd have to leave enough time. 'Shall we say in two hours? At noon.'

'I'll see you then,' the girl replied. Müller couldn't be sure, but there seemed a note of reticence. There again, passing the time of day with a police officer – especially in the Republic – probably wasn't every citizen's number one choice of activity.

Müller was a few minutes late. She'd overestimated how regularly supply vehicles would be heading to Sellin from Bergen, especially on New Year's Eve. As she opened the café door, and luxuriated in the sudden suffusion of warmth after the bitterness outside, she spotted Irma's shock of red hair. The girl was sitting in the corner, near the open fire. Seeing her, Müller almost felt maternal – she was glad that she appeared healthy, and hadn't succumbed to the latest craze of punk hairstyles which seemed to be being imported from the West.

Irma started to stand as Müller approached, and the detective moved towards her as though to offer a hug. Instead, Irma rather formally extended her hand, and Müller shook it, aware her own hand was still icy from the journey.

'Cold hands,' laughed Irma. 'At least you'll be able to warm them up in here.'

'It's good to see you after so long, Irma. You're looking well.'

The girl reddened under Müller's gaze. 'Oh, I don't know about that. Life's OK, I suppose. I'm still working at the campsite, though.'

'You didn't fancy university?'

Irma snorted. 'With my past, and my mother's track record? They would never accept me. You must know that, surely?'

Müller felt a tug of anger. The girl had done little wrong – well, perhaps that wasn't strictly true, given two people had died by her hand – and one of those killings, Müller had witnessed. But no charges had been laid. In reality, there was nothing that should hold Irma back, and she certainly used to be determined enough, thought Müller. But one of the shortcomings of the Republic was that the sins of the parents often led to disadvantages for their offspring. With her mother in jail for counter-revolutionary or dissident activities, Müller knew that Irma had little or no chance of entering higher education. It had been foolish to mention it.

'Sorry. It's ridiculous, but yes, I'm aware of your mother's situation and how that must affect you. You don't seem to be letting it get you down, though.'

The girl shrugged. 'I do all right for myself.'

'Anyway,' said Müller, rubbing her hands together in the direction of the fire to try to warm them, 'what would you like to drink? I'm buying, of course. And if you want to order something to eat too . . .'

'Thank you. But a coffee is fine.'

Once the coffees were in front of them, Müller turned the conversation round to the matter in hand – though she was aware she still had to tread carefully.

'Do you keep in touch with anyone from the *Jugendwerkhof*?'

Irma gave her a fierce look. Then mouthed a 'shush'. This time it was Müller's turn to blush. It had been stupid of her to ask the question while others could overhear. It was a period in her life that Irma would almost certainly want to forget. Attending the reform school was a badge of shame that she didn't want advertised, and Müller should have been more sensitive to the girl's feelings. She steered the conversation to neutral territory, asking about the weather, how Irma and her grandmother were coping. Irma asked Müller about her former husband, Gottfried. Müller gave a heavily abridged version of the truth, admitting that they'd broken up and that he had since unfortunately died – without going into the gory details as to how. She didn't want to remember the hooded excursion to the forest north of Berlin – to what Jäger had assured her was

Gottfried's execution site, despite the fact that she'd received a letter from her husband postmarked in the BRD indicating he was still alive. She could only assume, now, that his letter had been faked by the Stasi. The more she'd learnt of their methods, the more feasible that seemed.

Once their conversation was exhausted, Müller tried to finish the coffee as quickly as possible – hoping Irma would follow suit. When she had, Müller made it clear she was ready to leave.

'I'll walk you back to the campsite,' she said.

'Oh, you don't have to. I'll be fine on my own.'

'No, I insist,' said Müller. 'Conditions underfoot are awful. I couldn't forgive myself if you fell when it was me who urged you to come out to the café in the first place.'

Wilhelm-Pieck-Straße had been partially cleared of snow – or at least a pathway had been trampled down its midsection. There was little or no traffic venturing out, other than army vehicles.

As they fell into step together, Müller apologised.

'I'm sorry. That was stupid of me. You probably don't want your time there broadcast to all and sundry.'

'It's OK,' shrugged Irma. 'I guess you weren't to know.'

'If I tell you something, can I trust you to keep it secret?'

'Of course,' said Irma.

'The case I'm working on, it concerns the *Jugendwerkhof.*'

Irma didn't say anything. She seemed to be concentrating on watching where she was putting her feet, ensuring she didn't slip on the narrow and icy path cleared through the snowdrifts.

'It's someone you never got on with.'

Irma was still silent. *Isn't she curious?* thought Müller.

'You know the woman who was found dead near Binz?'

'I'd heard of it, yes, of course.' Irma was head down, as though feigning disinterest. Müller thought the girl's face had coloured up – but perhaps it was the icy wind coming in off the Ostsee.

'They're saying the woman hasn't been identified. But I knew who it was as soon as I saw the body in the mortuary. If I tell you, you mustn't repeat it, and you mustn't say the information came from me.'

'Perhaps it's better I don't know, then.' It wasn't the reaction Müller was expecting. She'd anticipated a little inquisitiveness on the part of the girl. Whatever, Müller was determined to tell her – and hang the consequences. If Irma still had any connections with former reform school inmates, they might have heard whispers about their former deputy director's fate.

'It was Monika Richter.'

Irma said nothing in response, continued trudging along the path, seemingly watching her step even more carefully.

'I was wondering if you knew anyone . . . anyone that had a particular grudge against her.'

The girl stopped dead, and stared Müller down. 'You're not suggesting I did it, I hope?'

Müller sighed, shaking her head. 'No, of course not. And officially she died of natural causes.'

'And that's why they sent you all the way from Berlin? Pull the other one!'

Müller exhaled slowly, then continued to walk. 'OK. You're right. But you must not talk to anyone about any of this. And to return to my question, do you know anybody who would wish Frau Richter harm?'

Throwing her head back so that her red hair escaped from the anorak hood, Irma shook with laughter. 'Oh my God. The list of people who'd want her out of the way would probably stretch from here to Sweden.' She turned to Müller, her face deadly serious. 'You've met her. Other than Neumann, the old director, I find it hard to think of a nastier, more vicious person. I didn't do it, but if someone else did, I'm glad. If you find them, please introduce me. I'd love to buy them a drink to celebrate.'

'So you don't think you can help?' pleaded Müller.

'I'll have a think. I owe you that, I suppose. But I can't promise you anything. I have nothing to do with that place any more, thank God, and don't want reminding of it.'

Müller understood the way Irma felt, though her vehemence was a little surprising. By now, they'd reached the run-down white clapboard house that served as Irma and her grandmother's home, as well as the campsite reception.

'I guess this is goodbye,' said the girl. 'Thanks for the coffee. If I do think of anything, is there a number I can call you on?'

'Just ask for the FDGB Heim Rugard in Binz. Room 1041. If I'm not in, leave a message and I'll ring you back at the campsite.' She smiled at the girl. Her maternal feelings were back. They'd been held in captivity together on the slopes of the Brocken, and faced what looked like certain death together. *Maybe I'll always think fondly of her*, thought Müller. She pulled the girl – now a young woman – in for a hug.

'Look after yourself, Irma. You'll make someone a fine wife one day.'

'Ha!' laughed the girl. 'That should be the limit of my ambitions, should it?'

'No, of course not.' Müller squeezed her hard. 'That's not what I meant.'

Irma pulled away but continued to hold the policewoman's gloved hands. 'I know it wasn't. And thank you. Actually, there is someone.' She grinned shyly.

'He's asked you to marry him?'

'No, of course not. It's far too soon. But he's nice. You'd like him. He's a bit of a rebel like me, though. He wouldn't approve of me having a policewoman as a friend.' She gave Müller a broad smile.

'I'll be seeing you, Irma,' said Müller as she turned to go.

'Maybe. Who knows?'

Once she was back at the hotel in Binz, Müller made a point of tracking down Schmidt. She'd asked him to liaise with Dr Tritten and go over exactly what the young pathologist had discovered.

She found the forensic scientist in his room, at the back of the hotel, overlooking the road. Both he and Tilsner seemed to have drawn the short straw – it was a smaller room, without a view. Unlike Müller's, which was more the size of a suite with private bathroom, balcony and magnificent view of the prom-enade and – through the trees – the frozen Ostsee.

'Ah, Comrade *Major*. Just the person I wanted to see,' said Schmidt as he opened the door. Once he'd closed it, he asked if she and Tilsner had made any progress with the inquiry.

'Remarkably little, Jonas, I'm afraid. What about you? How did you get on with Dr Tritten? I phoned her earlier and asked her to co-operate fully with you, with my authority.'

'Yes. She was open and helpful. Or at least, that's the way it seemed to me.'

Müller surveyed Schmidt's room. It was a mess already, with papers strewn over the desk. 'But did she have anything new to tell you, anything that might lead us to a breakthrough?'

'Not really. But there were one or two interesting things.'

Müller sat on the bed, while Schmidt took the chair by the desk. 'Go on. Tell me more.'

'Well, in her view the level of succinylcholine used had been precisely calculated. The correct level to induce almost complete paralysis.'

'Does that tell us anything?'

'Possibly not,' said Schmidt. 'But it might be an indication that the perpetrator had some sort of medical training. Perhaps as an anaesthetist.'

'In a hospital?'

'Who can say, Comrade Müller?' Müller mentally winced at her forensic scientist's continued refusal to use first names. It grated on her – but he was never going to change. She'd tried hard enough. 'It's one possibility, of course,' he continued. 'But not the only one.'

'Anything else of interest?'

'Yes, there was. Although at this stage it's only speculation.'

'There's nothing wrong with speculation, Jonas.'

The *Kriminaltechniker* pushed his thick spectacles back up his nose. Their heaviness caused them almost immediately to slide down again. 'No, of course not. But I chewed the fat with the young doctor over where someone might get hold of sufficient quantities of this succinylcholine.'

'Presumably in a hospital?'

'Well, yes. But interestingly, that wasn't Dr Tritten's first answer. I think it was because I asked her where the *nearest* place would be where one might find stocks of the drug.'

'And where's that?' As she asked the question, Müller could predict the answer. And perhaps it made Frau Winter's account of what she allegedly saw a little more believable.

'At Prora, Comrade *Major*. The People's Army barracks at Prora. Army medics need to carry stocks in case of injuries in battle, and while we're not – of course – at war at the moment, and heaven hope we never will be, they need to have supplies in case they have to operate in the field.'

Prora. It was a guess, of course. But Hitler's unfinished, monolithic holiday camp had a nasty habit of rearing its head at every opportunity. For Müller, it was a lead worth pursuing.

14

We're back in the room below the lighthouse. It amazes me that Dieter, Joachim and Holger feel this is a safe place to meet. It's a new light – unmanned and automatic – but I would have thought it's still of strategic importance to the Republic, surely? Someone must keep an eye on it. But the boys seem confident no one will disturb us once the construction brigade's shift is over, and the guard has disappeared for the day.

Dieter lights a candle again – like the last time. I assume it's going to be another round of dope smoking – if so, I've said to myself that this time maybe I'll take a few hits to show I'm one of the gang. I don't want Dieter thinking I'm a square.

But I'm surprised when – instead of taking a block of hash from his pocket – Joachim pulls out a sheaf of papers.

'Should we really be writing things down?' asks Dieter. 'Isn't that asking for trouble?'

Joachim glares at him, flicks his eyeline towards me. '*Asking for trouble*, as you put it, is having her here. I thought we'd agreed it was just us three? The more of us there are, the harder it will be.'

'I don't want to do it without her,' counters Dieter.

Joachim looks at Holger. The other youth shrugs. 'We need Dieter's expertise.'

There's a long sigh from Joachim, as though he knows he's outnumbered. 'Very well. Have you told her anything about it? How do we know we can trust her? How do we know she's not a 110-per-cent-er, living and breathing all the propaganda lies?'

I feel my face burning at the insult. At least, I think it's because of the insult. Perhaps it's more the guilt. They don't know that – at least officially – I already supply information to the authorities. They have no idea that less than half an hour after our last 'meeting' here, my Stasi handler had sidled next to me on the bus, placed his hand on my thigh, and given me explicit warnings about mixing with 'their sort'.

'You can trust me,' I lie. I wish it were true, and I hate myself that it isn't.

'There,' said Dieter, squeezing my thigh in the same place as Steiger did, but with affection – not the sadistic malice shown by the Stasi captain. 'You have the word of a lady.' He looks daggers at Joachim. '*My* lady.'

Joachim throws his arms in the air. 'OK. Have it your way. You'd better tell her what it's all about then. But as soon as she knows, she's in. There's no backing out. We won't let her. Are you sure you want that, Irma?'

I meet his gaze and give a slow nod. Whatever their venture, they don't know who I am. They don't know what I've done.

They don't know that – whatever they're planning – it will be more dangerous and risky to include me. I'm a marked woman. I'm a watched woman . . . by the Stasi. And by taking me into their confidence, little do they know they'll be sharing their scheme with a Stasi informer.

'We're planning to steal a boat,' says Dieter, with a deathly serious look on his handsome face.

'*Steal* a boat? Are you mad?'

'Ha!' exclaims Dieter, slapping his thighs. 'Mad, perhaps. Desperate, perhaps. But I like to think we're determined. Determined to build a better life away from this shitty little country, where we're all trapped behind barbed wire-topped walls and fences equipped with anti-personnel mines. What sort of country does that to its own citizens?'

I know how Dieter feels. I feel it myself. But they don't know that I was once somewhere much worse than a People's Army construction brigade – and I had a better reason than they ever would to want to escape.

And that I tried.

I failed.

And two of those I escaped with ended up dead.

They don't know that, and I'm not going to tell them. And they don't know how much extra danger that puts them in.

'Do you want in?' asks Dieter.

'I told you,' interrupts Joachim. 'As soon as you tell her, she is in. She has no choice. Not unless she wants to end up floating in the harbour alongside the boats.'

Dieter rises to his feet, and grabs Joachim by his lapels. 'Don't you dare threaten her,' he spits.

I lay an arm on my boyfriend's shoulder. 'It's OK. Let him go. I understand. And yes, I want to be a part of it. I desperately want to be a part of it. I hate this fucking country – hate it with all my heart.'

Dieter gives Joachim a final glare then lets him go. Holger sits quietly in the corner, and rolls his eyes at me. I give him a grin.

The band of brave brothers has been joined by a sister.

15

Binz, Island of Rügen, East Germany
New Year's Eve 1978

As she was getting ready for dinner, there was a knock on Müller's door.

'Just a minute,' she called out, grabbing her hotel robe and wrapping it round her underwear-clad body.

Opening the door a fraction, she was surprised – and slightly annoyed – to see it was Jäger.

'Sorry, Karin. Can I come in?' She saw his eyes flick down her body, or what could be seen of it through the narrow gap she'd left in the door. His look didn't improve her mood.

'As you can see, I'm changing for dinner.'

'No matter,' he said. 'I wanted to bring you this.' She realised that he was holding something behind his back. He brought it out and offered it to her. She looked at it quizzically. 'It's a mask – there's a masquerade ball for New Year in the union holiday home next door.'

'We're in the middle of a serious case, Comrade *Oberst*. I'm not really in the mood for celebrating New Year.'

His hand was still outstretched, offering the mask to her. 'It's not optional, Karin. There's a reason for this. Let's meet at that bar again in half an hour's time – bring Tilsner and Schmidt along. I'll explain then.' He held up his other hand, in which he was holding a shopping bag. 'I've got their masks in here – I'll hand them over in the bar.' He still expected Müller to take her own. She made a grab for it, feeling her robe start to fall open as she let go of one lapel – then she slammed the door in his face before she revealed more of herself. She couldn't help thinking that was what he'd planned all along.

'Why do I want to go to a fucking masked ball, in an end-of-the-line town like this one?' moaned Tilsner as they trudged through the snow to the bar. 'You wouldn't see me dead at one in Berlin – and at least in the Hauptstadt there might be some specimens worth dancing with.'

'For once, Comrade Müller, I'm in agreement with Comrade *Hauptmann* Tilsner,' said Schmidt. 'As you can imagine, it's not my sort of thing either. And I can tell you now, I won't be dancing.'

Müller stopped in her tracks and turned to the two men. 'Look, I can assure you, a night out with you two isn't my idea of fun. Neither do I enjoy being ordered around by Jäger, who we don't even officially work for. But we're here, we're doing it, so let's try to enjoy it. It will probably be the nearest thing to enjoyment we'll have all trip.'

She turned and resumed the march to the bar.

'Why all the sour faces?' laughed Jäger. 'I'm glad you'll be wearing masks for the evening – it might be an improvement.'

'There had better be a good reason for this, Comrade *Oberst*,' said Müller, taking off her coat and drawing up a chair. Jäger had already annoyed her with his antics outside the hotel room – not to mention dictating how they should be spending their New Year's Eve. In Müller's view, they'd be better off having a meal and thrashing out the various strands of the case. Her mood had been worsened further by Tilsner and Schmidt's attempts to blame her for the evening's agenda.

'Actually, there is.' The previous evening when Müller had met him here, the bar had been empty. Even now, there was only a handful of customers on what – if it hadn't been for the atrocious weather – should have been one of the busiest nights of the year. But Jäger lowered his voice – he evidently didn't want to broadcast what he was about to say. 'I've got an idea how to advance this case. It involves wearing these masks, I'm afraid.' He waved the two he'd brought for Tilsner and Schmidt – a harlequin jester, and a horned red devil. Müller wondered who'd be getting which. 'The other option was to not go out at all. But I thought we'd all find that a little dull.'

He called the bartender over. 'What will you all have to drink? On me, of course.' Müller doubted that was the case – the expenses would no doubt be met by the Ministry for State Security.

Once they'd put in their drinks orders, Jäger – *sotto voce* again – started to explain his scheme.

'I think you'll agree we may be best served by concentrating our limited resources on Prora. The victim was the director of the *Jugendwerkhof* at the eastern end of the complex. But at the western end, we have the army barracks. Now there are some suggestions – albeit very tenuous – that there might perhaps be a link there. The barracks house a *Fallschirmjäger* company, and the medics attached to that would have access to the medical agent used in . . . the murder of Frau Richter.' The final five words were uttered in a whisper that even Müller struggled to hear. What was more interesting to her was that Jäger seemed to be repeating a speculative theory only voiced to her a short time earlier by Schmidt, who in turn had discussed it with the junior pathologist. Had Jäger worked it out for himself? Or had Dr Tritten – or Schmidt even – briefed him separately? And why was Müller letting him dictate the course of the inquiry?

'There's also, as you know, a People's Army construction brigade housed there. I don't need to tell you that, when we're considering who may be enemies of the Republic, the finger of suspicion points quite readily towards construction soldiers. They're not prepared to fight to defend their homeland, are they? So why should we trust them?'

As he said this, Jäger seemed to be staring pointedly at Schmidt. The forensic scientist was avoiding his gaze. *What's going on here?* thought Müller.

The drinks arrived. Jäger took a sip of his beer, as though to lubricate his voice for the next part of his speech. Tilsner demolished half the contents of his glass in two large gulps. The cola in front of Müller was left untouched. She wasn't thirsty and was avoiding alcohol. The combination of that, a masked ball, and the lecherous look she'd seen on Jäger's face at her hotel room door, spelt danger. Danger she wanted to avoid.

'We're going to need to do a little undercover work if we're going to make any progress. Karin, I've checked which of the staff and inmates at the *Jugendwerkhof* would recognise you. There's been a big turnover of both since all that trouble with the previous director. We've worked out there's only one staff member, and quite probably *none* of the pupils still there. And that staff member is currently on leave.'

'I don't like the sound of this,' said Müller.

'Well, you expressed an interest in teaching. You wrote a very compelling application.'

She could see Tilsner looking at her aghast across the table. She hadn't told him about the plan to teach at the police university – a plan which Reiniger, and no doubt Jäger himself, had thwarted.

'That was at the police university,' she hissed. 'Not a *Jugendwerkhof*. Why would I want to go there? My ex-husband Gottfried actually did teach there for a short while. Look how it ended up for him.'

Jäger's expression was deadpan. 'It's not an option. This has been cleared at the highest levels. With Reiniger. With plenty of people higher than him. Higher than me, even. You will spend a few days undercover at the *Jugendwerkhof*, posing as a new teacher.'

The heat suffused Müller's face. She'd never felt so furious. How had the tables turned again so quickly? She knew about Jäger's past in the war; she'd threatened to expose it to the western press to get a hold over him, yet here he was taking charge again. Treating her – supposedly a major in the People's Police, an organisation he wasn't even part of – like one of his underlings.

'The other part of the plan is a little problematical, although I expected it to be more straightforward.' Müller noticed Schmidt was still staring down at the table, although now his untouched beer was in his eyeline. For some reason, he wouldn't look at Jäger. 'Tilsner is going to be drafted in as a captain in charge of one of the units of construction soldiers. There's one particular group we've been keeping an eye on who're involved in repairing the harbour wall at Sassnitz. Now normally that wouldn't pose a problem. I wouldn't expect any of them to recognise him – why would they, unless they've fallen foul of the criminal police in Berlin at some stage, and we don't think any have. Unfortunately, one of their number is known to him.'

Jäger paused. The silence hung heavily over the table, even though the Stasi colonel's monologue had – so far – been conducted in little more than a whisper. Schmidt shuffled in his seat next to Müller.

'Do you want to tell them, Jonas,' continued Jäger, 'or shall I?'

'It's nothing I'm proud of, Comrade *Oberst*.'

'No, I'm sure it isn't.'

Schmidt looked up at Müller, then across at Tilsner, with a defeated expression on his face. It was something, unfortunately, that Müller was having to get used to. Their last two cases together had seen not dissimilar times when the forensic scientist had appeared thoroughly ashamed, either of his own actions or those of his family.

'It's Markus,' he explained. 'My son, as you both know. He refused to do his National Service in the People's Army – so he was assigned to a construction brigade. He's part of the unit at Prora.'

Müller laid a hand gently on Schmidt's arm. 'Why didn't you say before, Jonas? Standing up for your principles is nothing to be ashamed of, as far as I'm concerned. You should be proud of him.'

'Hmm,' harrumphed Jäger. 'Thankfully, *Major* Müller, most people don't take such a liberal view. Otherwise how would we man our armed forces? How would we defend our republic against the counter-revolutionaries?'

'Jesus!' exclaimed Tilsner. 'Give it a rest.'

Jäger glared at him. 'Anyway, as you can imagine that presents us with a problem. We will be having a word with Markus Schmidt about his desire to return to his university studies once he's served his time. And whether that happens or not will be dependent on him not giving the game away. If you get the chance, Jonas, some fatherly reinforcement wouldn't go amiss.'

'Of course, Comrade *Oberst*.'

'Which doesn't explain,' said Tilsner, picking the devil's mask from the table, and throwing the jester's towards the portly *Kriminaltechniker*, 'why you're expecting us to prance around in these stupid things. Presumably that's not an integral part of your scheme?'

'Yes,' added Müller. 'Why?' She fingered her own mask, in front of her on the table. She wasn't sure what it was supposed to be – it looked either like a cat without whiskers, or a witch with feline ears.

Jäger slapped his hands on the table, and laughed. 'Why shouldn't we have a bit of fun on New Year's Eve? Do you like mine?' He held it up to his face by its handle. Müller could see it was meant to represent a wolf. It seemed appropriate. Then the Stasi colonel put it down on the table, adopted a serious look again, and lowered his voice.

'Although most people won't be venturing out and about to parties tonight, some will try to. And Binz – being a resort town – is likely to be the centre of activities. It's also, of course, the nearest town to Prora. Given two of you are about to go undercover, I don't want either of you recognised by any staff of the *Jugendwerkhof* who have the night off, or indeed any of the soldiers, or construction soldiers, who've been allowed to join in the revelries. It's nothing more than that. I saw there was the ball at the FDGB holiday home next door. It's an opportunity to enjoy ourselves for once, but to be able to do it incognito.'

Once the revelries got under way, Jäger seemed to delight in the chance to strut his stuff on the dance floor, picking partners from the local females with impunity – and without the disapproving gaze of his wife. The others nursed their drinks at a corner table. Müller was desperate for the whole evening to be over, so she could go back to her room and make a late-night call to Helga wishing her a happy New Year. She doubted Jannika and Johannes would still be awake – unless her grandmother had allowed them to stay up specially.

'He looks a right idiot, doesn't he?' said Tilsner, surveying Jäger on the dance floor with his latest partner.

'You'd be a better dancer, then, would you, Werner?' Müller remembered the times – twice only – that she'd ended up in bed with him. She couldn't understand how she'd allowed herself to do that.

'Do you want me to demonstrate?'

'Not particularly.'

'It might be better than sitting here like lemons.'

Schmidt, who seemed to have been in a sulk since Jäger had prompted him to reveal Markus's latest indiscretion, gave Müller a nudge. 'Don't mind me if you two want to dance. As you can imagine, it's not my sort of thing. Well, certainly not without my wife.'

'Shall we?' asked Tilsner.

Müller rolled her eyes but allowed him to pull her to her feet.

'So, what's the verdict? I'm a better dancer than he is, don't you think?' asked Tilsner, once they were on the dance floor. Müller cursed that he'd managed to lure her there despite it being a slow number. It meant they were dancing cheek to cheek – as far as their respective masks allowed.

'I haven't had the pleasure of accompanying the Stasi colonel yet. And hopefully he won't ask me.'

Tilsner pulled her in closer. With her arms round his waist, she noted again how much weight he seemed to have piled on, and how his once toned body had turned to fat. She'd always found him boorish and a little too fond of playing Jack the Lad. But now even her physical attraction to him had faded. From what she was feeling, it didn't seem as though it was mutual, however. She inched away.

'Remember that time on the way to the Harz?' he whispered.

'Don't flatter yourself, Werner. It was very forgettable, I assure you. And don't try anything either. Your groin would make a lovely target for one of my boots and I assure you, I have a fierce kick.'

'Lovely,' he laughed. 'I like a bit of spirit in my women.'

She pulled her head back. 'From the smell of your breath, *you've* already got too much spirit inside you.'

As she was planning to end the dance and make her way back to Schmidt, she saw Jäger tap Tilsner on the shoulder.

'My turn, I think,' said the Stasi colonel. 'We can't have you hogging the major to yourself, can we, Comrade *Hauptmann*?'

Müller found herself being steered away by Jäger to a quieter part of the dance floor. She shrugged at Tilsner, who looked crestfallen. Jäger tried to pull her close like Tilsner, but once bitten, twice shy. She locked her arms at her elbows as she held his hands in hers, making sure they kept their distance and they moved to the music – some sort of DDR reversioning of a recent hit from the west. Something about love not living here any more. In Müller's case it was true; love – romantic love – had been absent from her life for too long. She wasn't about to let Jäger fill that void – but she hoped the coming year might lead to an upturn in her fortunes. Already in her thirty-third year, it was high time she was settled down with a husband she could trust.

Immediately the New Year celebrations began, and once she'd given her best wishes for the coming twelve months to Tilsner, Schmidt and even Jäger, Müller pretended to go to the ladies – but instead got her coat and made her way back to her neighbouring hotel.

In her room, she dialled the Strausberger Platz apartment. Helga picked up almost immediately.

'Happy New Year, Oma!' she yelled down the phone.

'Thank you, *Liebling*. And a Happy New Year to you too. But don't call me Oma – it makes me feel old. And another year passing doesn't help.'

'Nonsense, Helga. You're still young at heart. Are the children still up?'

'No, no, of course not. They don't really understand what it's all about. I put them to bed at their normal bedtime. You know what they're like the next day if they don't get enough sleep. I've been watching television – the fireworks looked lovely. What about you, and how's the case going?'

'The case?' Müller thought about it. The honest answer was 'slowly' – they'd made virtually no progress, and now the next steps had been taken out of her hands. Jäger had arranged for her to introduce herself as a new teacher at the *Jugendwerkhof* the next day. She wasn't sure what she was qualified to teach. Jäger had made vague mutterings about 'Citizens' Education'. But there was no need to give Helga the truth. 'It's going fine. Hopefully it will be wrapped up soon.'

'But did you manage to get any time off to celebrate tonight?'

'After a fashion. I don't think I'd describe it as my most exciting New Year's Eve, though.'

'Well, if you do get chance, try to ring us tomorrow evening at suppertime. We'll be in then, even if we go out for a walk and play earlier, so you can wish the twins a Happy New Year.'

The thought of her children and grandmother seeing in the New Year without her tugged at Müller's heart. She felt her eyes prickling, but she didn't want Helga to hear her crying.

'I'll try to, Oma,' she said as brightly as possible, pushing her feelings to one side. 'Love you.'

When she put the phone down, Müller kicked her boots off and flopped onto the bed. She let the tears fall. The weight of loneliness overwhelmed her. Was this really what she wanted from her life? By herself, marooned in a hotel room, hundreds of kilometres from her family. She knew it wasn't. Something had to change.

16

'Thank you for coming in to see us, Wildcat.'

I hate him using their code name for me. It makes it seem like a stupid, childish game. In reality, I know it's deadly serious, and I'm worried. This is the first time I've seen Steiger face to face since the meeting on the bus in Sassnitz. In the meantime, I haven't sent him any reports. I suspect he's going to read the riot act, although his pasty, moon-like face always looks the same – I can never tell if he's angry or not.

'I'm a little disappointed you haven't given us any information on your new boyfriend or his colleagues. That's a very useful contact you've made there. We need to know some of their thoughts and actions in their private lives. Construction soldiers can't always be trusted, you know. You'd be doing him a favour. His friends might be leading him astray. There's nothing you want to tell me now, is there? Aside from the odd bit of dope smoking. We're not too bothered about that. But you need to be careful. If soldiers serving the People's Army are prepared to break the law like that, what else might they do? Anything you want to say?'

I think back to when he appeared as if by magic on the bus in Sassnitz, immediately after we'd been in the lighthouse. Did he know about that? Had he followed us along the harbour wall? Perhaps that room at the bottom of the lighthouse is bugged. Maybe he already knows about Dieter and his friends' plans to steal a boat. Perhaps this is all a trap.

I shake my head. 'Nothing I can think of. We do the usual girlfriend and boyfriend stuff. I'm sure you don't want chapter and verse on that.' But then I remember Steiger's hand high on my thigh in the bus – maybe he's another Neumann. Perhaps that's what he *does* want.

'We're always appreciative of any reports,' he says. 'After all, you managed to go into elaborate detail about Frau Kästner's fish-buying habits and Herr Schlender's coal deliveries.' I feel myself going red in the face. Maybe they've finally rumbled me. 'Actually, come to think of it, there's someone here from Berlin for the day who wants to talk to you about your reports, and see if they can perhaps be improved. He's an old friend of yours.'

My heart starts beating madly. I know who it will be. I don't want to see him again. I don't want any more reminders of what happened. Steiger picks up the single green phone on his desk. 'Could you show the colonel in, please.' *Colonel?* I don't know any colonel. That wasn't the rank of the man I'm thinking of. But perhaps he's been promoted. 'Oh, and Wildcat, he'll want to sit on that chair, I expect. There's a stool over in the corner for you.'

I'm being humiliated. It's part of the game Steiger likes to play with me. Really, they shouldn't have a hold over me any more. I'm too old at twenty to be sent back to *Jugendwerkhof* now. But my mother's in one of their hated jails. I know if I don't co-operate they'll make life even worse for her, or extend her sentence even further.

There's a knock on the door.

'Enter!' shouts Steiger.

Another man comes in, and I realise it is him after all. The one who looks like that West German TV newsreader – although of course we shouldn't know what any of the West German news-readers look like. Steiger rises, all obsequious now. 'Good morning, Comrade *Oberst*.'

Jäger flicks his hand at him, as though he's swatting away a fly, although presumably he's indicating to the man to sit down. He ignores him and turns to me. 'Why are you sitting on that stool, Irma? Come and sit here.' He gestures to the chair that Steiger had ordered me to vacate. 'Would you like a coffee or something, Irma? And don't look so frightened. This is just a friendly visit.'

He wants me to drop my guard. Nevertheless, I *would* like a coffee.

'That would be nice, yes please.'

Steiger looks affronted when Jäger turns to him, and says: 'Two coffees, please, Comrade *Hauptmann*. I'll have milk and one sugar in mine, please. Irma, how do you take yours?'

'Black, no sugar, thank you,' I say.

Steiger shuffles off, his face blushing like a beacon. I allow myself a little smirk. It's good to see the bullies being bullied once in a while. As soon as the Stasi captain gets up, Jäger takes the vacated chair for himself.

'So, Irma,' he says, leaning forward, his arms on the desk. 'You've continued to produce reports for us since we made our deal – what was it? – nearly four years ago now, wasn't it? However, there hasn't been much that is of use.'

'I can't help that,' I say. 'I can only tell you what I witness with my own eyes, or what I hear from others.'

'That's true. But *Hauptmann* Steiger says you didn't inform us about your new boyfriend, he had to find out for himself. That's not following the spirit of our agreement, is it? Also, you've been getting a small allowance from us. We can't continue to pay that if what you're providing us is useless.'

I feel a thickness in my throat, as though I'll struggle to say anything in reply. I pull my arms into my body. There it is in black and white, laid bare by this Stasi colonel: I've taken money to betray people, even my own mother.

'I have written several reports for *Hauptmann* Steiger.'

Jäger bangs his file on the desk. I flinch. 'I don't expect our own agents to have to find out you have a new boyfriend. I expect you to report that to us, and tell us all about him. What's his name?'

'It's . . . ' I hesitate. I don't want to be disloyal.

Jäger jabs his finger on the file. 'Let me help you, it's Dieter Schwarz. Why is Schwarz on Rügen?'

'He's a . . . '

'Come on, Irma. Spit it out. He's a construction soldier. You know what they are, don't you?'

'Y-y-yes.'

'*Y-y-yes,*' he mocks. 'They're people who refuse to fight to defend the Republic. What sort of a person is that to be mixing with? Anyway, it's not up to me to decide who you choose to have as a boyfriend.' He looks up as Steiger returns with the coffees. The man puts the mugs down on the table, shuffles from one foot to another, put out that Jäger is in his seat, but not daring to say anything about it. 'Thank you, *Hauptmann* Steiger. I'll deal with Irma here. I'm sure you've got other work to be getting on with.' It's a dismissal. Steiger reddens again and withdraws from the room. He won't meet my eyes, clearly uncomfortable about being humiliated in front of me.

Jäger's gaze fixes on me again. 'Before he became a construction soldier, what did he do?'

'He was hoping to become a university student.'

Jäger snorts. 'Well, that won't be happening now. What did he want to study?'

'He hasn't told me.'

'Oh, come on, Irma. Do you think I was born yesterday?' He shuffles through his file, peering at the contents. 'Ah yes. Well, that figures. Both his parents were hospital doctors, and received highly specialised training at our expense. Their son initially wants to follow their example, gets some basic work experience in his school holidays, and then throws it back in our faces. You know what I'm talking about, Irma, don't you?'

I don't reply. But my silence is enough of an answer.

17

Müller was grateful she'd turned down Jäger's exhortations to see in the New Year in a fug of alcohol. Other than a glass of Sekt when the clocks struck twelve, and a beer earlier in the evening, she'd stuck to colas and fruit juice. Over the breakfast table, it was clear Jonas Schmidt had followed her lead – he was as bright as ever. Tilsner, on the other hand, looked like death warmed up. Although given the still freezing temperatures outside, perhaps that warming wouldn't last long.

'You're not hungry, then, Werner?' she asked.

He looked at her, hangdog, through heavy lids. 'We can't all be Miss Goody Two-Shoes. Although Jonas makes a good fist of it. Has Jäger told you? He wants us to start after breakfast.'

'Start what?' asked Müller.

'Our *missions*. You at the *Jugendwerkhof*, me at the construction soldiers' barracks, and Jonas attached to the *Fallschirmjäger* medical team. Why are you letting him order us around again? You're supposed to be the boss, aren't you?'

Müller glared at him, even though the criticism was justified.

Schmidt came to her aid. 'The Comrade *Major* had already made those decisions, Comrade *Hauptmann*. She told me about them last night.'

It wasn't true, of course. Jäger had indeed taken control, and Müller had let him. It wasn't something she was proud of, but at least Jonas Schmidt had allowed her to save some face.

Müller's attempts to hitch a ride on army transport to the reform school fell flat. She wasn't – ostensibly – a murder squad detective, but a lowly stand-in teacher. She would have to strike out on skis to the *Jugendwerkhof* alone. It was about the first thing that had transformed Tilsner's hung-over expression into something approaching a smile. He was playing the part of a newly drafted-in People's Army captain. It trumped a teacher in the emergency pecking order by some distance. Schmidt, too, seemed to be getting a lift. Müller's deputy gave a sarcastic wave as their troop truck exited the hotel car park, while she was struggling with her ski bindings.

The going was slightly easier than when the two detectives had set out on their aborted house-to-house search. By following the army vehicles' tracks through the snow, the route towards Prora approximated a pisted *langlauf* track. Towering pines lay between her and the sea, their branches loaded and drooping from the ubiquitous blanket of white. It felt to Müller much like a winter expedition through the forested hills of Thuringia, where she'd grown up. The difference was the lack of any significant inclines, and the fact that every few minutes she had to sidestep on her skis out of the way as a personnel carrier roared by.

The shape of Prora gradually took form through the morning mist, rising like a huge dark wall, casting its menace between her and the frozen Ostsee coastline. Hitler's holiday camp built for Nazi workers, but never finished, and never used by them. Almost four years since she'd last seen it – other than when they'd arrived from Greifswald in the helicopter. That was to the other – western – end, where Tilsner and Schmidt had gone, some four kilometres distant from here: the blocks given over to *Jugendwerkhof Prora Ost*. An involuntary shiver pulsed down her neck. She knew the evil that had gone on here. Irma Behrendt had told her during those long nights of captivity in the Harz mountains what she'd had to suffer. She'd seen first hand the evidence of the attempt to frame her ex-husband Gottfried – God rest his soul – for something he hadn't done, the way that the Stasi had used that to break him for something he *had* unwisely become involved in: the fraternisation with dissidents linked to the Church. But nothing, surely, warranted the fate he'd been dealt in that forest near Berlin? Learning about that had almost broken her faith in this small socialist republic. Certainly, she had started to wonder if the West really was the root of all evil. This side of the Anti-Fascist Protection Barrier it was apparent that – at times – the forces of darkness held sway.

She choked back her tears. If she was to play her part of a teacher on secondment at the reform school effectively, it wouldn't help to arrive with smudged eyeliner and a tear-blotched face. But that – she knew – would be how most of the female pupils of this institution would look on their first day.

After unclipping her skis, she picked them up, slapping them together to rid them of excess snow. Then, holding them upright by her side like a soldier on parade, she rang the buzzer at the front entrance. This part of Prora – unlike the rest of the monolithic building – had a high-walled forecourt. Inside, she knew, lay the exercise yard where Irma Behrendt had nearly fallen to her death.

Entryphones were something of a luxury in the Republic, but for security reasons the *Jugendwerkhof* had one. No doubt, thought Müller, it would also have spy cameras checking who was outside. She looked up and around but failed to identify them.

'Please wait. Someone will be there to let you in in a moment,' a disembodied voice announced amid crackles of static.

Müller started jogging on the spot to try to keep the warmth of her blood circulating around her frozen body. At some point, surely, the weather would have to break.

The clang of the spyhole in the metal door being slammed open made her jump. She heard a key turning in the lock.

A serious-looking middle-aged man appeared before her once the door was opened, his gaunt features swamped by what looked like an oversized winter coat.

'Frau Herz, welcome,' the man said, unsmiling, as though an actual welcome was the last thing on his mind. For a second, Müller was thrown by the use of her fake surname. Then she gathered herself.

'Thank you,' she said.

The man closed the huge metal door behind her, then relocked it. Müller suddenly felt herself a prisoner. Images of her time – albeit brief – in *Bautzen II* jumped into her mind. For the young inmates here, the regime was likely to be remarkably similar.

The man inspected her and her skis curiously. 'You skied here?' His tone was incredulous. 'If you'd have telephoned, we could have arranged transport quite easily.'

In her mind, Müller cursed Jäger. The Stasi colonel had insisted she would have to get to the reform school under her own steam. It was another example of him toying with her. It was happening too often.

She tried not to betray her thoughts. 'It's fine. The fresh air and exercise did me good. Especially on New Year's Day morning.'

'Aha,' said the man, pushing his spectacles up his nose. 'I trust you weren't partying too hard last night.'

'No,' said Müller, giving a weak laugh. 'You?' She realised the man had failed to introduce himself, as though she ought already to know who he was. It was a failing of Jäger's plan – she'd been too thinly briefed.

The man's frown deepened. He brushed his hand through his thinning strands of greasy black hair. 'No, no, of course not.' He stiffly extended his hand for Müller to shake. 'Comrade Peter Trautmann. I'm the deputy director here. Our director, Monika Richter, is . . . ' He paused, staring hard at Müller. His dark eyes seemed to regard her with suspicion. Perhaps a new teacher arriving on New Year's Day by ski was almost too unbeliev-able for him to swallow. 'She's . . . taking the festive period as an extended holiday. As you can imagine, I was unable to get away for the New Year festivities.'

The man had started walking quickly across the exercise yard, which Müller noticed had been cleared almost completely of snow.

'I will show you to your room.' He turned and examined the rucksack on Müller's back, without breaking his stride. 'Is that your only luggage?'

'For now, yes. The rest will follow by train, when the line's back up and running.'

The man nodded, then turned away as though he hadn't been interested to start with.

Müller paced her room from door to window – little more than four strides, fewer across. This – presumably – would have been one of the holiday rooms proposed by Hitler for his faithful Nazi workers to reward them for their efforts for his short-lived fascist empire. To Müller, it felt little more than a cell. She looked out of the window across the white-grey of the frozen Ostsee – ice and snow as far as you could see, like an extension of the land. To do so, she had to stand on tiptoe to avoid her eyeline being blocked by the iron bars obstructing the lower portion. *To keep out intruders, or imprison those inside?* Müller knew the answer.

After she'd quickly unpacked her few belongings, she tried to retrace her steps along the corridors and down the stairs to the ground floor. At one point, she got lost and passed what appeared to be a dormitory. In a room about twice the size of her own, she saw three, maybe four sets of metal bunk beds, each one three tiers high. Surprisingly, all were occupied by teenage girls, heads down, reading books or magazines. Was this the sort of dormitory Irma Behrendt had been incarcerated in? Yet here the door was open. Perhaps New Year's Day brought special privileges.

Once she was on the ground floor, she started to get her bearings from her previous visit four years earlier. She negotiated her way towards Trautmann's office – or at least the one he was occupying as a result of Richter's demise – and knocked on the grey metal door.

'Enter!' he barked. 'Ah, Comrade Herz,' he said, rising to his feet and pulling out a chair for her. 'I trust you are happy with your room. I made sure you were assigned one on the coastal side.'

Müller gave a cursory nod. 'Indeed, it has a lovely view.'

'Hmm. I'm aware, of course, the facilities are a little basic, certainly for someone like yourself, fresh from the Hauptstadt. Anyway . . .' he said, rubbing his hands together, '. . . we're not here on holiday, are we?' He fiddled with his spectacles and opened a file on his desk. 'You come very highly recommended for your knowledge and teaching of Citizens' Education, and as you can imagine with the kind of children and youths we have in here, re-education in their duties as citizens is central to our aim of reshaping them into valuable members of our socialist Republic. I can't see from your background that you've ever worked in this kind of establishment before, however.'

'No, that's true.' Müller furiously tried to remember where her curriculum vitae said she *had* taught. She'd only had a few minutes to study it before, and during, breakfast.

'Children such as ours often need a firm hand, Frau Herz. Monika Richter was . . . is a staunch believer in that.'

The way Trautmann corrected the tense of his assertion had Müller wondering how much of his former boss's fate the man was aware of. Did he know Richter would never be coming back? Was that why he'd been so quick in occupying her director's office?

'Now the teacher who'll be showing you around has, shall we say, not fully taken that on board. She'll be here in a moment. All I would say is, if you find her being too soft with the pupils, please let me know. Give them a couple of centimetres, and well . . . I'm sure you get the picture, Frau Herz.'

Müller's eyes were indeed drawn to a picture: the photograph of Erich Honecker, staring at her from above Trautmann's head. It was almost as though wherever she went in the Republic, the eyes of the chairman of the State Council followed her.

There was a knock on the door.

'Enter!' shouted Trautmann, in the same didactic tone he'd used a few moments earlier.

Müller turned in her chair. As she did, she had to fight to stop the shock registering on her face. She had no doubt the woman standing in the doorway recognised her, despite the passage of those four years. Yet she, too, hid that in her expression.

'You wanted to see me, Herr Trautmann?'

'Yes, Frau Schettler,' he said, rising to his feet. Müller mirrored his move and stood. 'This is Frau Herz, the new teacher I was telling you about the other day. She's here temporarily on attachment from Berlin. Could you perhaps show her round?'

The detective knew her cover was blown. Schettler was the one person who would recognise her from the 1975 case. Someone who Jäger had insisted was on extended leave and would – therefore – not be in a position to undermine their operation.

Yet here she was standing in front of Müller, extending her hand, her face masked with a thin smile but otherwise a deadpan expression.

'Welcome, Frau Herz. We may as well be going straight away.'

Again, the face, the tone of voice betrayed nothing.

It was only from her hazel eyes that Müller could tell anything.

She may have been mistaken.

But what she saw there was a look of pure and abject fear.

18

We'd arranged to meet this evening in the room at the bottom of the lighthouse again. Dieter had told me to bring a knapsack full of warm clothes and provisions. Normally, that sort of thing would alert the suspicions of the authorities: someone in a coastal area with a rucksack, no matter that they were locals with passes. I can only think there is one reason for the instruction – that tonight is the night. Tonight we steal the boat.

But I look outside the window of my grandmother's apartment, above the campsite reception. It won't be happening. Already snowdrifts are building up against the front door on the ground floor. I won't be going anywhere – Oma and I will have to sit it out. Surely, Dieter and the others will be doing the same, won't they? My hand hovers over the telephone. I want to try to ring his base, to warn him. But I know it's too dangerous. The Stasi watch what I do – they will almost certainly listen to what I say by tapping the telephone line too. And after the warning from Jäger and Steiger at the offices in Bergen, I can't be too careful.

'What's wrong, Irma?' Oma asks. 'You seem all on edge. It's nothing to worry about, you know. It was even worse in the winter of 62/63.'

I try to raise a smile, poised over the phone receiver. *Dare I?* I know I can't. 'I was hoping to go out tonight,' I say.

'To meet that new boyfriend of yours?'

I give a little nod.

'I don't know what was wrong with Laurenz. I liked him. It's embarrassing now when I bump into his mother at the shops. Still, that's young love, I suppose.' She grins a gummy, false-teeth grin at me. Oma can never really be angry with me. She's already lost her daughter. She doesn't want to push me away too.

I give a start as the phone suddenly rings. I'm too frightened to answer it, so I let Oma do it.

'People's Camping Site Sellin,' she says in the slightly posh, affected voice she adopts when answering the telephone, as though she runs some sort of high-class hotel in the West. 'I'll see if she's available.'

She puts her hand over the mouthpiece. 'It's that boy of yours. Do you want to talk to him or not?'

'Of course, Oma.'

She passes me the handset, frowning. I make a face at her. What's it to her who I talk to on the phone? Why wouldn't I want to talk to my own boyfriend? But something in her manner makes me more nervous than usual.

'Hi,' I say to Dieter.

'Change of plan because of the weather.' His tone is urgent. No time for mutual endearments.

'OK. I thought there would be. I'm pretty much stuck here at the campsite.'

'Can you get out at all? What about to the end of Wilhelm-Pieck-Straße, by the steps to the demolished Seebrücke?'

I try to think how I'll be able to fight my way through the drifts. Then I remember the old snowshoes in the storeroom. Oma must have had them since this winter she keeps going on about. The really bad one. In 1962 or 63. I have a vague memory of making an igloo with Mutti, the excitement of crawling inside. But I can't have been more than about three years old.

'I can try. But how are you getting there? Aren't all the roads blocked? That's what we heard on the radio.'

'Don't you worry about that. Be there at eight o'clock.'

'OK.'

'Promise?'

'Of course. Should I bring the things?'

There's a pause on the line.

'Yes. And a bed sheet. A white bed sheet.'

'A *bed sheet*? Why?'

But there's a continuous tone in my ear. Dieter's put down the phone.

Oma hears me scrabbling around in the storeroom, and comes to see what I'm doing.

'Irma, what on earth are you up to?' She's holding a flickering candle on a saucer for light, because I've got the only torch. The power's been cut. Probably something to do with the weather.

We heard the power lines had been felled by the weight of the snow in Binz – now it looks like it's our turn.

'I'm trying to find the snowshoes!' I shout from deep inside the cupboard. 'I'm sure they're in here, aren't they?'

I hear Oma sigh, and then the sound of a door unlocking. 'You won't find them in there!' she shouts. 'I got them out earlier and put them in the office – I could see one of us was going to need them.'

I get up from my crouching position in the store cupboard, where I'd been lifting various bits of junk to try to find them, and close the room's door. Oma is standing there, with the battered snowshoes in one hand, a stern look on her face.

'Why do you want them? I hope you're not going to try to go outside tonight. It's awful out there.'

'I thought you said it wasn't as bad as 1963?'

My grandmother's reply almost sounds like an angry growl. But she knows she won't be able to dissuade me when my mind's made up. She knows because she's the same. Mutti's the same. That's what's always landing her in trouble.

'It's not. At the moment. But it might soon be, young lady. I hope this isn't just to see that boyfriend of yours? I thought he was based at the other end of Prora? There's no way you'll be able to get there, Irma. You'll get yourself killed if you try. Believe me.'

I pull her into a tight hug, feeling then how much weight she's lost. She's skin and bones – all the worry over Mutti being in prison, I expect. I hold her by her shoulders, and look into her eyes. Seeing her wisdom, knowing she's right.

'I'm not going to Prora, silly. Just into town. To Sellin. It's only a few hundred metres.'

'Yes, but it's a blizzard, Irma. People will die out there, believe me. And I don't want one of them to be you.' She gives a slight sob, and I in turn give her another squeeze.

It's harder going than I imagined. I have to fight to get the front door open. Finally, I manage to force it open about half a metre. Snow flies in my face from the wind, as the top of the drift falls inwards.

'You cannot be serious, Irma!' shouts Oma. 'It's worse than I thought.'

I am beginning to have second thoughts. But what if that's Dieter's plan? That all the coastal guards will have been diverted to help with the rescue and emergency efforts, delivering food and that sort of thing. Maybe it's just the time to steal a boat, and perhaps Dieter, Joachim and Holger have decided that Sassnitz harbour is too much in the eye of the authorities. Perhaps Sellin is a better bet.

These thoughts race through my brain, but in an instant I'm out of the door before Oma can stop me. I try to jam it shut behind me before she can argue further.

As soon as I let go, I feel the wind trying to blow me off my feet, and the snow is like grit in my eyes. This isn't fluttery, pretty, snowball snow. The snowflakes are more like shotgun pellets. I don't think I can go along the coastal path along the cliff edge – I won't be able to stand up.

But at least the snowshoes do their job. I'm walking on the drifts mostly, rather than sinking into them. It's horribly cold, freeze your bones sort of cold, but it's such an effort to move that it somehow keeps me warm enough. That and Oma's woollen *Strickpulli* underneath my anorak, and the shirt and vest under that. I gave in to Oma's nagging to borrow her long thermal underwear.

I manage to get as far as the lamppost outside the campsite entrance, cling on and try to get my breath back, each inhale like a knife to the heart, the air is so bitter.

Holding on to the lamppost works. But there aren't any more lamps on this bit of the coast path. I look around in a panic, gripping fiercely on to the torch. I can't keep it on all the time – the battery won't last. Just short bursts to try to memorise the terrain. I realise the only way I'm going to be able to do this is by going from object to object and clinging on, like a drunken passenger on the deck of a boat in rough seas. All I can think of is to use the pine trees. The woods give some shelter from the snow and the wind, and – moving from tree to tree – I begin to make some slow, staggering progress.

There's an eerie blackness at the end of Wilhelm-Pieck-Straße. I cling on to the telescope at the top of the steps down to the ruined Seebrücke with one arm, and with the other use my teeth to pull my sleeve so I can see my watch. The luminescent dial tells me it's already ten past eight. I'd underestimated how long it would take me to get here. I've no idea how Dieter was planning to come – how the hell would he get here from Prora? – but even if he made it, I'm so late he's probably given up and gone again.

Then suddenly I hear someone going '*Psst!*'

There's a figure hiding at the edge of the veranda of the nearest building. He comes out for an instant so I can recognise him, then beckons me with an urgent wave. I look around to make sure no one is watching, then make my way across the snow into the shadows.

'Ha!' He kisses me full on the lips – his skin still warm, as though he's just come out into the cold. 'Snowshoes. Great idea. We should have thought of that.' I see Joachim and Holger are skulking behind him. Joachim has a sour look on what bit of his face I can see that isn't covered by the hood of his white camouflage suit. He's never forgiven Dieter for involving me in their plans – he doesn't trust me. He's got good reason not to, of course, but neither he nor the other two know that. All three are wearing the same white winter army suits.

'We were sent here to clear snow in Sellin,' says Dieter. 'But no one's keeping a proper lookout in this weather. We managed to slip away. Did you bring the bed sheet?'

I nod, pointing to my backpack. 'Are we doing it tonight?' I ask.

'Maybe,' says Dieter, mysteriously. 'Not the boat, though. Come on.' He beckons me again. The other two have slipped into the shadows. Dieter pulls me along by the hand. I realise we're going to the shoreline – not down the steps to the pier, but trying to follow a path through the snow-covered undergrowth. In summer, this would be sandy but relatively easy to climb down. Now, it's a nightmare. In the end, the other three give up trying to stay on their feet, and start sliding down on their bums, using the bushes as handholds so they don't skid out of control. It's even slower going than my tree-to-tree trek from the campsite, but eventually we make it to sea level.

I realise we're heading *under* what remains of the Seebrücke, out along the snow- and ice-covered beach. In this light, or rather dark, it's hard to see where the beach ends, and the frozen sea begins. Despite the snow and heavy cloud cover, the lamp-light from the pier illuminates the iced-up sea. And that is all that is visible, I suddenly realise.

Ice, ice as far as the eye can see.

Dieter pulls me close and hisses in my ear. 'Get the sheet out and wrap it over your head.'

I don't understand why, but then I look at Joachim and Holger further ahead, and how their camouflage suits blend in with the dark whiteness of the ice, the dim lighting above giving it all a twilight, evil feel.

And then I realise at last what the sheet is for.

It's my camouflage suit.

It's my escape ticket.

We're going.

Now.

Across the ice. To Sweden. To Denmark.

It doesn't matter where.

Anywhere but here.

And anywhere with Dieter.

19

Sassnitz harbour, Rügen, East Germany
New Year's Day 1979

Tilsner found it hard to believe they were doing this on a day which should be a public holiday. But it was happening nonetheless. He hunched his shoulders, trying to get the army greatcoat they'd provided him with to cover more of his body as the wind sliced in from Siberia across hundreds of kilometres of frozen sea. The problem of Markus Schmidt had been temporarily solved by getting the People's Police to arrest him on a trumped-up charge. He'd be kept in a cell until this had all blown over – then Tilsner had assured Schmidt his son would be freed without a stain on his record. It was a hollow assurance – but the important thing was he was kept out of the way.

'Right!' he shouted. 'You all know what you're supposed to be doing! Now let's get on with it!'

In formation, they began to march along the harbour wall. The first part had already been partially cleared of snow – or at least enough snow had been cleared to provide a narrow passageway. Tilsner was marching behind his motley group – a regular army sergeant taking the front. In between was a gang of about twenty construction soldiers. Three of them he'd been asked to keep a close eye on by Jäger. One – a certain Dieter Schwarz – was the boyfriend of Irma, the girl who'd been caught up in the *Jugendwerkhof* case four years earlier. Müller seemed to have a soft spot for her, but to Tilsner she spelt trouble, and therefore it was a fair bet her boyfriend would be of the same ilk. From what Jäger had said, that was indeed the case. A Stasi officer had seen them gain illegal access to a room under the lighthouse at the far end of the harbour wall. He'd later inspected it and found evidence that it was being used as some sort of illegal drugs den. In Tilsner's view, it sounded like the man's report had been over-egged – as though he was trying to get a gold star for his homework. A bit of dope smoking wasn't anything to get excited about. But Jäger seemed convinced that there was some link between the army base at Prora – either the construction soldiers' barracks or those of the regular *Fallschirmjäger* – and the murder of Richter. With luck, Schmidt might succeed at his end of things – in the warmth of the medics' unit – and pin down what was going on. Then they could all get out of this godforsaken shithole and back to Berlin. It might be OK in the summer – Tilsner himself had taken girlfriends to the beaches on summer camping holidays in the dim and distant past – but now in the winter it was unremittingly awful. Still, he thought, patting his stomach with his gloved hands, the weather might present opportunities. There might be other possibilities. He used the thought to try to cheer himself up.

Their official mission was twofold: to liberate some of the tools and construction materials at the end of the harbour wall that had been abandoned when the Arctic conditions suddenly closed in, and use them – and what other tools they had – to clear away more of the snow and ice from the harbour wall. The aim: to enable all the crew of the fishing boats and other vessels berthed here to get out and inspect their vessels to guard against ice damage.

For Tilsner, though, this stated task was window dressing. His objective was to watch, and listen. To find out if whatever Dieter Schwarz and his friends were involved in was anything more than rolling up a few joints and getting off their faces.

On both sides of the wall, ice stretched as far as he could see.

The lee side – the actual harbour – was relatively smooth and covered with a thick layer of snow, like a blanket. Dotted around the harbour, and particularly at the quayside, lay scores of fishing boats, iced in and going nowhere, every exposed surface that wasn't near vertical coated with either frozen sea spray, snow or a combination of the two.

The angular shape of the wall had been rounded off by frozen spray. On the far side of the barrier, the Ostsee was a much wilder picture. The vast expanse of sea ice was far from smooth. The waves and wind, the force of the water as it froze into larger sections, had produced weird, irregular patterns of white and grey – almost like a moonscape.

As they continued along the wall, it became clear they couldn't walk in formation. In fact, walking at all was near impossible. Instead they were clambering, sliding over blocks of ice and layers of snow. How the fuck they were going to clear all this, he had no idea. They would have to do the best they could.

'Watch yourselves!' he shouted. 'Don't take any risks. I don't want any daft bugger falling through the ice into the harbour. You wouldn't last five seconds.' Although as he said it, and peered at the icy surface, he doubted anyone would fall through that. It was solid. Tens of centimetres worth. Perhaps a half metre thick, or more, he had no idea. Even the icebreakers seemed to have given up following day after day of sub-zero temperatures.

Tilsner felt exhausted by the time they got to the lighthouse, and they hadn't started the real work yet. With the extra layers he was wearing, even though his extremities – fingers, toes and nose – felt like they were about to drop off from the cold, the rest of his body was too hot. Under his arms, the sweat felt sticky and uncomfort-able. The pickaxes, shovels, sand and cement were stored below the automatic light, in the room Schwarz and his mates seemed to use as their illegal smoking den. After a group of the young men cleared away the snow with a combination of boot kicks and hand shovelling, the sergeant got out a key. He unlocked and opened the door with a groan and screech of unoiled metal.

He saw Dieter flick back his overlong fringe and exchange a sly grin with his two buddies. He tried to remember their names – Joachim was one, and – Holger! That was it. But seeing them grin at each other took him nowhere. What he needed was to overhear conversations. To find out what – if anything – was really going on.

'Right – everyone either take a pickaxe *and* a shovel, or a bag of sand – and then let's get to work.'

He grabbed the smallest pick and shovel he could see for himself before anyone realised he was taking the easy way out. Dieter, Joachim and Holger meanwhile lounged in a corner – as though they were hoping by the time it was their turn, the equipment and material would have been claimed. As the other soldiers made their choices, Tilsner stood off to one side with the sergeant. Like Tilsner, he'd got in quickly and found a small pick and a shovel that was hardly bigger than a child's beach spade. Neither of them were leading by example, but then – themselves apart – these were all construction soldiers. Refuseniks. As near to being a counter-revolutionary you could get to without being labelled that. They wouldn't be inspired by good deeds for the Republic. They'd already made their choices.

Out of the corner of his eye, Tilsner kept watch on his three targets. All the picks and shovels had gone. They finally slouched towards the bags of sand, and made half-hearted attempts to pick up a bag each.

'I can't do this,' said Dieter. 'They're too heavy.'

'No, me neither,' said Joachim.

Holger shrugged, standing with his hands on his hips.

Tilsner moved forward. 'This is how you do it,' he said. He bent and lifted the bag of sand, trying not to stagger under its weight. Then he edged it up over his shoulder. 'Like that,' he said, glaring at Dieter, and lowering the bag to the floor again. The youth made a half-hearted attempt to copy, but dropped the bag to the floor.

'I can't do it,' he whined.

Joachim made an even more feeble attempt, dropping his bag with a thud at Tilsner's feet.

The detective sighed. 'OK. Take a bag between two of you. But I want all these five bags brought down to the other end of the harbour wall. Holger, you stay and sweep up after everyone.' He handed the youth a brush that he saw propped in the corner of the room. 'And then you can swap round – so one of you is always here, and two of you are always carrying the bags. No slacking though. Sergeant Adler and I will be watching you.'

He saw Dieter give a small grin to his friends, as though that's what they'd been planning all along. To make sure they had time on their own, away from the rest of the group. To do what, though? Perhaps they really were just dope heads and once everyone else was gone their plan was to roll up another joint.

Tilsner left them to it. He lifted his own pick and shovel, and followed the rest of the gang to the other end of the harbour, where they planned to begin their efforts to drive a clearer route towards the lighthouse.

After he and Adler had set the company to work, and Dieter and his cronies had – with almost deliberate slowness – brought the first two of the bags of sand, Tilsner decided to follow them back.

It was Dieter and Holger: their friend, Joachim, had been left on sweeping duty. To make sure they didn't see him, Tilsner tried to keep up in a crouch on the seaward side of the wall. The path here was even less clear. But with the sea silenced by its icy covering, he could make out snatches of conversation from the other two.

'What do you make of that new captain?' asked Holger.

'He's a lazy fucker,' replied Dieter. 'Did you see how he picked out the two smallest and lightest tools for himself? And like the rest of them, he follows orders like a fucking sheep.'

'Do you think he suspects anything?'

'Why should he?'

'I dunno. It seems strange, him suddenly turning up like this. Why did we need a fucking captain, anyway?'

'Maybe they don't trust Adler. Let's face it, Adler's a soft touch. We usually manage to twist him . . . '

The conversation died away on the wind. Tilsner realised they must have been making better progress than he was. He saw some ice- and snow-encrusted steps which led to the other side of the wall, and risked climbing one then raising his head. The two youths had put more distance between themselves and him – some thirty metres or so. Tilsner knew he wouldn't be able to catch them up without climbing over to their side and giving himself away. Instead, he carried on his struggle on the seaward side, knowing any slip would be more dangerous than sliding onto the ice in the harbour. The ice on the seaward side would be thinner. Fall on that and it could be certain death.

When he reached the lighthouse, Tilsner had half-expected two of the youths to meet him on their way back with one of the remaining bags of sand. But as he waited out of sight by the door, he could hear not a lot was happening. The three of them were just talking – by their raised voices it sounded like an argument – but Tilsner had missed half of what they were saying. He struggled to understand what it was about.

'I've told you,' said Dieter. 'Not without Irma. And we're not prepared.'

'Dieter's right,' said Holger.

Tilsner heard a sarcastic laugh. 'You've changed your tune.' The accusation came from Joachim.

'There's another problem,' said Holger. 'I don't know how, but that Markus guy seems to have found out what we got up to in Sellin.'

'*Scheisse!*' shouted Joachim.

'Shhh!' hissed Dieter. 'That Tilsner fucker could come back and check on us at any moment.'

'So what do we do?' asked Joachim. 'If he knows about Sellin, does he know the rest? And who the fuck told him? Was it your girlfriend?'

'Don't be ridiculous. He doesn't know her. He must have found out from one of us. Anyway, I don't think Schmidt will be a problem. He's gone AWOL. The word is he's been arrested.'

'How do we know that?' asked Holger. 'He might be one of their spies. And even if not, he could have already blabbed, which means others might know.'

A moment's silence followed. Tilsner was tempted to burst into the room, and use strong-arm tactics to find out what they were on about. But he knew that would be futile. A waiting game was better.

'So is that the end of everything? Do we give up?'

'No we fucking don't,' insisted Dieter. 'We'll have to bring everything forward. It'll have to happen tonight.'

'Where?' asked Holger.

'Here,' said Dieter.

It seemed to be the end of the conversation. Tilsner heard scrabbling and swearing – they were picking up another bag. As quickly as he could, he climbed out of sight to the seaward side of the wall, and started the long journey back to the rest of the company.

His struggle over the snow and ice gave him plenty of opportunity to chew over what he'd discovered and try to make sense of it.

What was it in Sellin that Markus had discovered?

What was it they planned to do tonight at the lighthouse?

And – perhaps most importantly – did it have anything to do with the murder of Monika Richter?

20

I hear the crack first – like a bullet. Then another, then another.

I whip my sheet-covered head round. *Surely they wouldn't open fire on us?*

There's no one there. Just blackness.

Then more cracking sounds.

I squeeze my eyes shut and try to run but I feel the ice collapsing beneath me. My brain has time to register that was what the bullet-like cracking noise was.

Then I'm falling.

Into the sea.

The sudden cold shoots through my entire body. I try to shout out, but the icy water rushes into my lungs. Then I'm flailing, fighting for breath.

A huge blackness is trying to claim me.

I know it's Death.

Its fingers clawing at me.

I start to black out. Then something does grip me. By the shoulders. It's painful – I try to shrug it off and realise through semi-consciousness that someone is trying to save me. Dieter. It must be Dieter.

Huge hands manage to haul me back up onto the ice. But it's so very, very cold. Like an ice devil has licked me all over and wants to devour me, my body convulsing like someone has put electrodes on my legs.

'*Scheisse!*' yells Joachim.

'Keep your voice down and help me,' hisses Dieter. 'We've got to get her somewhere warm. Quickly. Otherwise she'll die.'

The three of them prop me up. I can't put one leg in front of another. I'm dimly aware of them dragging me towards the beach, then to the sea wall. They let me rest on a bench. Giant shivers are coursing through my body.

'What do we do?' pleads Joachim.

In the fug of semi-consciousness, I can feel Dieter start to undress me. 'We've got to get these wet clothes off her.'

'Someone's going to see us from the bit that remains of the Seebrücke if we're not careful,' says Holger. 'They'll think we're raping her or something.'

I think I must be slipping away into dreamland, the dreamland before death, because I see a dark silhouette approaching. I realise it's a person – a woman – we've been caught. Even if I survive, they'll lock me up again just like my mother.

My nightmare gets worse when the silhouette starts to take human form.

Now I know we're finished.

It's her.

'Hello, Irma,' she says, smiling and friendly to them, but to me I see her leering at my half-undressed body.

She's like a wolf bitch, licking her lips. Salivating at what she's stumbled on and how she can use it to her advantage.

I want to warn the others. It's the woman of my nightmares, as bad as Neumann, if not worse. But I can't speak. As I try to, my mouth blubbers and shivers; no words come out.

'You four look like you need some help,' she says. 'My summer house is at the top of the cliff. I'm staying there for Christmas. It's warm inside. I can give her dry clothes. She knows me. I used to be her teacher.'

They believe her, I can see it in their eyes even though I'm pleading for them to understand.

But they go along with her suggestion.

They deliver me into the wolf bitch's lair, and there is nothing I can do about it.

Nothing at all.

21

Once they were safely away from Trautmann's office, Müller turned to thank Frau Schettler.

'You could have blown my cover straight away. You didn't. Thank you. But why?'

Schettler just put her finger to her pursed lips, and gave a shake of her head.

'I'm going to show you some of the facilities you need to be familiar with now, Frau Herz.' The woman was refusing to acknowledge what Müller had said. She must have her reasons, thought the detective.

Schettler was pacing ahead, her mousy hair bobbing as she walked, her thin frame full of energy all of a sudden. Müller realised she was being led outside, into the exercise yard, the place where Irma Behrendt had nearly met her death in trying to save her friend, Beate. In the end, her efforts had been in vain – but not until several months later.

'I want to show you the isolation cell,' said Schettler, a look of shame plastered across her face, her hands pressed against her cheeks. She sighed, as though showing Müller the 'facility' wasn't her intention at all. Müller had heard about it anyway from Gottfried – but seeing it first hand would be another thing entirely. As they approached, she noticed the low, wooden structure seemed to have burn marks on the outside.

Schettler saw her inspecting them. 'They're cigarette burns. If someone's locked up here that the others don't like, sometimes they throw cigarettes at the bunker from the windows up there in an attempt to set fire to the whole thing.'

Müller gasped in horror. 'Doesn't anyone try to stop them?'

Schettler stared at her – a grim look on her face. She lowered her voice to a whisper. 'I think you've met our director on your previous visit. Does that answer your question? Or should I say our former director. But Trautmann is little better. It's like Neumann all over again.' She started turning the dials of a combination padlock. 'Anyway, let's go inside. There's barely enough room for one, never mind two, but at least we can talk freely in there.'

Müller crouched so as not to hit her head on the low lintel at the entrance, and followed the other teacher inside.

Schettler sat on the bench-like bed, and Müller squeezed alongside her.

'It's good to see you again, *Oberleutnant* Müller. Sorry for that little charade. But I didn't think it was safe to talk in the school.'

Müller gave a nod. 'It's *Major* now, actually. Not that that's important. And while I'm here, it has to absolutely be Frau Herz.'

'I understand. But *why* are you here?'

From the way she'd referred to her in the present tense, it seemed as though Schettler – unlike Trautmann – wasn't aware of Richter's fate. Perhaps it was in Müller's interests not to tell her just yet.

'As you can imagine, it's an inquiry. On Rügen.'

'A murder inquiry?'

Müller nodded. 'And you might be able to help me. It's useful having a friendly face here.'

'It's something to do with the *Jugendwerkhof*?'

'I'm the one who's asking the questions, Frau Schettler. All I'd ask is that you do nothing and say nothing that might reveal my real identity.'

'Of course.'

'What interests me,' asked Müller, 'is why you're still here. Four years ago, you seemed as horrified as I was about what had been going on. I would have thought you'd have taken the first opportunity to leave for a new job. You seemed about the only person here with any sense of decency.'

'Other than your husband.'

'*Ex*-husband.'

'Oh, I'm sorry to hear that.'

'It doesn't matter. The relationship had run its course, but yes, he was a decent man.' As she said this, she found her voice catching. Schettler picked up on the emotion, and laid a hand round Müller's shoulder, thinking she was mourning the break-up of a treasured union. It was, of course, much worse than that. He was dead – executed by the Stasi. But Müller wasn't about to enlighten her.

'So tell me, Frau Schettler, why *are* you still here?'

The woman didn't answer for a moment. Then replied with a single word – a surname.

'Richter.'

'*Richter*. Director Richter? I don't understand.'

'You've met the woman. You know she's evil. It's a blessing to have her away for a few days on annual leave.'

Müller still didn't reveal what she knew about the woman's fate.

'And?'

Another pause, this time a longer one. Eventually, Schettler did speak – but in such a low whisper, Müller struggled to hear.

'She has something on me. If she revealed it, well . . . let's say my career would be as good as over.'

Müller weighed up whether it was worth enlightening the woman. It might at least put her out of her misery, knowing that Richter could no longer harm her career prospects. Whatever this mysterious '*hold*' was that she'd had, she'd never be able to use it against the teacher again.

'OK. I'm going to trade some information,' she said. 'I will tell you something about Richter – in return you have to tell me what it is she had on you. Deal?'

'*Had?*'

'Yes, very much *had* – in the past tense.'

Schettler clasped her hand over her mouth. 'Oh my God!' she cried through her fingers. 'It was her, wasn't it? She's not on annual leave, is she?'

'No,' laughed Müller, cruelly. 'It's now very much permanent leave.'

'And you're here, so she was—'

'—murdered? Yes, we think so.'

Schettler gasped. Then realised which way the conversation was flowing. 'I hope you don't think it was me, after what I told you. You know, about her having this hold on me. It was nothing as serious as that.'

'I'm sure it wasn't. And if we had to arrest everyone who had a grudge against Frau Richter, we'd have half of Rügen behind bars. So no, you're not a suspect. But I do want to know what it was that you were in her debt over.'

The woman sighed. 'I suppose that's only fair. To be honest – and I know it's a terrible thing to say – but to me, your news is a relief.'

Only now were Müller's eyes starting to grow accustomed to the dark in the confined space. She gazed around at dank, dirty walls. Breathed in the smell of stale sweat and other, worse bodily odours that had been faintly masked with disinfectant. She couldn't believe youths and girls – little more than children – were locked up in here for days at a time. Yet Gottfried had insisted that was what happened – something he had been deeply ashamed of. She waited for the woman to reveal her secret.

'You see,' Schettler continued, 'Richter knew all about me, because she was one too.'

'One what?'

'Can't you guess?'

Müller probably could by now, but she wanted to hear it from the woman's lips. She sighed and waited.

'She was a lesbian. I'm a lesbian. Theoretically, of course, that isn't a problem in the Republic. But we know that's really not the case, don't we? And as a teacher, too, well, news like that doesn't go down so well.'

'And had you two been involved?'

Schettler seemed to shudder. 'Goodness. Of course not! But we had, shall we say, a mutual friend. A mutual close friend. Or at least, she was a good friend of mine once.' The woman sounded wistful all of a sudden. Müller decided to try to fill in the missing information.

'And did this friend . . . did she end your *friendship* . . . and begin one with Richter?'

She felt Schettler give a silent nod. Müller wondered if another jealous lesbian love rival could be the one responsible for this murder – someone they hadn't yet found.

'Where does this other woman live?'

'*Lived*. She's dead.'

'Dead?'

'Uh-huh. Not only that, Richter inherited their love nest. It's a summer cottage, bang on the coast at Rügen, right by the former Seebrücke. In the West, it would be worth a fortune. There must have been some underhand dealing to let her get away with it.'

'*Get away with it?*' Müller's thoughts were beginning to race. Had Richter been guilty of some sort of crime? Had she killed this other woman in order to inherit what sounded like a desirable house? One that, in Sellin, would be coveted even by the great and good in the Republic, never mind the director of a questionable *Jugendwerkhof* that in reality was little more than a youth prison.

'No, I don't mean anything like that,' said Schettler, as though she could guess the way the detective's mind was working. 'It's that the property should have gone to the state, or her blood relatives, yet Richter seemed to manage to snaffle it. That's where she was over Christmas.'

'Yet her body was found not far from here, on the edge of Binz,' said Müller.

'Ah,' said Schettler, seeming to understand. 'So, she *was* the woman on the news? This mysterious shopper. Walking out in the snow with a shopping bag. That doesn't sound very like her at all.'

'What doesn't?'

'The walking bit. She was a lazy bitch, she wouldn't walk anywhere if she could avoid it.' Schettler's voice was full of menace and hatred, so much so that Müller was revising her opinion that the woman was incapable of murder.

Her own training told her that, in the right circumstances, with the right provocation, anyone had the capability to kill.

And kill in a premeditated fashion.

Even Frau Schettler.

And from her own mouth, the woman had expounded what sounded like a plausible motive.

22

Sellin, Rügen, East Germany
28 December 1978

They've left me alone with her, and I couldn't get the words out to tell them not to. I tried to use my eyes to plead with Dieter, but he seems distracted. Almost mesmerised by Richter. They are worried about themselves. If they don't get back to their barracks, and quickly, they will have some explaining to do. They were supposed to be clearing roads here. Surely, by now someone will have discovered they've sneaked off? For a moment, Dieter looks as though he will stay with me, but the other two try to drag him off.

'Don't worry about your girlfriend,' Richter coos, as though butter wouldn't melt in her mouth. She's worked out the signals and can tell Dieter and I are an item. 'I'll look after Irma. She can have a hot bath to warm herself up, and when she's ready I can walk her back to her grandmother's campsite.' It freaks me out that Richter has been spending time here, a few hundred metres along the coast, and I never knew. I wonder if she's been spying on me. I wonder, but I don't voice the thought aloud because – probably because of the shock – my mouth won't allow me to speak.

Dieter starts zipping up his camouflage suit. I try to speak. *Don't leave me with her. She's evil.* That's what I'm trying to tell him. But all that comes out is a gargling sound.

'But don't go back out on the ice, boys,' she laughs. 'Goodness knows what you were trying to do. Irma's very lucky. You could have all been killed.'

This is said with uncharacteristic jollity. I'm the only one who seems to be able to hear the subtext under the words. And that subtext is: *I know very well what you were trying to do. And unless you let me get my own way, I will report you to the authorities and you'll all be facing a nice long stretch in jail.*

That's what I hear. But they see the friendliness. The faux concern. It's what Dieter wants to hear – and the other two want to get back to barracks as soon as possible to try to avoid any scandal.

The door closes behind them.

At that point, Richter drops her mask. She locks the door. I look round frantically to see if there is another way out. Even if there was, I know my legs are like jelly. I'm still traumatised by whole body shivers. There's no way I'd be able to run. And nowhere to run to.

I try to cower from her, shrinking to one side of the sofa. I'm still half-undressed, with only my soaking underwear and Richter's winter coat covering me. In other circumstances, I'd want to luxuriate into its fur.

But here, as it rubs against my still damp skin, it's like the caress of a rat.

'Don't be frightened, Irma. I want to help you.' She's coming close. Looming over me. Her breath warm on my trembling face. She starts to open the fur coat. 'You need a bath to get the warmth back into your bones. It'll work wonders. Trust me. You're still numb from the cold and shock. Let's get you out of those wet things.'

I try to shrink back further, but I'm powerless as she eases her arms behind my back and unclips my bra.

She draws the material away slowly. I realise I've stopped shivering. Instead, I seem frozen to the spot. Petrified – like a reclining statue for her to admire.

She looks at me for a few short seconds.

'You've grown into a beautiful woman, Irma,' she says, then she closes the coat again, as though she doesn't have an ulterior motive after all. All of a sudden, I think I've misread the situation. Perhaps it was the shock, the cold, playing tricks on my mind. Perhaps she really does want to help me, to help us, to make sure none of us get into trouble.

She strokes my cheek.

'There. That's good. You've stopped shivering. You stay here and I'll run the bath. Then I'll make you a nice hot drink. You'll be feeling better in no time.'

I find my voice. And I don't shout for help, I don't tell her: *No, I want to go home immediately*. I don't because my addled brain tells me not to. She's got a duvet from somewhere and draws it over me. Some warmth starts to get back into my body.

'Thank you,' I say instead. 'Thank you for being so kind.'

She smiles at me. It seems like a genuine smile. 'It's a pleasure, Irma. You're not in the *Jugendwerkhof* now. You're an independent young woman with your whole life in front of you. And I'd very much like us to be friends.'

I think I doze off for a moment, then she's back in the room. Something is different though. She's changed into a dressing gown and pulled her dyed black hair up into a bun. She's not an attractive woman – but here, in her home environment, she no longer seems as fearsome as she did in her reform school role.

'Come along, sleepy head,' she laughs, grabbing the duvet off me. Then she's pulling me to my feet. I stagger, uncertain on my legs, trying to stand for the first time since falling into the ice. She helps to hold me up, her arm under the coat, rubbing my back gently almost in a motherly way. I realise how much I miss my own mother. Whether it's still the shock or what, I find myself trembling again, then sobbing into her chest. Big heaving sobs, like the shivers before, and I can't seem to stop them. And I can't stop the tears either.

'Oh, Irma,' she purrs, her hand gently stroking my back. With her other hand, she lifts my chin, and looks into my eyes. I close them to avoid the intensity of her stare. It seems full of love. It's confusing. 'Don't cry, silly girl. You're safe now. You miss your Mutti, don't you?' she says, kissing me lightly on each of my closed eyelids.

I nod, my head against her towelling robe-covered chest.

She strokes my back, her hand moving lower. I make no move to stop her. I wonder what's happening, get frightened for a moment again, then everything becomes clear. She's feeling the dampness of the outside of my knickers, plastered as the fabric is against my bum.

'Goodness,' she laughs. 'No wonder you're still shivering.'

She opens the fur coat, exposing my skin to the warm air of the room. Then her fingers are inside the elastic waistband, easing the sodden material down my legs, until they puddle to the floor.

She doesn't close the coat, but instead looks at me for a second or two. I feel myself reddening, the blood coursing around my body again.

'There's no need to be ashamed, Irma. No need at all.'

I luxuriate in the almost too-hot bathwater, stretching on my back, and ducking my head under. I feel glad to be alive. Maybe I've had a lucky escape not just from the ice, but from a stupid decision. It was reckless. Ill thought out. And I'd allowed Dieter to drag me along with him. Now, someone I'd always hated as a teenager seems to be showing me kindness.

There's a soft knock on the door. With my ears full of water from my head ducking, I almost don't hear it.

'Come in,' I say.

Frau Richter is there in her nightgown, carrying a hot mug of something.

'I thought I'd make you a cup of hot chocolate,' she says. 'I hope it's not too sweet but I thought an extra couple of spoonfuls would help with the shock.'

She crouches by the side of the bath and offers it to me. But I've got both my hands over my breasts, and she can see that I don't want to move them.

'Don't be silly,' she coaxes, pulling one of my hands towards her to take the drink. I slide my other hand over to make sure I'm still covered, and bring the mug up to my mouth.

The sweetness hits the back of my mouth, but there's a slightly bitter aftertaste too. I can't help give a little grimace, then feel ashamed that I'm seemingly throwing her kindness back in her face.

'Sorry,' she says. 'It's dark hot chocolate, which I prefer. You youngsters are probably used to the milk chocolate version.'

I take another, bigger gulp. It's not so bad really. 'No, it's lovely,' I lie. 'I was worried it was a bit too hot and that I might scald my mouth. But it's perfect, honestly.' I lick my lips, then place the mug down on the bathside table.

'I'll help you wash your hair,' she says. Her voice is all echoey. Louder, commanding.

'There's no need,' I try to say. But it comes out as a slur. I feel sleepy all of a sudden. I try to stand, but nearly fall back. Frau Richter kneels alongside the bath, and coaxes me into the water again. Her hands feel so strong as she begins to massage the shampoo into my wetted hair. It brings back memories of Mutti doing the same for me all those years ago. I feel safe, warm, wanted . . . but so very sleepy.

She squirts some more liquid into my hair, and begins to rub it into a lather with one hand, while the fingers of her other hand lightly brush the hairs on my arm, so gently it's almost like the delicate touch of a butterfly's wings.

I feel myself drifting off on a cloud of pleasure.

Then she's whispering in my ear.

'Did you used to have baths like this with Mutti, Irma?'

'Mmm,' I murmur.

'But she was taken away from you, wasn't she? That wasn't very fair, was it? But if you want, I can be your new Mutti. You'll like that, Irma, I'm sure you will.'

I fall into a semi-conscious sleep feeling loved, feeling happy, still with a woozy buzz – the sort of feeling you get when you've been out on a winter's night, you've had too much to drink, and then you get back to the warmth of home.

The next thing I'm conscious of I'm lying on a bed. I feel all tingly, almost like a need to go to wee. But it isn't that. I must have been dreaming of Dieter – what our life might have been like if our futile escape bid had succeeded.

I must be in his bed. I see a dark head of hair between my legs.

Then, the head rises up. The eyes meet mine.

Immediately, the shame, the hatred comes crashing in.

It isn't Dieter's face.

It's Richter.

I start screaming and try to wrench myself away, but she's tied my hands.

The tears stream down my face as I try to prise myself free, and I let out an animalistic howl of hatred.

I hate her.

I have always hated her.

There is no way back from this. I will have to kill her.

She will have to be my third victim.

And all of them – each and every one of them – have deserved it.

23

Müller went through the motions for the rest of her induction day. Her instinct told her Schettler's information should be acted on immediately. But what if it came to nothing? What if Richter's secret house and her sexual inclinations, her takeover of Schettler's lover, were nothing to do with why she'd been killed? She couldn't immediately wreck Jäger's undercover plans – not without something stronger.

Two things changed her mind – both of them telephone calls, conducted from the payphone in the *Jugendwerkhof* when she was sure no one was eavesdropping.

The first was to Tilsner, who sounded from his whisper like he was having to be equally discreet, although he insisted he was squirrelled away alone in the officers' quarters.

'I overheard something Dieter and his crew were talking about.'

'Irma's boyfriend?'

'That's right. One of them said, "*That Markus guy seems to know what we got up to in Sellin.*"'

'*Sellin?*' hissed Müller.

'Yes. And it sounded like something pretty fucking serious.'

'Can't we lean on Markus? I thought we'd taken him in for questioning to get him out of the way?'

'Not *we* exactly. The People's Police in Bergen. Do you want me to get over there now? The thing is, the conclusion of their rather heated argument was: "*It'll have to happen tonight.*" So they're up to something all right, and have already been up to something else in Sellin.'

'OK, that does it,' said Müller. 'I'll get on to the People's Police in Bergen, and get them to put pressure on Markus, if indeed he does know anything. I'll also get them to arrange transport for you and Jonas, and for myself. I'll ring you back in a few moments to let you know when they think they'll be arriving.'

'Why? Where are we off to?'

'To Sellin. To try to find out what those three were up to. If I have to force it out of Irma Behrendt, I will, don't worry. Also, I've discovered Richter had a secret hideaway on the island.'

'Where?'

'Where do you think? Sellin, of course, and only a few hundred metres from Irma Behrendt's grandmother's campsite.'

The ploughs had worked their magic on the roads and limited amounts of non-military traffic were starting to move around the island again. Müller was unsurprised when an unmarked police

Wartburg arrived to pick her up outside the *Jugendwerkhof*. At the wheel, the local murder squad captain, Günther Hummel. She could see Tilsner and Schmidt in the back.

She wasn't sure she wanted to share everything with Hummel at this stage, but if she wanted the co-operation of the People's Police, rather than having to rely on Jäger and his cronies, she would have to give him some bits of information.

'We've found another address for the victim. A house she apparently owns in Sellin.'

Hummel creased his face in confusion. 'Sellin? But we were told she lived in at the *Jugendwerkhof*. We don't have any record of her owning or renting property in Sellin.'

'Well, apparently she did. But she didn't like it widely advertised, only a select few know.'

'Do you want uniform backup?'

'Not at this stage, Günther, thank you all the same. Let's do things with as little fuss as possible.'

They drove in silence the few kilometres to Sellin – although it took twice as long as normal because of the snow- and ice-covered roads. It was so cold that the salt and grit didn't seem to be making much impression.

'It seems to handle well in the snow,' said Müller, to lighten the atmosphere. 'You can't be used to conditions like this?'

'No, that's true. This is the worst I've known it since I was at school, years ago. Sixty-three, I think it was.'

'That's correct, Comrade *Hauptmann*,' interrupted Schmidt from the back seat. He seemed in a remarkably good mood considering his son was currently being held for questioning. 'The winter of 1962 to 1963 was indeed the worst in recent memory – well, since the forties, at least. But I don't think they had such a big downfall of snow in such a short space of time. It was colder though, and for a longer period.'

'Colder than this? I can't remember it being that bad,' said Tilsner. 'And you should see it at Sassnitz. It's not just the harbour that's completely frozen – it's the Ostsee too. As far as the eye can see.'

'Anyway,' said Müller, 'I don't care which was worse. This is bad enough. I was simply complimenting *Hauptmann* Hummel on his driving.'

'It's nothing to do with me,' laughed Hummel as he slowed and pulled over to let a military vehicle pass. 'The depot had a few spare sets of winter tyres – I managed to bag one of them. I spent this morning fitting them. Bloody freezing it was too.' He flexed his fingers on the steering wheel. 'I'm not sure these will ever recover properly – I think I've got frostbite.'

'I doubt it, Comrade *Hauptmann*,' said Schmidt. 'If you had, they'd have turned black or fallen off by now.'

Schettler had described to Müller where Richter's house was situated, so they found it with ease. The description of a summer cottage was something of an understatement, however. This was a grand, white painted lodge – with its verandas and balconies in the traditional Baltic *Bäderarchitektur* style enjoying sumptuous views over Sellin's wooden pier and the Ostsee itself beyond. Schettler's estimation that something like this in the West would be worth a small fortune was not far off the mark.

Tilsner approached the glazed front door with gloved fist poised, as though he was ready to do a bit of breaking and entering.

'You might as well check if it's open first, Werner,' cautioned Müller.

As he pushed at the door, she saw she'd been right. It swung open a few centimetres, then seemed to get stuck. Tilsner forced it further. '*Scheisse!*' he cried. 'There's half a snowdrift in here already. It's probably been open to the elements since it happened.'

Müller cursed silently to herself. If the door had been open, foxes, stray dogs and other animals could have got inside, destroying or at least contaminating any forensic evidence Schmidt might be able to isolate.

She approached the front door. Tilsner had already gone a few metres inside, and seemed to have stopped. 'What a fucking mess. We'd better suit up, boss. Jonas is going to have a field day in here.'

Once Hummel had provided them with protective suits, overshoes and gloves from a sealed bag in the boot of the Wartburg, the four of them entered and set to work.

Müller's eyes were drawn to what had presumably caused Tilsner to shout out. One of the front curtains was missing, and from the mangled rail and debris of broken plastic curtain hooks, it looked like someone had wrenched it off.

'Jonas,' she called out. 'Could an animal have done that?'

Schmidt snorted. 'A bear perhaps. And I don't think they have bears on Rügen, at least not nowadays. Otherwise, no. That's the work of a human hand or hands, I'd lay money on it.'

'Everyone. Have a look around. Let's see if we can find this missing curtain anywhere.' Müller had a horrible feeling she knew where it had gone. Frau Winter might have thought that sled had a tarpaulin that at one time had covered up emergency supplies of food. But the old woman had admitted her eyes weren't too good these days. Müller's suspicion was it had been no tarpaulin, and it hadn't been covering sacks of potatoes or boxes of bread. For her money, it was Frau Richter's own curtain that she'd been wrapped up in, and it had been her own body underneath.

'Boss, come here quickly!' Tilsner's shout came from further in the house, up the stairs.

She found him standing in the woman's bedroom, or what appeared to be her bedroom, complete with unmade, soiled bed sheets.

'What have you found?'

Tilsner was pointing to the bottom sheet of the bed. 'Just there – that hair. I thought Richter was described in the autopsy report as dark-haired?'

'*Dyed* black hair.' Müller looked more closely at the area where Tilsner was pointing.

'Well, that's not a black hair, dyed or otherwise. It's also not from someone's head, it's a—'

'OK, Werner. You don't need to spell it out. I can see for myself.' She picked up the coarse curly hair, and held it up to

the light. Was it Irma's? If so, why had she been in Richter's bed?
'We need to get Jonas to bag it up and examine it properly. But,
yes. It's from a redhead. Any others?'

Tilsner pointed towards the rumpled pillows.

Müller moved up the bed. From the pillow, she picked up two
longer strands of head hair, again holding them up and letting
the light shine through.

They were both a gingery red colour. As clear as night is day.

'Jonas!' Müller shouted. After a few seconds, Schmidt ran
into the room, panting. Müller had a horrible thought. They'd
found the evidence too easily. It smacked of other cases she and
Tilsner had been involved in – other cases in which the hand
of Jäger and the Stasi seemed to have played all too big a role.
Something made her look at each corner of the ceiling, at the
lightbulb. Were they being watched?

'What is it?' frowned Tilsner.

She shook her head. 'Probably nothing. Jonas, I want you to
bag these hairs up. These ones I found on the pillow are from
the head of a redhead. Werner has found a similar coloured one
from another part of the body – probably the same body – and
almost certainly not Frau Richter's.'

'No,' agreed Schmidt. 'I remember the autopsy report. Her
head hair was described as dyed black, but her pubic hair –
I assume that's what you mean, Comrade *Major* – that was
described as natural black, with flecks of grey. Though, and
I don't know if this is relevant, there was only very short stubble
there. So, I doubt we'll find any of her pubic hair at all, except
on her razor.'

'Can you bag these up and look for any that match – or indeed don't match? In the bathroom, kitchen, lounge. Check the bath, sink, taps and door handles for fingerprints too.'

Müller returned to her earlier musings. The hairs had been too obvious, hadn't they? And what Jäger had said about Irma working for his ministry also had her thinking. Had she annoyed them in some way? Had she failed to supply the reports she'd promised in her role of unofficial informer? And was the Stasi now paying her back, with Müller and her team as their stooges? She wouldn't put it past Jäger. She wouldn't put anything past Jäger. She was surprised he hadn't turned up at the scene. This was normally the time he put in an appearance.

With Schmidt and Tilsner hunting for more hairs, or anything else they could find, she asked the forensic scientist another question.

'Did you keep the samples you took during the graveyard girl investigation four years ago, Jonas?'

'Of course, Comrade *Major*. I never destroy anything. It's all in filing cabinets back at Keibelstraße.'

'And would that have included samples of Irma Behrendt's hair?'

Tilsner looked at her askance. 'Aren't we jumping to conclusions? It's too much of a coincidence, surely?'

'Maybe, maybe not. We already know she hated Richter. We know her boyfriend was involved in *something* in Sellin. Something highly dodgy. What if they plotted it together, with the help of his mates, and then Irma and Dieter celebrated by romping on Richter's bed?'

'Hah!' laughed her deputy. 'You must have your TV tuned to the West. You've been watching too many American police dramas.'

Müller found herself reddening. The accusation was a little too near the truth. 'Anyway, Jonas, would we have samples of her hair?'

'We did. I got some when we took a sample of the wool her grandmother used to knit that jumper. There was a hairbrush in her bedroom at the campsite. But they'll be on file—'

'Why do you need the bloody file from Keibelstraße?' asked Tilsner. 'The campsite's up that path. Let's go there and get another sample now.'

Müller and Tilsner left Hummel and Schmidt at Richter's house, while they exited and got out of the protective suits and into their winter gear.

As soon as they were out on the street, Tilsner began to talk.

'OK, let's assume your theory for a moment is correct.'

'It's not really a theory. I was thinking aloud. Those hairs seemed too easy to find – as though it might have been staged. As though someone might have wanted to put Irma in the frame for Richter's murder. And we know who that someone might be, or at least which organisation.'

'OK. I agree. It could be one of Jäger's games. But I got the impression he was as in the dark as we are about the culprit or culprits. That's what he claimed anyway.'

They'd left the dimly lit main street behind and were walking rapidly along the coastal path. In a few days, life had begun to get back to normal. Emergency generators had been brought online to provide some electricity, and footpaths that had been impassable were now well-trodden.

'But what about the conversation I overheard earlier at Sellin lighthouse?'

'What about it?'

'Well, let's say they did do it. Or maybe Irma did it, and Dieter helped her cover it up. Then the others found out about it, including Markus. They wouldn't hang about, would they?'

'What do you mean, *they wouldn't hang about*?'

'I was out there today. On that harbour wall. That's where I heard all this. But I looked around. Ice and more ice – as far as the eye could see. Thick fucking stuff. Not just in the harbour. The sea itself. It's like an extension of the land. I don't know how far it goes, but . . . '

'But what?'

'As you know, geography's not my strong point.' Müller remembered him mixing up the two Frankfurts, although she'd thought at the time it was a joke. Perhaps it hadn't been. 'But even I know it's not far across that sea to Sweden, or indeed Denmark. People have been known to try it in boats. You don't hear about it in *Neues Deutschland* of course, but then there's not much in that rag except Party propaganda.'

They were nearly at the campsite now. Müller wished her deputy wouldn't so freely dispense his anti-Republic wisdom, at least not in public. He was sounding like a would-be *Republikflüchtling*.

'They're up to something tonight. At the lighthouse. I heard them discussing it. Perhaps they're just rolling cigarette papers and whacky baccy again, but after we've been here I think we ought to nab Hummel's Wartburg and drive out there. We can always ask Drescher to send out a patrol car to pick up Jonas and Hummel. There may already be one out in Sellin.'

'OK,' agreed Müller, as they rounded the corner into the campsite entrance. Already she could feel the snow had got inside her boots – they were squelching as she walked. At least they hadn't frozen yet, but Müller suspected that would only be a matter of time.

Tilsner rapped on the front door. They saw a light turn on in the hall, and the sound of slow footsteps.

'Just a moment!' a woman's voice shouted.

They heard the lock turn, then Frau Baumgartner peered out, without taking off the safety catch. She saw Müller, and opened the door wide.

'Come in,' she said, frowning.

'Hello, Frau Baumgartner. It's nothing to worry about,' said Müller, stamping her boots on the mat. 'Is Irma in?'

The woman ushered them in, then closed the door behind them to keep out the cold.

'She's not, I'm afraid. There's nothing wrong, is there?'

'No, no. Nothing at all,' smiled Müller. The lie came easily. 'Do you know where she is?'

'She said she was going out with her new boyfriend. They've not been able to see as much of each other these past few days.'

Müller wasn't as certain about Irma's grandmother's assertion, but she let it pass. 'But the buses have started running again now, well, a few of them anyway. She's gone out to see him. She went a couple of hours ago.'

Tilsner arched a knowing eyebrow at Müller. She ignored him.

'Would it be OK to take a quick look in her room, Frau Baumgartner? It's nothing to worry about.' Müller could tell from the old woman's sour expression that she didn't believe her.

The woman shrugged. 'I don't really have a choice, do I?' She held Müller's gaze. 'I thought you said you were her friend.'

Tilsner slapped his hand against the wall. 'Just show us to her room.'

The two detectives found what they were looking for – a hairbrush with strands of Irma's telltale ginger locks. Putting her gloves back on, Müller took the brush and sealed it in a plastic evidence bag. She knew it would have the girl's fingerprints too – again circumventing the need to get them from Keibelstraße.

'Anything else worth taking?' asked Müller. She could see Tilsner rifling through the drawers of Irma's desk.

He shrugged and pulled out a flower-patterned exercise book. He flicked through it, then proffered it to Müller. 'Looks like her diary. Might as well bag it in case it's of any use.'

Müller turned, and saw Frau Baumgartner standing, sentry-like, in Irma's bedroom doorway. 'Isn't that a bit personal?' the woman said in an accusatory tone.

'I can assure you, Frau Baumgartner, all we're trying to do is to make sure Irma is safe – as long as she hasn't broken any laws.'

'And if she has?' shouted the woman, as Tilsner shoved her out of the way and the two detectives half-ran downstairs.

'If she has,' Tilsner yelled over his shoulder, 'then that's her own lookout!'

They opened the front door, then slammed it shut behind them, hard enough to make the old building shake. A huge slab of snow dislodged from the roof and narrowly missed them as it crashed to the ground, covering them in a cloud of ice particles.

Müller wiped the snow off her face and rushed to catch up with her deputy.

24

Sellin, Rügen, East Germany
28 December 1978

I feel sick to my core about what's happened. Richter can tell I've got my wits about me again – she's seen the murderous look in my eyes.

As she unties me, I can see she's wary in case I lash out.

'I'm sorry,' she says. 'I thought it was what you wanted.'

I give her such a look of disdain that I can see her wither in front of my eyes. She drops her gaze. Not to look at me. The old pervert has sated her lust. But to look at the floor – in shame at what she's become. What I know. What I can use against her.

'I'll get your clothes and boots. They should be dry by now – I've had them over the hot water tank.'

I pull the duvet around myself to hide my nakedness. She will never look at me again. The smell of woman assaults my nostrils. I almost gag. Did I encourage her advances? No. But still the shame pulses through me. It's almost as though I'm frozen to the spot – that I've been reduced to the function of a machine, and what's more – thanks to her – a machine that no longer works properly. How could she have done this? How could Dieter have left me alone with her? *I thought it was what you wanted.* Does she really believe that? She's violated me, and I will get my revenge. She's ruined me too, I've no doubt. I'll never want to have sex again – not with Dieter, Laurenz, not anyone. And never, ever with another woman.

She leaves me alone to get dressed and retreats downstairs. I can only guess what she is doing – perhaps contacting some of her Stasi friends to try to construct a story, in case I decide to go to the police.

Once I'm dressed, I make my way downstairs – avoiding her bathroom. I want to have a bath, a shower, I want to scrub myself till my skin bleeds raw. But I'm not doing it with her soap, in her bath. I want nothing more to do with her.

She's holding something behind her back. I shouldn't be surprised if it's a knife or heavy object, arming herself in case I suddenly lunge at her. I ignore her and continue towards the door.

'Irma. Don't go straight away. I want to give you something.' *You've already given me quite enough, you fucking bitch.* 'It's a peace offering.' She holds out the object. It's a beautiful, delicate, porcelain figure – a nude. The flesh tones are pale, like my own skin. The hair, of course, is red. A miniature version of me. Perhaps that's what I was. Perhaps she'd obsessed on finding her own real red-headed porcelain doll to play with.

She turns it round to show me the base. 'It's Meißen. A very special friend gave it to me. I want you to have it – it's priceless.

If you ever got into trouble you could sell it – you'd never have to worry about money again. Although, of course, I hope you'll keep it, to remind you of me.'

I take the figure and let out a huge manic laugh.

The woman is so deluded. She has no idea what's coming to her.

For a few seconds, I humour her and pretend to admire the figure, turning it round and round in my hands, smiling sweetly at it.

Then I tighten my grip. I can see the look of fear in her face, thinking I'm about to smash it over her head.

Instead, I hurl it at the wall and watch it fracture into a thousand pieces.

25

Rügen, East Germany
Late evening, New Year's Day

Müller braced herself, gripping the Wartburg's dashboard as the car was thrown this way and that. Tilsner seemed determined to test the snow tyres to their limits.

'I appreciate we're in a hurry to get to Sassnitz, Werner!' she shouted. 'But it would be better to get there in one piece.'

She watched as he leant out of the window to attach the magnetic blue light to the car's roof, hunching down into her anorak as the cold rushed into the car. 'We will, don't worry!' he yelled above the roar of the tyres and vibrations. By now, the caterpillar tracks of military vehicles had torn up much of the smooth, impacted snow on the roads – leading to a bumpy ride. He closed the window. 'But maybe we should have done this first.'

'Why?'

'To head them off before they try and leg it across the ice.'

'*If* that's their plan. In any case, we're investigating a murder, not mounting an anti-*Republikflucht* operation.'

'You've seen the evidence,' said Tilsner. 'If Irma's with them, by stopping them escaping we kill two birds with one stone.'

They skidded to a halt in the car park by the quayside, at the beginning of the harbour wall. Just before Sassnitz town limits, Tilsner had detached the flashing blue light. They didn't want to lose any element of surprise, in case Irma, Dieter and their friends hadn't set off yet.

'We're on foot from here on,' he said, climbing out of the car door. He leant back to give her a warning. 'Just watch your footing in the dark. We cleared a lot of it earlier today, but it's probably refrozen.' He opened the rear door, pulled out a small rucksack, and swung it over his back. 'A People's Army portable radio,' he explained. 'It might come in useful. I've retuned it to the People's Police frequencies.'

Müller followed in his footsteps in a crouching run. The wall curved round slightly towards the sea, following the shape of the coast. In the distance, Müller could see buildings on the shoreline illuminated at regular intervals by the rotating light. They were like ghosts of buildings – there one second as the bright light hit them, gone the next as darkness reclaimed them.

On and on they ran. The harbour wall seemed endless, its strange-shaped covering of sea ice and snow looking like frozen slime when it – in turn – was lit by the rotating beam. All Müller could hear was the panting of her own breath, and their footfalls, softened by the ice and snow.

'How much further?' she asked, between gasps. They'd come to a dead stop.

'Another couple of hundred metres. But it gets harder now. We'll have to crawl. Is your Makarov ready in case we need it?'

Müller checked her shoulder holster and nodded. Tilsner passed her something. It felt cold to the touch, even beneath her gloves: a spare magazine for the gun. 'I got a few from the barracks gun room, in case.'

Müller had never used the full eight of her semi-automatic's bullets. The thought of having to carry spare ammunition made her shudder. 'Shouldn't we get backup from uniform? Or the army even?'

Tilsner had started to crawl forward again, but more slowly, using his hands to cling to the wall. 'You know the answer to that,' he whispered. 'If we ask for backup, what we'll get is Jäger and his mob. I'd rather arrest them ourselves if we can, and persuade them to confess.'

They were within fifty metres of the lighthouse. Tilsner risked lifting his head above the parapet of the sea wall. Müller followed suit. She could see the lighthouse beam and its regular flash, and at the base of the structure – each time the beam passed – a group of figures going in and out.

'Looks like they're there. And looks like they're preparing something.'

Müller strained to see. Tilsner got his field glasses from his breast pocket. 'Jesus,' he said. 'Take a look at that.' He handed her the binoculars.

The figures were clearer, larger now. She could make out Dieter and Irma. But what made her heart sink was what they were doing: loading a sled with various boxes. Poking out from the open top of one of them, she could see what looked like the barrels of rifles.

26

I rush to the yellow phone box – the one I used four years earlier to ring *Hauptmann* Steiger. If Richter is watching, she probably thinks I'm about to ring the police this time. But I'm not.
Instead I ask the operator for the People's Army construction
soldiers' barracks in Prora. What I want to do is wash myself at
Oma's. Wash all the evil away. But first I need to act otherwise
it will be too late. Richter could already be on the phone to the
Stasi – constructing lies about me. I know Ministry agents will
be listening to this call – at least they will hear the truth.

I put my coins in, dial the number, but have a struggle persuading them to bring him to the phone. Eventually he comes
on the line.

'Dieter,' I sob. 'Something terrible's happened.'

'What, *Schatzi*?'

'At Frau Richter's. I can't say over the phone.'

'If I don't know what's happened, how can I help?'

I shiver in the phone box. Snow is falling heavily outside. I breathe in deeply and tell him my story despite my terrible shame.

I shelter further down Wilhelm-Pieck-Straße in the veranda of a house that doesn't look like it's occupied in winter, and wait for him. He said someone at the barracks owed him a favour and he'll try to get a vehicle and come right away. He's bringing a couple of his friends.

He says we need to make her pay for what she's done to me.

They arrive and pick me up, then we drive to the end of the road by the cliff and the phone box. Right by Frau Richter's house. They set up warning barriers and 'Road Closed' signs, as though they're a roadworks crew. That's what they're dressed as too. Dieter takes me by the hand, and drags me through the freshly fallen snow to Richter's front door. In his other hand, what looks like some sort of toolbox. The others hide each side of the door.

I'm not sure I want to be part of this any more. I want her punished for what she's done but I don't want to involve the police and have it raked over again. But this feels evil – more evil, even, than she is. In the heat of the moment, I'd told myself I wanted her dead. Now I don't think I do.

Dieter looks around, making sure there are no witnesses. Richter's house isn't overlooked – except by the sea and beach, and no one will be out there on a night like this. He knocks on the door.

Richter comes to it, but sees me and him, and doesn't open it.

'It's all right, Frau Richter. Irma would like you to come out and apologise to her in person, and then we'll say no more about it.'

I see the relief on her face. It's what she wants to believe.

As she steps out onto the threshold, as though to take my outstretched hand, Dieter's friends act. One drops a corded sack over her head and clasps his hand over her covered mouth; the other wraps what looks like webbing round her torso, immobilising her arms. She tries to kick back, but another set of webbing is wrapped round her legs. She's taken on the appearance of a partially unwrapped Egyptian mummy. She's trying to struggle against her bindings, but there's nothing she can do.

'Irma says you drugged her, Frau Richter. Drugged her, then molested her.'

The woman is shaking her head, trying to mumble 'No, no.' That's what I think she's saying.

Dieter has another look round to check no one has seen, then he points inside the house. 'Let's go and check, shall we?'

'I think this has gone too far, Dieter,' I say. 'We've given her a fright, as long as she agrees not to go to the police, let's leave.'

But he looks at me fiercely. 'This isn't just about you, although that's bad enough.' He's almost spitting with venom. 'She saw what we were trying to do under that demolished pier. That puts us in danger. We have to see this through to the end. Otherwise she'll report us.'

Joachim and Holger have lifted her inside. Dieter drags me after them.

I can't understand what he's doing. He seems to be rooting round in the kitchen. He emerges, clutching a dirty mug. It's the one I drank the hot chocolate from – there's a dark residue in the bottom. He smells it.

'Just as I thought, Frau Richter. But if you go around spiking drinks, it's not advisable to do it to the girlfriend of someone whose parents are both hospital doctors, and had hoped to go to medical school himself. It might come back to bite you. You might get a taste of your own medicine, almost literally.'

The other two have replaced her makeshift hood with webbing round her mouth. She still can't shout for help – but she can see, and that seems to be Dieter's intention. He's rifling through his 'toolbox', preparing something.

He brings out a hypodermic needle, with a colourless liquid inside. He looks at the woman's fingers, and spies one with a fat ring on it.

'Irma, can you get the washing-up liquid from the kitchen?'

'I don't like this, Dieter. Let's go, please.'

'Just do it,' he spits.

'She's right, Dieter,' says Joachim. 'We ought to be on our way. It's like a blizzard outside. Soon we won't be able to get back.'

'Shut up, Joachim. Remember, she's seen what we were trying to do. At any moment she could tell someone.' He looks up at me. 'Do I have to get it myself, Irma? You heard Joachim, we need to get back quickly.'

I don't have any option, though I don't understand what he wants it for. I hope he's not going to pour it down her throat. I go to the kitchen, find the washing-up liquid propped by the taps, bring it back and hand it to him.

He squeezes some around the ring then, using a cloth, works the silver band off her finger. He pinches her skin together, and plunges in the needle.

I see a damp patch around her groin, and realise she's pissed herself in her terror. But she doesn't seem to be struggling any more. 'Can you hear me, Frau Richter?' She doesn't nod, she doesn't blink her eyes. But they're still open.

It's like she's turned to stone.

Dieter uses a knife to cut free the webbing around her mouth, torso and legs. She doesn't move.

'What's wrong with her?' I ask, panicking.

'I've used a drug to paralyse her. But don't worry, Frau Richter. It's only temporary. It'll wear off after a few hours.' He gets close to her ear, and almost snarls into it. 'Just like whatever you gave Irma, but she'll have the memories of that for ever.'

It's true. But I didn't ask him to do this. I didn't want it to go so far.

He stands, and looks around, his eyes settling on the curtains. 'Holger,' he says. 'Help me rip it down.'

'Why?'

'We can wrap her up in it. Use it as a kind of stretcher.'

The two of them yank down the curtain. Part of the rail comes away from the wall. They wrap her body in it, but Dieter is careful to leave her face uncovered.

So that she can see everything that is going to happen to her.

It's clear I'm not going back with them to Prora. Whatever their plans for Richter, I'll never know.

'Don't do anything stupid,' I say to Dieter as he hugs me, after he and the others have lifted her body into the back of the truck, together with all their roadworks apparatus. I can see other equipment in the back too. Boxes. What looks like a sled. A tarpaulin.

'Don't worry, Irma.' He squeezes me tight. 'Whatever happens, remember it's to ensure your and our safety – and to pay her back for what she did to you.'

I feel a terrible dread settle over me as I trudge back to the campsite through the snow. The wind has begun to howl, and drifts are already forming. I wonder if they will get back to Prora, or whether they'll be snowed in with their semi-comatose cargo. What would happen then?

I won't answer Oma when she asks where I've been. I slam the front door behind me and run up to my room. I tear off my clothes and stuff them into a plastic bag in the wardrobe. I never want to see them again. I'll burn them if necessary.

I run naked carrying a towel to the shower. I don't want to put on my dressing gown – I don't want it sullied with her scent.

I run the shower as hot as possible, till it's almost scalding my body.

I scrub and scrub, every part of me, until my skin stings and burns.

The next day, when the snow is metres high, I hear that there has been a fatality because of the weather.

A middle-aged woman has been found, lifeless, under a drift near Binz.

Apparently she'd been out shopping, judging by what she'd been carrying, but had been caught out in inappropriate indoor clothing when the snows fell.

They're already calling it a hundred-year winter.

A 'catastrophe winter'.

I know I should be horrified by what Dieter's done, by what I helped him do.

But I'm not. Instead I feel a lightness of being, a fuzzy warmth, as though the world has been rid of an evil spirit.

And, perhaps, it has.

27

Briefing by the Minister for State Security, Erich Mielke

'Welcome, Comrades. Thank you for giving up your evenings for this meeting. As you're aware, we have a critical situation because of the weather along the Ostsee coast. Some of our officers will be joining us by conference call from there, but I'm sure you've seen the weather reports. In fact, you only have to look outside this window. But I can assure you, things are much worse in the north. The first person we're going to hear from is Comrade *Oberst* Klaus Jäger who joins us from Binz on the island of Rügen. Jäger? Mielke here. Can you hear us?'

'*Yes, receiving you loud and clear, Comrade Minister.*'

'Go ahead with your report, Jäger. I understand there have been some new developments since we last talked to you?'

'*Yes, Comrade Minister, the situation is very serious here. According to helicopter reconnaissance, the Ostsee is almost completely frozen as far as Denmark and Sweden. Only a narrow shipping channel is being kept relatively clear by icebreakers, but*' *we don't know how long they can continue operating. The situation is equally bad further west along the Republic's coast, at Rostock, Warnemünde, and Boltenhagen.'*

'And what's your assessment about what this means for us? Have any *Republikflüchtlinge* tried to take advantage of the conditions? What about that cell you've identified within the construction soldiers' barracks? Presumably you've sorted that by now?'

'There's been a complication, Comrade Minister.'

'I don't want to hear about complications, Comrade *Oberst*. You're aware of your orders and duties.'

'The complicating factor is that some members of the cell are suspects in a murder investigation being carried out by the People's Police.'

'The *Kriminalpolizei* on Rügen? Just tell them we're taking over.'

'No. It's the Serious Crimes Department from Keibelstraße.'

'Not that Müller woman again, Jäger? I thought I'd told you to make sure you deal with her. I thought she'd resigned.'

'She did, or rather she tried to. Reiniger at Keibelstraße refused to accept her resignation.'

'Well, he's a buffoon, Comrade *Oberst*. I'll get in touch with his boss at the People's Police and pull him into line. Anyway, I thought we had one of ours working in that department?'

'We have, Comrade Minister. Her deputy.'

'I don't understand, Jäger. What is the complication?'

'We intercepted a radio message from Müller and her deputy Tilsner sent to the People's Police in Bergen, from where they've

been staking out the cell at Sassnitz harbour. It appears the suspects may be about to make a run for it across the ice. Müller and Tilsner want to follow to try to arrest them, and were asking for backup from uniform.'

'It's not a matter for the *Vopos*, Jäger. We should be dealing with it. Us and the coastal *Grenztruppen*. A helicopter gunship would sort them out.'

'The weather's about to take another turn for the worse, Comrade Minister. My understanding is helicopters and other aircraft have been grounded until further notice. Shouldn't we give Müller and Tilsner permission to begin the chase at least, until reinforcements arrive?'

'I'm not interested in this nonsense about arresting the culprits. Tell them to wait for backup for the time being. But if the criminals attempt to flee the Republic, they should be shot on sight.'

'As you wish, Comrade Minister. All I would say is that a trial might be to our benefit, given that it would expose construction soldiers for what they truly are, and at the same time prove what we've always been saying. That Republikflüchtlinge are almost always criminals trying to evade justice in the Republic.'

'I'm not on the ground, Jäger. You are. You must do as you see fit, but you will face the consequences if anything goes wrong.'

'Of course, Comrade Minister. That goes without saying.'

'Thank you, Jäger. You'd better stay on the line to hear the rest of it. Gentlemen, you've heard an example of the seriousness of the situation first hand from *Oberst* Jäger. As a result of the weather emergency we're facing, the State Council has issued the following decree: a special zone is to be created – a band along the Republic's northern coastline twenty kilometres in width. No citizens who do not have residence rights within this zone will be permitted to enter. Anyone who defies this and does not have the necessary identity papers will face immediate arrest. Port cities such as Rostock, Stralsund, Warnemünde, Boltenhagen and their ilk will be designated closed cities with roadblocks and checkpoints at all entrances. In addition, the coastal border guards have been given instructions to shoot to kill anyone venturing onto the frozen sea with a view to escaping the Republic. You can take it from me, that instruction also applies to any of your agents in the field. That is all, Comrades. Get to work.'

28

Sellin, Rügen, East Germany
Earlier, evening of 1 January 1979

I get the call from Dieter at about 6 p.m. Things have been a little strained since the business with Frau Richter, so I'm pleased to hear from him. Overall, I think I've managed to put the Richter stuff behind me quite well, considering what happened. I was a bit nervous when that policewoman, Frau Müller, turned up. But I think she put my weird mood down to my anger at her mentioning my time in the *Jugendwerkhof* at the café. No one wants to be reminded of that sort of thing, especially in public. You don't know who's listening, you don't know what they'll try to use against you.

'Irma,' he says. 'I need you to come over tonight. We're going on a little walk. You know what you need to bring.'

A little walk.

That's the agreed code.

Tonight must be the night.

I said I would never attempt anything like this again, and I thought the discovery of the body might blow over, that they might believe it was down to natural causes. I suppose I knew as soon as the policewoman arrived that wasn't going to be the case. But something must have changed. Something bad.

'OK,' I reply. 'Some of the buses are running again. It shouldn't be a problem. But it could take me an hour. Perhaps longer.'

'We'll wait for you in the usual place. Don't forget anything.'

On the bus, I chew my nails, and glance round furtively. Steiger may have had his men tap into Dieter's phone call. I shouldn't think construction soldiers are trusted, and I know – from my 'interview' with Steiger and his superior, Jäger – that I'm certainly not. They've probably detailed an agent to follow me to the rendezvous with Dieter, Joachim and Holger in the bar. Then they'll move in and arrest us all. I've been expecting that, really, every minute since we knocked on Richter's door four nights ago.

When I get to the bar by the quayside, I'm surprised to see Dieter sitting alone. Joachim and Holger are nowhere to be seen.

'Ah, Irma,' says Dieter, getting up to hug me. 'I thought from what you were saying about the buses you might be later.'

'I don't know how long they'll keep running. Heavy snowfall is imminent again, apparently.' I worry for a moment how I will get back to Sellin. Then I remember. I'm not going back to Sellin. A small shiver of fear courses through me. Dieter sees it, I think, and hugs me tighter.

Dieter doesn't know that I've done this sort of thing before. Well, not over the ice. That will be even worse. But I've made an escape attempt before – and I know how strong, how determined, how bloody-minded you have to be to make it work. And you have to plan, meticulously. That's what I fear is missing here. The evidence is that first aborted attempt under the remains of the pier at Sellin.

It was madness.

This is madness.

Yet, still I'm going through with it. Last time, it was desperation. This time, it's for love. I don't want Dieter to go without me.

'Where are Holger and Joachim?'

'They've gone on ahead. Getting things ready for the party.'

The party. Another of Dieter's favourite code words. God, how I wish we were going to a party. I think Dieter, Joachim, and Holger are in for a horribly rude awakening.

29

'What did they say?' asked Tilsner.

Müller had removed the headphones after using Tilsner's portable radio set. She knew they were far enough away from the lighthouse that Irma, Dieter and their friends wouldn't have heard her making contact. The noise of the wind howling in across the frozen Ostsee would have made sure of that. Back in the mountains of Thuringia, a winter wind was often a warmer one – a harbinger of a thaw. Here, snow was falling again – although from the angle it was being blown into their faces, perhaps *falling* wasn't accurate.

'Berlin have told the police in Bergen that ideally they want us to wait for backup, as I suspected. A detachment of border troops should be on their way.'

'Why?'

'Because they're armed. Two of us against four of them? Even if we're professionals and three of them are construction soldiers – rather than the real thing – they don't want us to chance it. And that's my view too, Werner.'

She watched Tilsner blow out his cheeks and kick a mound of icy snow in his frustration. He took the radio and head-phones from her and repacked them in his rucksack. 'What happens if they *do* make a move? Do Berlin's orders cover all eventualities?'

Müller wiped the objective lenses of her field glasses with her gloved fingers, then raised the eyepieces to her face. Through the smeary picture, shrouded in a darkness regularly pierced by the rotating lighthouse beam, she could just about make out the entrance to the bottom of the structure. She wasn't going to tell Tilsner at this stage about the relayed message from Mielke. 'There doesn't seem to be any sign of them setting off yet, if indeed that's what they're going to do. Perhaps they're preparing.'

'I still say we ignore Berlin and go in and arrest them now. We've seen them loading their guns. Let's act now, *before* there's a bloodbath. *Before* they escape, if that's their aim.'

As the snow drove in at almost ninety degrees, Müller wiped the binoculars again, then took another look.

'*Scheisse!*' she screamed. 'They're setting off.'

'What are we waiting for? Let's go!'

Müller moved to try to hold her deputy back, but he was already clambering up the uncleared part of the sea wall path; stumbling, crouching but moving quickly.

She didn't have time to weigh up whether it might still be safer to wait for backup.

For good or bad, she and Tilsner were a team on this operation. She shoved the binoculars away and started to follow.

Immediately they were out on the iced-over sea, Müller was filled with a sense of panic and dread. What from a distance had looked relatively flat and solid, now seemed like a death trap. As the rotating beam highlighted the figures they were trying to follow – some two hundred metres ahead – it also revealed huge distortions in the ice. Jagged blocks left to refreeze by previous futile attempts to send in the icebreakers. Crests and curves where waves appeared to have frozen as the surf broke. And all the time she was thinking, *Why?* Why had they come out here without proper supplies, without backup and – most importantly for her – without contacting her loved ones back in Berlin? She'd sworn she would never again put Jannika, Johannes and Helga in danger. Yet she was the bread-winner – being out here was putting everything at risk.

Furiously, she tried to speed up to catch Tilsner. To tell him they ought to turn back. But he was too far ahead, pressing on towards the escapees. *This is madness*, she thought. *I have to put a stop to it right now.*

'Irma Behrendt, Dieter Schwarz and you others!' she shouted at the top of her voice. 'This is the police! Put your hands above your heads and stay completely still!'

She wasn't sure they could hear her – perhaps they were already too far away. Through the driving snow, it was getting more difficult to see. Tilsner, twenty metres or so ahead, must have heard but seemed to be pressing on.

As she continued to run, she fumbled inside her camouflage jacket to get the Makarov from her shoulder holster. She held the gun in her left hand, while she tried to pull her right-hand glove off with her teeth. Even in the gloves, the ends of her fingers were so cold she could hardly feel them. Now her right hand was exposed to the cold and snow, she felt it shaking. She came to a halt, passed the Makarov from one hand to the other, then raised it as she fought to control her shivering.

'This is your final warning! Stop and wait for arrest, otherwise I'll fire!'

Tilsner was starting to disappear from sight. She no longer had any visual contact with Irma and Dieter's group.

Aiming in the direction of their last position, but making sure she fired into the air, she squeezed the trigger. Once, then again.

The two shots rang out in quick succession.

Tilsner had stopped in his tracks, but she wasn't sure about the suspects.

Then – from behind them – the sound of a loudspeaker boomed across the frozen sea, echoing harshly against the ice, repeating virtually word for word her own warning for Irma and Dieter's gang.

'Stop immediately! Raise your hands above your heads! You are violating the borders of the Republic and are under arrest!'

Even as Müller struggled to obey, first dropping the Makarov into the snow, she heard the telltale tack-tack-tack-tack-tack of automatic fire. 'We're police, don't shoot!' she yelled, as she thrust her arms upwards. In the bright searchlight that fought for dominance over the intermittent beam of the lighthouse, she saw Tilsner adopt the same surrender position.

She waited for thud of a bullet in her back.

Hoping, praying, that they were firing warning shots into the snow clouds above.

'Where are they?' demanded Jäger, once he'd convinced the border guard captain not to arrest Müller and Tilsner.

Müller pointed in the direction she'd last seen them. She could have predicted that the Stasi colonel wouldn't be far behind.

Dressed in the same snow camouflage suit as the two detectives and the border guards, Jäger ordered the searchlight to be shone in the direction Müller's finger pointed. He raised a pair of binoculars to his eyes.

He shook his head. 'This is a complete mess. You were ordered by Berlin to wait for backup, unless the criminals attempted to escape. In which case, the orders were to shoot them on sight. You defied those orders.'

Müller shrugged and stamped her boots to try to keep her blood circulating, but said nothing.

It was left to Tilsner to defend their action. '*Major* Müller did indeed order me to wait for reinforcements. But I saw the criminals trying to escape the Republic. I felt it was my duty to try to stop them. The major did not defy your orders – she tried to stop me.'

She could see Tilsner staring Jäger down. Jäger's boyhood friend might, officially, only be a captain in the police but he wasn't prepared to cede ground to the Stasi colonel. The closely held secret that bound the two of them – their past history in the Hitler Youth at Gardelegen, and what they had done there in the war – was something neither of them wanted to be made public.

As Jäger dropped his eyes momentarily, Müller could tell her deputy's gambit had worked.

The Stasi colonel turned instead to the captain of the border guard detachment. 'What do you think, Comrade *Hauptmann*? Is it safe to try to follow them?'

Slinging his recently fired Kalashnikov over his shoulder, the man stamped on the ice. The action caused Müller to think once more about what she'd left behind in Berlin, and how much better off she'd have been continuing with the teaching job application. The layer of ice beneath was all that stood between them and an almost certain death – although she noted one of the guards' sleds was carrying an inflatable boat, the others had the searchlight and what looked like boxes of supplies.

'The ice seems solid, Comrade *Oberst*. There's no sign of a thaw. But it's a risk.' Müller saw him glance towards the inflatable. 'My orders were to follow the criminals, arrest them if we can, but not hesitate to shoot if we must. The boat offers us some protection if we encounter a break in the ice – although we won't all fit in it. We're going to carry on – at least while it seems safe underfoot.'

As he said the words, he started waving his men onwards. There were twelve guards in total – four per sled – pulling them along with harnesses like Arctic expedition dogs.

Müller glanced at Jäger. 'What about us?' she asked.

'Suit yourselves,' said Jäger. 'I need to get back to shore to brief Berlin. Both of you have messed up enough already. The only way you're going to save face is if you arrest or kill them.' The lighthouse beam suddenly illuminated his face, split by a cynical smile. 'But if you do decide to press on, you may end up killing yourselves.'

30

The frozen Ostsee
Night of 1 January 1979

At first, as the adrenalin courses through me, it seems exciting, exhilarating – and the bitter cold has little effect. Out here on the ice with the man I love – escaping to a new life of hope in the West. As I trudge behind the sled, watching it periodically highlighted by the lighthouse beam, I allow myself to fantasise for a few seconds. A fantasy seems appropriate given the ghostly look of the others – like me, covered in white bed sheets, a procession of ghouls.

Where will we live? Will we prefer to stay on the Ostsee coast, but on the western side? Or would one of the big BRD cities make a more suitable home? The lights and nightlife of Hamburg and the Reeperbahn had looked so inviting on that short, illegal visit four and a half years ago. Perhaps this time we really will get to Sweden? Each faltering step across this frozen winter wasteland is a step nearer to the Swedish coast. That's where I'd been aiming for, after all, with that last escape by boat.

My hopes are shattered when I hear the female police officer's shout.

'What should we do?' I hiss to Dieter. The cold cuts through my outer layers and I find myself trembling.

'We carry on,' he says, sounding unflustered. He points out a jagged mound of ice that's been pushed up by the sea, and urges us to head behind that.

Here, we're in shadow. We can tell because the lighthouse beam no longer illuminates us.

We follow that narrow band of shadow, further into the iced-up sea.

Then more shouts from the woman police officer.

We keep walking.

Two shots ring out.

Dieter falls again to my side, to check I'm OK.

He pulls the bed sheet back so he can whisper in my ear. 'Ignore it. They can't see us. We're protected by that mound of ice. By the time we're out of its shadow, they'll have lost us.'

He pulls something from his pocket and offers it to me.

'Eat,' he orders. 'We need to keep up our energy.'

I look at it suspiciously, but it is a sandwich.

I take a bite. It's like someone's forgotten the filling and put in too much margarine instead.

Dieter holds my other hand, pulling me along, trying to hurry me up.

'It's disgusting. Who made it?'

'I did,' he laughs. 'Margarine sandwiches. A construction soldier speciality. Fat is the best energy source when you're in an environment like this. Butter would be even better, of course, but . . . '

His sentence trails off. Then I jump nearly out of my skin.

The ack-ack-ack of automatic fire echoes across the ice.

Scheisse! The seriousness of the situation we're in sinks in.

I may not get to taste that butter after all.

I stuff the rest of the margarine sandwich into my mouth and gulp it down, even though – without a drink – I'm struggling to swallow it.

I try to savour it, like the last meal of the condemned.

31

'What is it, Jäger?'

'There's been a further development, Comrade Minister.'

'Go on, I'm listening, although really I want to get some sleep. You realise what time it is?'

'The criminals have – as we suspected – made a break for it over the ice.'

'So I'd heard, Jäger. Why didn't your people stop them? You realise the seriousness of this, don't you? It has the potential to become an international incident if the BRD or anyone else in the West gets to hear about it.'

'They won't get away with it, Comrade Minister. There is a unit of armed border guards in pursuit, with a number of our agents amongst them.'

'What about those *Kriminalpolizei* buffoons?'

'They are tracking them, too, Comrade Minister.'

Mielke banged his schnapps glass down on the table. 'If they get in the way of justice being done, Jäger, mark my words, it will be you who pays the price.'

'*I understand that, Comrade Minister.*'

'Meanwhile I've got some news for you. Our Soviet friends may be able to come to our rescue, although I'm not sure allowing them to is such a good idea. We'd never hear the end of it.'

'*Come to our rescue in what way, Comrade Minister?*'

'There's a Soviet icebreaker fighting its way through the Ostsee at the moment. It went back to Shipyard 189 in Leningrad for repairs – but now it's on its way back to the Arctic. The Soviets had already agreed to make a small diversion to reopen the channel to Rostock to free some of our shipping. As you can imagine, Soviet icebreakers are much more powerful than ours. You may have heard of this vessel, the *Arktika*.'

'*That's one of the new nuclear-powered icebreakers, isn't it?*'

'Precisely, Jäger. It can smash through ice up to five metres thick which it regularly encounters in Arctic waters. Although the Ostsee ice may look thick to you, it's nothing like that. It might be a metre at most in its thickest parts, so the scientists tell me. We've persuaded our Soviet friends to make another slight detour before they reach Rostock. They'll be visiting Rügen, somewhere we like to go in the good weather – not so much now, eh, Jäger?'

'*No, Comrade Minister.*'

'The border guards will give the Soviet captain the necessary co-ordinates for this diversion. But as you can imagine, it's not some tourist jolly. The *Arktika* will smash everything in its path. Including our little band of criminal *Republikflüchtlinge*. And, with a bit of luck, our *Kriminalpolizei* friends too.'

32

The frozen Ostsee
Early hours of 2 January 1979

Tilsner seemed to need no encouragement to continue the chase. He might have put on weight, but he seemed to have regained his zest for the job, and Müller was thankful for that. She'd been impressed, too, by the way he'd backed her in the confrontation with Jäger. It didn't alter the fact that she'd never be able to completely forgive him for his role in those events in the Nazi period, but more than ever now, she was prepared to give him the benefit of the doubt. In an environment like this – where at any moment an ice fissure could open up and claim them, or they could be the victim of a stray border guard bullet – she needed him on her side.

She struggled to catch him up, feeling like a manic duck as her attempt to run in her snowshoes resembled more of a waddle. But after a couple of minutes of exertion, with sweat breaking out on her face despite the bitter cold, she drew level with him.

'You shouldn't do that, you know.'

'What?'

'Try to run on the ice. Just keep up a steady pace, otherwise you start to perspire.'

She wiped a mixture of sweat and snow away from her forehead. 'And what's the problem with that?'

'It's the worst thing possible if you want to avoid frostbite. If you sweat into your gloves or boots, in extreme cold the sweat then freezes. Then your fingers and toes fall off.'

The snow had cleared slightly. Sassnitz lighthouse was behind them, but they knew they were going in the right direction because they could occasionally see a bright light – the searchlight on the border guards' sled – and it was getting nearer. Travelling with less equipment than the troops, they were managing to catch them up. As long as the *Grenztruppen* were on the right trail, they were too.

'I can still feel myself sweating!' shouted Müller.

'We're going to catch up with the border guard detachment soon,' panted Tilsner. 'The advice about perspiration and frostbite was stuff I read about Arctic and Antarctic expeditions. It's fucking cold here – but it must be ten times worse at the North and South Poles.'

Müller wasn't so sure. The conditions *were* Arctic – that was where this weather front had come from apparently – blown in from the Arctic Soviet wastes – and now settled over the north of the Republic and the Ostsee, with no sign of it breaking.

What she found more interesting was Tilsner's admission to reading serious books – and books about polar expeditions. Nothing like the erotic novel she remembered him hiding under the covers of his hospital bed, when he'd been recovering after the shooting in the Harz during the graveyard girl case. That incident seemed like a lifetime ago. Yet it was less than four years earlier, and at one time he'd been teetering on the edge of death.

When they finally caught up with the border guards, Müller was surprised how pleased she was to see them again. Perhaps it was the false reassurance of the inflatable boat on their sled. The small generator powering the searchlight, with its bus engine-like diesel rattle, also gave a hint of a better-prepared operation. Or perhaps it was the thought of safety in numbers, even though all of them were just – what? – tens, scores, at best perhaps a hundred centimetres above an icy grave.

'My understanding, Comrade *Major*,' said the captain, not stopping to welcome them, 'was that you had gone back to shore with *Oberst* Jäger. If anything goes wrong, we've already told you, there won't be enough space on our dinghy.'

Müller shrugged as she kept pace with him. Despite his words, the captain's craggy face – brought into sharp relief as one of his troops sliced the searchlight through the never-ending blackness – had a confident air. 'We'd better make sure nothing does go wrong, then, Comrade *Hauptmann*,' she replied. 'Have you seen the criminals?'

'Now it's stopped snowing again, we've found their tracks – even though they seem to be trying to disguise them by dragging a blanket over them. Visual contact is more difficult. They're obviously camouflaged – they blend into the ice.' He clapped his gloved hands together. It looked like he was applauding the ingenuity of Irma, Dieter and their colleagues. Müller knew, however, he was trying to keep the blood circulating in his extremities. 'We think they're wearing white bed sheets or something like that,' he continued. 'Before we set off, we were warned it was a trick they might use. Criminals used similar sort of things in attempted escapes documented in 1962/63 – the last time the Ostsee froze over so completely.'

'It could be a long chase. Won't you have to stop to camp at some stage?' asked Tilsner, sounding out of breath. In the gloom, Müller could see him looking hopefully at the supplies on the back of one of the sleds, no doubt trying to work out if there was a tent.

'Perhaps. Although my best guess is that the criminals will try to get as far as possible at night. They'll know that, with the snow clearing, once daylight comes there'll be helicopters and spotter planes out looking for them. So while we think they're still on the move, we need to be too.'

Müller saw that the officer was holding a compass in one hand, and studying it with a torch held in the other. 'Where does it look like they're heading?'

'I'm not certain they've thought it through. If they wanted to reach the West, Sassnitz wasn't the best place to start. Strike out at ninety degrees from the coast here, and you end up back in the Republic, or at best in western Poland. Clearly they're not doing that. They've already turned in a more northerly direction.'

'So, the Swedish mainland?' asked Tilsner.

'Perhaps. Or there's Bornholm – an island in the middle that belongs to Denmark, even though it's nearer Sweden. But to reach either of them you're talking a walk of at least a hundred kilometres. Maybe more like a hundred and fifty. They're not going to do that in a single night – not across this stuff. You're talking more like three or four days.'

Müller's geography wasn't a lot better than Tilsner's. But she knew the captain was right. Irma, Dieter and friends would have been better off if they had staged their escape attempt from the coast near Rostock. There, they would have faced a trek of some fifty kilometres, perhaps less. That might have been doable in one exhausting twelve-hour night, although Müller doubted it was possible across this ice. Further west in the Republic, there would be routes across the ice to the BRD which would just be a few kilometres. No wonder this part of the coast seemed to be more lightly patrolled.

'Which means they'll have to stop to rest at some point,' said Müller.

'Exactly,' replied the captain. 'My plan, therefore, is to keep going as long as we can unless we lose their trail. My guess is they will push themselves to the limit, and then perhaps dig in, make an igloo out of the snow, disguise it and try to get some sleep.'

'Unless,' suggested Tilsner, 'their plan isn't to reach the West at all – but to hitch a ride on a Western boat.'

Tilsner was correct, of course. Whichever route was chosen, Müller knew Irma and her fellow escapers would face an insurmountable problem: crossing the shipping lane. Even if the weather meant that – by now – the Republic's and Western icebreakers hadn't managed to keep it ice-free, the frozen surface would be much thinner, more treacherous. But as Tilsner had intimated, their plan might be to *reach* the shipping lane, rather than cross it. Hoping that some ships – *Western* ships – would be managing to fight their way through. On their way to, or from, northern Sweden or Finland.

The border guard captain and his troops continued their relentless pace, even though Müller was tiring. 'That's a likely scenario, *Hauptmann*,' he said to Tilsner. 'I doubt they would manage to get that far in one night. The main shipping lane is almost exactly halfway between here and Bornholm. But there's another reason they might not get that far.'

'What's that?' asked Müller.

'We got a message from Berlin. The Soviets may be coming to our rescue.'

33

When I feel my leg collapse, for an instant I think I'm being sucked into the icy sea like at Sassnitz. I tumble into the snow, my snowshoe trapped by something. Dieter comes to my aid, and starts to help me up.

'Sorry,' I say. 'I should have looked where I was going.'

'Don't worry. It's dark – it's difficult. Here.' He offers his shoulder for me to lean on. 'Test your weight. Is it OK?'

I feel shooting pains from my ankle up my leg. It *isn't* OK, but I'm not going to admit that. I'll have to keep up with them; I can't risk falling behind or slowing them down. 'It's fine.' I smile reassuringly at Dieter. 'How much further?' Already it feels like we must have walked far enough to reach Sweden, though I know from that book Herr Müller lent me at the *Jugendwerkhof* that can't be the case.

Dieter returns my smile. 'While it's still dark, we need to keep going.' I see him glance backwards. From time to time, we see the beam of the searchlight of whoever is following us. Border troops, we assume. The lighthouse beam disappeared hours ago. 'And we don't want them to catch us. I've been try- ing to disguise the trail.' He holds up his bed sheet. The rest of us are still wearing ours, but he's been trailing his, hoping that by smoothing out our tracks as we go, we might confuse our followers and – eventually – lose them.

We resume our steady walk. I've been excused sled-pulling duties – the others share it between themselves, with two pulling at any one time, the others resting. If trudging at a fast walking pace across the frozen surface of the sea can be described as resting. I try to disguise the fact that I'm limping. Try not to show the pain on my face, even though no one would see it in this near-blackness, just the occasional star breaking through the snow clouds giving us a weak illumination.

'Once dawn breaks,' says Dieter, 'if we still haven't made it by then, we can rest a little if we think they've stopped following us. We might manage to get some sleep.'

'Where is it we're heading for?' I ask.

He hesitates before he answers. I have a sudden horrible thought it's because he doesn't know – that this escape attempt might be as badly planned as mine from the *Jugendwerkhof*, even though – against the odds – that actually succeeded. 'It depends on the conditions we encounter,' he says. 'Whether we can get across the shipping lanes or not.'

My foot slips slightly and I feel another jab of pain from my ankle. 'And if we can't?' I ask.

'Let's wait and see,' he says. 'If we're lucky, we might reach there before dawn.'

The others have moved ahead. I grit my teeth, try to ignore the pain knifing with each stride from my ankle, and increase my pace so we can catch them up.

Each stride is a step nearer to freedom.

Each bolt of pain is something I'm willing to endure for the goal at the end.

The dream of living a life in the West with Dieter, wherever that may be.

It's the lights we see first, in the distance. Initially, I think it's a town, that perhaps we've reached Sweden already. My heartbeat hammers in my ears in excitement, I start walking more quickly towards the lights, the renewed rush of adrenalin masking my ankle pain. It's almost as though my leg feels as good as new again.

Next, it's the noise. A low hum getting gradually louder.

Finally, I realise what – in my heart – I already knew. It's not the lights of a port or town – it's a ship. Heading straight towards us, slicing through the ice.

I feel elated. We must have reached the shipping lane. This might be a Western ship – we could flag it down and get it to take us to the West.

But it looms ever larger, bearing directly down on us.

Then we hear the thunder of ice cracking, as this massive vessel powers towards us.

It's almost as though the ice is moving beneath our feet.

Then I realise it *is*.

At the same time, I see the illuminated blood-red bridge of the ship.

The Cyrillic lettering. The hammer and sickle. From my Russian lessons, I dimly remember how to transliterate the ship's name – А Р К Т И К А – *Arktika*, I think it says.

Dieter is grabbing me.

'Quick, Irma, quick!'

We're running now – away to the side, the ice cracking under our feet as the blood-red monster charges forward.

Running back towards the Republic. Back towards the border guards. Back to where we've just escaped from.

Back to try to save our lives.

34

When Müller saw the lights in the distance, she immediately asked the border guard captain – who'd finally introduced himself as *Hauptmann* Heinrich Hartmann – what they were. Or rather where it was. She, too, at first believed it to be a building on a coastline.

'I said that Berlin had arranged for some help from our Soviet friends. This is it, I think. I provided them with the co-ordinates.'

As the lights grew closer, Müller could make out it was a ship. It had a searchlight sweeping over the frozen sea in front of it as it powered through the ice.

'It's one of their icebreakers,' said Hartmann. 'Normally it operates in Arctic waters. Luckily for us, it had finished being repaired in Leningrad and was on its way back through the Ostsee. It's taking a diversion.'

Hartmann appeared unruffled, but Müller found herself tensing as she watched the ship smash through the ice as though it wasn't there. She could hear a thunderous crashing as the frozen surface was broken into huge blocks which were swept aside in a relentless forward motion. Then – in the glare of the vessel's searchlight – she spotted silhouettes on the ice, running away from it.

'There they are!' she shouted.

Hartmann raised his binoculars. Then shook his head. 'I can't see them.'

Müller, too, realised they'd been plunged back in darkness and she could no longer make out the group. 'They were definitely there. At least, there were figures running away from the icebreaker.'

'That makes sense!' shouted Hartmann, above the crashing of ice and the roar of the ship's engines as it came ever closer. 'The aim was to smash a channel through the ice around them to cut them off.'

As he said this, Müller noticed Tilsner had started to run in the direction she'd seen Irma and Dieter's group running. She started to follow, then felt the ice begin to shake under her feet as though it was going to break off.

She glanced round.

Hartmann was yelling at her as the guards ran in the opposite direction.

Then she realised why.

The giant craft was bearing down on her, and the ice was cracking and giving way.

She began to run in panic, towards Tilsner, her loyalty to her deputy winning out over Hartmann's frantic beckoning.

Huge blocks of ice were rearing up in front of her.

The giant red bow of the ship was nearly upon her.

She knew she must get out of the way. Thoughts raced through her head of Jannika, Johannes, Helga – how she'd let them all down.

Selfishly putting herself in danger again.

As the red metal of the ship was nearly upon her, she threw herself to the side. A block of ice smashed into her back, slamming the air from her lungs. She fought for breath, for a foothold, felt icy water shower over her and almost immediately freeze in the air.

Then it was over.

She clawed her way up the ice block, and managed to get to her feet. She ran again. Trying to get as far away from the red monster as possible, as its giant hull slid by, almost – it seemed – as though it was within touching distance, although she knew that was an optical illusion.

Finally, panting, she stopped to catch her breath. The ice beneath her felt solid again. The freezing air was like giant icicles arrowing down her windpipe into her lungs as she hyperventilated, desperately struggling to get her body back in equilibrium. Shivering from the shock and the cold of the seawater churned up by the Soviet vessel.

She looked up.

The lights of the ship had passed. It seemed to be turning, in a wide circle. Some distance away, on the opposite side to the icy channel carved by the boat, she could see a light and the silhouettes of a number of figures. It must be Hartmann and his border guard squad. They'd gone one way, she'd gone the other. Their light swung round, and she had to shield her eyes as it settled on her, illuminating her for hundreds of metres around.

A booming voice came through a loudspeaker.

'Don't worry, Comrade *Major*. We're in radio contact with Berlin – we can get a message through to the icebreaker to make sure the crew stop to pick you and *Hauptmann* Tilsner up once they've finished their work. Just stay out of the way of the criminal gang. Do you have your gun?'

Müller cupped her gloved hands round her mouth, first having to clench and unclench her fists to try to shake off the frozen seawater that had rained down on her as the icebreaker passed. She shouted through her own makeshift loud hailer, hoping her voice would be amplified enough to be heard over the fading roar of the ship.

'Yes, I'll be fine!' She hadn't checked the gun to see if it had got soaked along with the rest of her, but it had hopefully been shielded from a soaking by her jacket. 'I'll try to make contact with Tilsner. He's got a radio – we'll communicate with you and Berlin via that.'

'Very well, Comrade *Major*. But do not engage with the criminal gang. You will be rescued very soon.'

Müller tried to believe his words. But she knew if she didn't get out of her damp clothing, she probably didn't have long to survive. She remembered Tilsner's warnings about sweat and frostbite. As her body began to convulse in huge involuntary shivers, she once again longed for the comfort of her apartment of Strausberger Platz, the embrace of her children and grandmother.

She wasn't sure she'd ever be able to enjoy that again.

The only hope until she was rescued was to force herself to walk. To tramp one foot in front of the other towards where she'd seen Tilsner disappear to. To try to get some warmth flowing through her body.

Otherwise, she knew, she was facing certain death.

35

We're huddled together, trying to work out what to do, when we hear the loudspeaker conversation.

Joachim seems excited. 'It sounds as though at least two of them are here with us. But they've been separated from the rest.'

I hear Dieter sigh. 'Yes, but don't you realise what is happening?' In the distance, we can still see the lights of the icebreaker. It's changed direction – almost as though it's going round in a huge circle. Then the meaning of Dieter's words become clear. 'It's obvious. The icebreaker is cutting us off – carving a channel around us. We're basically sitting, marooned, in the middle of the Ostsee.'

'How far to the shipping channel?' I ask.

'I'm not sure,' says Dieter. 'I've been using the compass, and trying to estimate distance by counting our paces. I think we've walked twenty, maybe thirty kilometres so far. It could be as much again. And we'd have to get across that.'

He points in the direction of the channel cut by the icebreaker, where we nearly lost our lives.

'In this weather, it's not going to take long to refreeze, surely?' suggests Holger.

Dieter gives a resigned laugh. 'Ha! Do you think they're going to let it freeze over again? Did you see the name on the side of that ship?'

'*Arktika*,' I say. 'At least, from my not very good knowledge of Russian, that's what I think it said.'

'Exactly right, Irma,' replies Dieter. 'Although what the fuck it's doing here, I've no idea.'

'What do you mean?' asks Joachim.

'The *Arktika* is one of the most advanced Soviet icebreakers, which normally operates in Arctic waters. It can punch through the thickest of ice – doing that for months, years even, without refuelling. You know why?'

Everyone was silent. I had no idea how Dieter knew this – but he'd hoped to become a medical student until he blotted his copybook by joining the construction soldiers. He must have studied science at school. Maybe the glories of our Soviet friends' icebreakers were part of his physics lessons.

Dieter answered for us. 'It's because it's a nuclear icebreaker. It's powered not by diesel, but by two small nuclear reactors.'

'Why does that make a difference?' asked Holger.

'If they have spare fuel rods on board, it could stay here for ever. Going round and round, making sure we never escape.'

'Why would the Soviets allow—'

Holger cuts off Joachim's question by clasping his hand over his mouth.

Then he drops his voice to an urgent whisper. 'Over there! Look. It's one of them.' Silhouetted against the lights of the ice-breaker as it swings back round towards us, there is what looks like a male figure clad in white camouflage fatigues. But what makes me shiver is what's in his outstretched hand.

A gun.

He is hunting something.

And all of us know what his quarry is.

We lie flat to the ground. Dieter and Joachim take charge, inching forward, staying low, shuffling along on their stomachs like walruses.

He orders me to stay back with Holger. But we – like the two guards – are armed, although I have no confidence in my ability to fire a gun, despite a quick verbal lesson from Dieter.

The icebreaker approaches again, but the crew seem to have trained its searchlight on the channel in front, rather than sweeping across our small ice island. There is enough light, however, for Holger and me to watch Dieter and Joachim shuffling towards the border guard, policeman, or Stasi officer. Whatever he is, we have no idea – all their winter camouflage outfits look the same. But I thank the fact that he seems to have replaced his gun in his holster. He's waiting there. Asking for it.

Dieter and Holger split up, curving either side of the officer, like big cats encircling their prey. I can see he has his back to both of them now – he seems to be staring up at the icebreaker, as it comes round in another swoop.

And then they pounce.

As Joachim distracts him from the front, Dieter jumps on his back. I hear the man's scream.

We see all this in silhouette, powerless.

Part of me hopes my boyfriend isn't slitting the man's throat. Part of me doesn't care.

The man works for this hateful Republic – determined to stop our dream of escaping to freedom.

If he pays for that with his life, perhaps that's simply him getting his just deserts.

36

Müller's blood turned colder still when she heard Tilsner's scream, audible even above the din of the icebreaker. She climbed a mound of ice in the direction of the sound – and saw everything silhouetted by the bright lights of the Soviet vessel.

They were near enough for her to shoot, and she was a good shot. She drew the Makarov from her holster, released the safety catch, and took aim.

But she knew it was futile. If Tilsner was still alive, she couldn't be sure of not hitting him – especially given the numbness of her hands from the cold. And one of the construction soldiers was holding something to her deputy's head. They might be pacifists, but this group seemed ready to use weapons. Because what was being pressed against Tilsner's temple as they shuffled away was the silhouette of a handgun.

As Müller tried to get her gun back in the holster, her shivering hands making it difficult, she felt a hand clasp around her mouth from behind.

Her arm was yanked up towards her shoulder blade, as her gun fell on to the ice.

She felt the prod of something hard in her back.

She didn't have the strength to resist.

Didn't want to.

'Hello again, *Major* Müller.' She recognised the voice of Irma Behrendt. Müller felt herself being turned round by whoever had her in their grip, until she was face to face with the former reform school girl. 'We don't seem to be able to stop bumping into each other, do we?' There was an attempt by Irma to make her comment sound flippant and throwaway. But Müller could detect something else in the voice, and on the girl's face.

The same thing she herself felt.

Fear.

37

Generaloberst Erich Mielke yawned and rubbed his eyes as the conference phone line from Rügen jolted him awake again. He looked at the clock. A few seconds past 5 a.m. The Soviet ice-breaker should have arrived. Everything should be in hand. Why the hell was that idiot Jäger contacting him again? Was he incapable of dealing with the situation himself?

He depressed the switch on the intercom panel. 'What is it, Jäger?'

'Good morning, Comrade Minister.'

Mielke looked at the clock again. He prided himself on being an early riser, a hard worker. But in his book, five in the morning was still very much the middle of the night. 'Spit it out, man. This had better be important.'

'I thought you would want to know, Comrade Minister, that the icebreaker has completed its work and the criminals are now completely cut off.'

'What about the border guards? Have they arrested them yet? Or are they coming up with a more permanent solution?'

'The border guard unit has the situation under control but I thought it safer for them if they remained on the main body of ice. We don't know how stable the island of ice the criminals are on is. It could break up at any moment.'

'Tossing them into the sea? Well, that wouldn't be any great loss – an ice grave sounds about right. What about the two detectives?'

'They followed the criminal gang on to the ice island, Comrade Minister. It's my expectation that they will already have them under arrest.'

'So what's the plan, Jäger? Wait till daylight and send in a helicopter to bring them out?'

'We could do that, of course, Comrade Minister, but that would depend on whether the snow closed in again or not. That was the reason for my making this call. My recommendation, if you can get the Soviets to agree, is to bring them all off on the icebreaker and hold them under arrest there. You said it was heading to Rostock to clear the shipping channel – it could make an unscheduled stop in port to drop off our prisoners?'

'I'll see what I can do, Jäger. But if we involve the Soviets even more closely, then it becomes doubly important nothing goes wrong. I'm sure you understand that and its consequences for your continued employment at a colonel's grade.'

38

Müller had been shocked at the way she and Tilsner had been overpowered by a group that – supposedly – was peace-loving, and unwilling to lift arms to defend the Republic. To escape the Republic, to defect to the capitalist world, in that case they seemed to have no qualms about *threatening* to use weapons. Although, from the nasty red mark and swelling on the side of Tilsner's face, it looked as though he might have received a pistol-whipping.

She tried to reason with their captors. 'Irma, you know this isn't going to end well. We're trapped here. The best thing is to give yourselves up, and hope you might get away with prison sentences.' Müller knew there hadn't been an official death sentence pronounced by a court for several years. But by attempting to flee the Republic, stealing weapons from the army, deserting *and* kidnapping two police officers, the death penalty might be a real option, at least for the three young men. She would speak up for Irma. She owed her that much from their past history together. She owed her too because the girl – just now – had persuaded her male colleagues to give up one spare set of clothing so that Müller could get out of her own freezing, soaked clothes, and into something dry. But, at the very least, the girl would be facing a long jail sentence.

Surely they could see that was better than risking death here on the ice?

'Shut up!' shouted Dieter. 'We don't need your advice.'

'Perhaps she's right,' ventured Irma.

'Be quiet!' Müller could see the hurt in Irma's face from the venomous put-down by her boyfriend. Perhaps he was losing it. Perhaps Müller and Tilsner could use that to their advantage.

Müller saw the one called Joachim scrabbling around in Tilsner's rucksack. 'Fuck, he's got a radio in here.'

Dieter's face suddenly lit up. 'Wonderful,' he said, considering. 'Let me explain what you're going to do with it, Mr Police Officer.'

Müller realised that Dieter Schwarz was devious enough to have made an excellent Stasi officer should he have chosen a different path. In many ways, his approach reminded her of Jäger's. When he made his radio call to the Stasi colonel, Tilsner was given a clear script – and with a gun to the back of his head, little leeway to deviate from it. Müller's deputy seemed to be being more compliant than necessary. Perhaps, like her, his main priority was to get back safely to the Hauptstadt.

'Can you hear me, *Oberst* Jäger?'

'*Go ahead, Comrade Hauptmann. What do you have to report?*'

'We've managed to apprehend the criminals and their weapons.' Müller watched Schwarz as Tilsner said the words. 'We're now requesting transfer back to the Republic. Could that Soviet icebreaker take us aboard?'

'We've already arranged with the Russians to let you board. The vessel should be coming to a stop any time soon and lowering a ladder for you to climb up.'

Müller wondered about the wisdom of this. Surely lowering a boat onto the surface of the ice would be safer? But perhaps it was a deliberate ploy to ensure everyone came onto the ship one at a time, and could therefore be searched. Schwarz's worried expression under the glare of the *Arktika*'s spotlights told her that he was concerned about this too. The young construction soldier's plan had been – no doubt – to escort the two detectives on board at gunpoint, while giving the impression that exactly the reverse was happening. In other words, that the detectives had the construction soldiers and Irma under armed arrest. This plan would be much more difficult to execute if they all had to climb a rope ladder at the same time.

Schwarz quickly scrawled a note and thrust it under Tilsner's nose. The one called Joachim flicked on a torch so Tilsner could read it.

'Are you there, Tilsner? Will that work?'

'Receiving you loud and clear, Comrade *Oberst*. There's one problem with that. One of those arrested has suffered a twisted ankle. I was wondering,' continued Tilsner, closely following Schwarz's script, 'if the *Arktika* has a helicopter on board? I believe it's equipped with a helipad.'

'That's correct, Tilsner. What are you saying? That you need an airlift?'

'That would be very helpful, Comrade *Oberst*.'

Tilsner's never usually so free with the honorifics, thought Müller. Perhaps that was his way of alerting Jäger that something was awry. She didn't get the feeling from his reactions that Jäger had picked up on it, however.

'*I'll see if it can be arranged. I'll come back on and let you know.*'

Dieter mouthed a 'good work' message to Tilsner. What he got in reply was a sarcastic smile, which earned Müller's deputy a jab in the ribs with the gun. Less than five minutes later, the radio crackled to life again.

'*Are you still there, Comrade* Hauptmann?'

'I am, Comrade *Oberst*, yes. What news?'

'*The crew were assessing how solid the ice looks in your part. They think it'll be OK. Get ready. The helicopter should be landing in a couple of minutes' time.*'

Müller found herself being forced to play a role – at gunpoint, like her deputy. Schwarz asked her to repeat to him what she was to say to the helicopter captain once they were on board.

Dawn was starting to break, so the aircraft was clearly visible as it took off from the ship's landing pad. Müller watched it pitch forward, rise in the air, then hover and settle on the ice in a whirlwind of snow. The construction soldiers – Dieter Schwarz and the one known as Joachim – jabbed her and Tilsner forward with their guns. The two detectives also had their Makarov pistols drawn, emptied of ammunition, and had been given instructions to hold them menacingly at the backs of Irma and the third construction soldier, Holger.

The convoy of people ran at a half trot towards the helicopter, Schwarz and Joachim bringing the sled of supplies at the rear. Müller had seen what some of the boxes contained at the harbour – rifles. In the few minutes before the helicopter's touchdown she'd also seen Schwarz checking over some of the other boxes. Her heart was in her mouth when she saw what they contained.

Once everyone – and the weapons – was on board, the pilot asked for the cargo doors to be slid shut. Schwarz prompted Müller forwards to speak to the pilot, keeping his gun hidden, but letting Müller know with a surreptitious jab that it was there.

'I have a request to make, Comrade,' she asked in her halting schoolgirl Russian, last used in the far east of the Soviet Union on the trip to meet her father. 'Would it be possible to fly us directly back to the coast. Would you have enough fuel for that?'

The pilot shook his head. 'No,' he said, tersely. 'In any case, it would have to be authorised by the captain. I will take you to the ship and you can discuss it with him.' As he was speaking, the pilot increased the rotor speed, then tilted the craft forward and they were airborne.

Müller asked one more question at Dieter Schwarz's behest. 'You'll be pleased to get back to the Soviet Union, won't you?' she said, lightly. Almost as though she was making conversation. 'Aren't you usually at work in the Arctic?'

'I wish we were on our way back. We're not. After this detour, we go to the polar ice.'

'Past Denmark and the BRD?'

The pilot nodded. 'Unless they've suddenly dug a new ship canal through Finland and Norway and failed to tell us, there's no other way.'

Müller expected Soviet troops to greet them on the deck, but the welcoming party were civilian. Civilian and remarkably trusting, considering there were nuclear reactors on board. Müller explained what they wanted, again following Schwarz's script, and again with him standing directly behind her with his hidden gun in his pocket poking into her back. They were escorted to a room which Müller explained they needed for their sole use, with the crew helping to carry the contents of the construction soldiers' sled.

After providing them with bedrolls and sleeping bags, the crew left them, saying they were welcome to join them in an hour's time for breakfast. Müller thought she'd be hungry, but all of a sudden tiredness overwhelmed her. All she wanted to do was sleep. That, and return to Berlin to see her children. Already Helga would be wondering why she'd been out of contact for so long.

She picked up one of the bedrolls and a sleeping bag, then threw a set to Tilsner.

'Presumably it's OK if we grab some sleep?'

Dieter nodded. 'Some of us may, too.' Then, checking the room door to make sure no one was looking through, he waved his pistol in the air. 'But at least one of us will always be awake and on guard. So don't think about trying anything.'

Tilsner shrugged and yawned. If he had an escape plan, it looked like he – too – was intending to get some sleep first.

'There's nothing we can do, Karin. This tub will be taking us back to Sassnitz – or maybe Rostock's more likely. Until we get there, we might as well get some sleep. I don't know about you, but I'm exhausted.'

Perhaps he was trying to lure their captors into sleeping too, hoping to disarm them. More likely he realised the odds were against them at this stage. Once back in a port in the Republic, it would be a different matter.

39

Things seem to be spiralling out of control, and I fervently wish I'd never thrown my lot in with Dieter and his friends. Yes, he's attractive, I still fancy him – but he's led me and the others into danger. There only seems to be one way out of this mess – kill or be killed. I find it impossible to believe his ruse has worked. That the Soviet crew has been duped into thinking we're under arrest when in fact it's the reverse – we've captured two police officers and are holding them at gunpoint, on a Soviet vessel, with boxes of guns and dynamite stolen from the barracks at Prora. The audacity of it is scarcely credible. The stupidity of it is scarcely credible. Yet, it's happening. Right now. And I'm trapped in the middle. What I'm hearing doesn't make me feel any more at ease. In fact, it has the precise opposite effect.

'OK, Mr Know It All,' says Joachim, speaking in a whisper so as not to wake the two detectives who've either gone to sleep or are making a good job of play-acting. 'For some reason, you seem to be an expert on Soviet icebreakers.'

'I remember learning about this one at school,' says Dieter. 'One of those interminably boring lessons about how wonderful our Soviet friends are. At least this was more interesting.'

'How many crew are we up against?' asks Holger.

'I can't remember. But it's more than a hundred.'

'A *hundred*?' echoes Joachim. 'How the hell can we take out a hundred of them.'

'We don't have to, do we? All we need to do is take control of the bridge. Force the captain to go where we want. It might not necessarily be suspicious. There's no way this vessel should be here.'

'What do you mean by that?' asks Joachim.

'It usually operates in the Arctic – we already heard from the helicopter pilot it's on its way up there. If we force it to divert to Kiel, Copenhagen or Gothenburg, then at least initially, that's not going to look suspicious.'

Joachim snorts in response. 'Good luck with that.'

Dieter glowers at him. 'I'm working on it. I've got us this far, haven't I?'

'Yes,' says Holger. 'From the shit into even deeper shit. I've had enough.'

'There's no turning back now, mate. I'm not going to face the death penalty – and I'm not going to let any of you stand in my way either.'

He isn't looking at me when he says this. He eyeballs Joachim and Holger in turn. But I know it applies to me as much. Perhaps more so. I suspect Dieter is beginning to think that Joachim was right to start with – that I never should have been allowed to join them on this trip.

With all my heart, I wish that had been the case.

40

'*We've run into difficulty, Comrade Minister.*'

'You, Jäger. *You've* run into a spot of difficulty. I warned you that if anything goes wrong, I'm holding you responsible.'

'*Be that as it may, we have a problem. The port authorities in Sassnitz have passed a message to me, from the captain of the* Arktika.'

Mielke gave a long sigh. 'Go on, Jäger.'

'*Müller and Tilsner gave the impression that they had the criminals under arrest, which is why the* Arktika *captain and the Soviets allowed them on board. At least, I think that's correct.*'

'That is correct, Jäger. Are you telling me the criminals are *not* under arrest?'

'*I can't say that for certain, Comrade Minister. What I can say is that the crew members are suspicious. One of them thought he spotted one of the criminals prompting Müller and Tilsner. Almost as though* they *were the ones under duress. He didn't spot a gun, but it was almost as though they were being jabbed in the back. There was an atmosphere.*'

'Yet Müller and Tilsner have guns?'

'*Yes, and they used them to bring the criminals on board and force them on the helicopter.*'

'It may be something and nothing, Jäger. Let's hope for your sake it is. Meanwhile, please instruct the captain to continue his course to Rostock whatever happens. If the criminals try anything, if they are in control, they might try to hijack the ship using Müller and Tilsner as hostages. If that happens, the captain should head for Rostock. The police officers are expendable as far as I'm concerned. Do you have anything to say about that, Jäger?'

There was a moment's silence at the other end of the line. '*No, Comrade Minister. I understand what you are saying. I will relay the message – but should it come from Moscow?*'

'Don't worry about that, Jäger, you pass that message on. I don't mind if you convey my thoughts about Müller and Tilsner, to underline the situation for the captain. I'll make sure the message is reinforced from the Moscow end of things, or from wherever the *Arktika* takes its orders. Do we know if there are Soviet troops on board?'

'*It's a civilian ship, Comrade Minister, so as far as I know, no, there aren't. Though according to the captain, they have access to a limited supply of weapons for emergencies.*'

'Please suggest to the captain he prepares himself as best he can. I'll talk to Moscow.'

41

The frozen Ostsee
2 January 1979

After a couple of hours' fitful sleep, Müller was prodded awake. She was disorientated; wondered where Helga and the children were. Then she remembered. She'd chosen to leave that life behind again, at least temporarily. A smaller flat, she now realised, would have been a fair price to pay for her safety and for continuing to be a fit and proper mother to her children.

Dieter was jabbing his pistol into her side again. 'Wake up. We're going on a visit to the bridge.'

Müller stood and dusted herself down. 'I need to go to the bathroom first.'

The young construction soldier tossed back his hair, as though he didn't care about Müller's bodily needs. Then he seemed to come to a decision. He moved over to Tilsner, who was snoring steadily, and kicked him awake. 'Get up. It's time for a bathroom visit.' He turned to Irma. 'I'll go with him. Irma, you go with her. And make sure you've got your gun.'

There were no women's toilets on a vessel where the entire crew was almost certainly male. Nevertheless, Dieter allowed them the courtesy of ladies first, while he stood watch over Tilsner outside. Tilsner was holding his empty Makarov, and Dieter's handgun was concealed in his jacket pocket.

As soon as they were inside, and the door was shut, Müller tried to reason with Irma.

'You can turn this round, Irma. I would vouch for you, say your boyfriend put you under pressure to do what you did.'

The girl wouldn't meet her eyes. 'Just go to the toilet if that's what you want to do. I don't want to talk to you.'

'Have you thought about how this is going to end? You're already waving a gun around. You're on a fast track not just to jail, but to the mortuary, Irma. Is that what you want? To end up like Beate, like Mathias?'

'Shut up. Otherwise I'll bring Dieter in here.'

Müller entered a cubicle, holding her nose to try to keep out the stink of male bodily functions and sweat. They didn't seem to have heard of cleaners. But it was a squatting toilet with hose attachment – at least she wouldn't be catching any diseases by sitting on the same seat as Soviet merchant sailors. She had to pull her borrowed camouflage trousers down, while trying to make sure they didn't fall in the filth. After relieving herself, she tried one final time to persuade the girl. 'Think over what I'm saying, Irma. I can help you, you can help us. This doesn't have to end in a tragedy, although Dieter seems hell-bent on making sure it does.'

'I don't know what you're planning,' Müller said to Dieter a few minutes later, as he used his jacket-covered gun to prod her towards the bridge. 'But when we get up there, I have one request.'

'What's that?'

'I want you to ask the captain to send a message to my children in Berlin.'

'I don't have a problem with that,' said Dieter. 'As long as you do everything I want. If you don't . . . ' He pushed the gun barrel into her ribs. Even though it was covered with two layers of material, it still hurt.

As they walked into the bridge control room, Dieter ended his subterfuge with the weapon. He held it against Müller's temple and pushed her along.

He began speaking in Russian. Almost fluent Russian – certainly too good for Müller, but he was evidently a well-educated young man; he'd chosen to throw the Republic's expensive medical training back in its face. She managed to understand the gist of what he said: *take us to the West, otherwise the lady police officer gets it in the head.*

The captain seemed unfazed.

'We can take you to Lübeck. But if there's any trouble we won't. That's all I'm willing to offer.'

Dieter nodded, and Müller exhaled in relief.

It seemed too easy, but when guns were being waved around, anything could go wrong.

42

Joachim has gone to the bridge with the male policeman – the one she calls Tilsner – so I'm alone with Holger in the room.

Everything *Major* Müller said to me in the toilets was true. I know that. Dieter is no doubt full of himself by now, thinking that he's taken over a Soviet ship. Believing that they will ferry us to our freedom. I want to believe that too – but I've seen how they work. And that's assuming that his ruse of using Frau Müller as a hostage has worked. Down here, Holger and I have no way of knowing.

'What do you think's going on?' I ask him.

He shrugs. He looks as fed up as I feel. 'It's spiralled out of control, hasn't it, Irma? Was this what you were expecting?'

I give a shake of my head. 'Do you think we can talk some sense into them?'

'Not really. Dieter might be a firebrand, but one thing he said is true. There's no turning back. If we give up, we're probably facing – what? – life in jail at the very least.'

I kick out at Dieter's bedroll. 'Or worse.'

'I don't want to think about that. We'll have to stick together, Irma. However this plays out.'

I feel myself stagger as the ship gives a lurch. 'What's that?'

He looks out of the smeary porthole window, wiping it with his sleeve. Once, twice, three times – as though he can't see. 'It looks like we're moving.'

Where to, though? That's the question. Has Dieter succeeded in his reckless gamble? Or is everything over, and we're being taken back to the Republic?

I slump to the floor, my head in my hands. Holger crouches next to me, prises my hands away and holds them gently in his. They're not the delicate, perfectly formed hands of Dieter. These are meaty, solid, industrial. As though Holger's real vocation should have been to stay in the East – working for the workers' and peasants' paradise. 'We'll be OK,' he says. 'I'm sure of that. You're a strong woman, Irma – not many would have been brave enough to come with us.'

I laugh bitterly at that. 'You don't know me, Holger. You wouldn't be saying that if you did.'

'I know enough,' he says. 'I know that Dieter's a lucky man to have you.'

We hear the door opening behind us. Holger drops my hands and his face suffuses with a guilty blush. I turn. It's Dieter – back from the bridge – this time with the male policeman at gunpoint.

He shoves the policeman into the corner, pulls me up to him, dancing me round for a couple of turns. 'We've done it,' he laughs. 'They're taking us to Lübeck.'

The West! I want to believe it like he does, so I smile, and let him spin me round. I want to dream of our new life there. But I've been on a boat like this before, full of hope as he is, only to see it dashed a few short hours after we'd thought we'd reached the promised land. What followed after that was far, far worse than what I'd had to suffer in the Republic as a child and then a teenager in the *Jugendwerkhof*. And I've seen his ruthless side – and it worries me. If he can be so cruel to others, who's to say it won't be me next?

'Where's Joachim?' I ask.

'Up on the bridge, with the policewoman. Making sure the crew do what we say.'

I smile and give him a slight nod. Doesn't he realise this is all too easy? The Soviets will not accept being humiliated like this. *'Our socialist friends'*, as schoolteachers like to call them, are in reality our masters. I know in my heart something terrible will happen, but in my face, in my actions, I try not to show it.

'How many hours to Lübeck?' asks Holger.

'The captain reckons five or six hours. We can take turns to get a few hours more sleep, but Holger, you need to take over from Joachim next on the bridge.'

'Shouldn't we make sure we're further west before we head into port?' I suggest. 'Kiel, for example. Copenhagen, even.' The idea of Lübeck worries me. From Geography lessons at school and in the *Jugendwerkhof*, I know the sea border bisects Lübeck bay. The East German or even Soviet navy could block us, board us . . . there are so many things that could go wrong.

Dieter looks at me as though I've farted from my mouth. 'Are you ever satisfied, Irma?' he asks, anger written over his face.

I don't think I am, no. But that's why we're here, doing this, isn't it? Because we weren't satisfied with our lives. We thought

we could change them, find a better way. It's the cherries in the
neighbour's orchard again. It's human nature.

I doze a little, cuddled up to Dieter. In my dreams, I'm back on
that cargo ship of four and a half years ago, watching the signs
pass as we travel along the canal, realising from the colourful
adverts that we're already in the West. And then I'm in Hamburg,
on the Reeperbahn, the lights are dazzling, and I realise my skirt
is too short. People are looking at me. *Men* are looking at me.
Sizing me up like a piece of meat. I try tugging my skirt down,
but someone's hand is on my bum. I feel myself panicking, wanting to escape, and then—

I wake. It's Dieter's hand on my bum. But not in a lecherous
way. He's rested it there as he sleeps. There's movement in the
room. Holger is getting up and waking the male policeman.

He sees me looking at him quizzically.

'It's time for me to relieve Joachim,' he explains. 'He should
be back down soon.'

The male policeman groans. 'Why do you need me to go with
you?'

Holger jabs him with the gun, but he looks as though his
heart isn't in it. Not like Dieter, who's now passed out from his
adrenalin high.

'You're our insurance policy,' says Holger. 'It's just the way it is.'

After they've gone, I decide I've had enough of trying to
sleep. I move to the porthole to see what sort of view there is.
The sun's come up – its brightness dazzling on the ice; I have
to shield my eyes. This must be the right-hand side of the ship.

I can make out the chunks of ice pushed to the side by the icebreaker's bow, but otherwise it's a frozen white wasteland. Sunlight spells danger for us. Without the snow clouds as cover, helicopters will be flying. Who's to say that the Republic's *Fallschirmjäger* aren't already in one of them – in mid-air – ready to storm the vessel? That's why I know this isn't going to work. Why people like that Stasi colonel Jäger and his ilk will never let it work. They're humouring us for the time being. They are still in control.

Joachim is back, along with the male policeman who looks thoroughly down in the mouth about being pushed around by people he no doubt regards as worse than dog shit.

'It's worth taking a look on the other side,' says Joachim. 'You can see the coastline.'

'The BRD already?' I ask, hopefully.

'No, still the Republic, I guess. We've only been underway a couple of hours. But still, it's interesting to see it from out at sea. And see it for the final time.' He slaps me on the back. 'We've done it, Irma. Are you excited?'

'I will be,' I say. 'Once we're safely in the West.' I don't tell him that I fear this is all a trap, and we'll never get there. Or if we do, it will be like last time.

The male policeman snorts in a derisory manner.

Joachim aims a kick at him. 'What's that, Vopo? Was there something you wanted to say?'

The man shakes his head, but has a sly grin on his face. 'No, no. I was clearing my nose.'

When Joachim turns away, the male policeman gives me a wink. I'm not sure what he intends it to mean. But to me, it signifies what I've feared all along.

We're not as in control as we think we are.

At some stage soon, the tables will turn.

43

Müller was hoping no one would do anything stupid. Neither
the construction soldiers, the Soviet crew, nor she hoped – down
on the deck below – her deputy Werner Tilsner. Dieter and his
gang had already proved themselves, if not trigger-happy, then
more than willing to threaten to use weapons. The irony of it,
when they were in fact little more than conscientious objectors,
wasn't lost on her.

Her first priority, though, was to get a message through to her
family in the Hauptstadt. Even though the Soviets' radio systems were likely to be more advanced than the Republic's, she
doubted she'd be able to talk to them, unless there was some way
of patching a radio link through to the telephone system.

'I've agreed to let her send a message to her family,' Dieter
said to the captain. All the while, he kept the pistol barrel at
Müller's temple. But oddly, she didn't feel frightened for herself.
Instead, she was suffused with a steely calm – trying to imagine
this was happening to someone else. There was no point provok-
ing them. It was already a powder keg situation. Thankfully, the
Soviet captain appeared equally unmoved.

'We can probably pass something on,' said the captain. 'Get her to write it down and I'll make sure it's delivered to the wireless room.' The conversation was in Russian, but again Müller managed to understand the gist of it. The captain handed her a pad and pen, and she began a short message to try to reassure Helga, and at least give her grandmother something to read to the children.

But as she started to write, Müller found her emotions overwhelming her. She'd been shown to a desk at the side of the wheel, with Dieter standing behind her – the gun no longer at the side of her head, but at her back. In case she'd forgotten, from time to time he poked her with it.

High above the ice-covered sea, she could see into the far distance and the coast of the Republic. It hammered home to her just how far away from her children and little family she was. She swallowed back her tears and began to write a short note of love and reassurance.

The guard changed with regularity. Approximately every hour or so, Tilsner would be brought up at gunpoint, so that first Dieter, then Joachim could be relieved. The third one, Holger, seemed different. More thoughtful, less gung-ho. Dieter and Joachim gave the appearance of adrenalin junkies – as though they enjoyed teetering on the edge of calamity. Holger had a more stolid air – almost as if he knew things weren't going to turn out well, but that he was resigned to his fate. It was a more realistic approach – and mirrored the way Müller felt.

He was less edgy with her, sitting next to her rather than forcing her to stand, letting her and the crew know his gun was there – but not constantly proving it with jabs of the barrel.

'It's still not too late to give yourselves in, you know,' she said to him.

He gave a long sigh. 'I don't mind talking,' he said, 'but let's not talk about that. It's not going to happen.'

She tried to think of another approach. Perhaps being positive was the way. 'What are your plans when you get to the BRD?'

He eyed her suspiciously, no doubt wondering what she was angling at. He shrugged. 'Nothing very interesting. I just want to be left alone to live my life.'

'What tipped you over the edge? Was it having to join the construction soldiers?'

'Not particularly. I'm a mechanic by training. I'm used to getting my hands dirty.'

Müller looked down to inspect them – an almost Pavlovian reaction to check a suspect was telling the truth, even though this was hardly a standard interrogation.

'As in cars?'

He nodded. 'I like to find old bangers and restore them. I guess I'll do something similar in the West. I haven't really thought about it.'

'Any relatives in the BRD?'

He nodded. 'My uncle's family live in Munich. Maybe I'll head down there. I quite fancy the idea of going south, near the mountains. If I can't get a job as a car mechanic to start with, maybe I'll look for something in a ski resort. Repairing the lifts, that sort of thing. And get a bit of skiing in on the side. Do you ski?'

Müller laughed.

The young man looked confused. 'Sorry, did I say something funny?'

'No, sorry. I was thinking about the bizarre nature of this situation. Me, a police major, being held at gunpoint. You . . . '

'A deserter . . . an escaper . . . a kidnapper. Take your pick.'

'And we're talking about skiing, smashing through a frozen sea on a Soviet icebreaker . . . '

'Which, in effect, we've hijacked. It doesn't look too good, does it?'

She looked at him with a shake of her head. 'It doesn't, Holger – if I can call you that – it doesn't at all, I'm afraid. They won't let you get away with it. You've come to realise that, haven't you?' She could see it was true in his face. Müller decided to take a calculated gamble – it was disloyal to Irma, but she didn't owe the girl, or rather young woman, anything. In fact, Irma was in her debt. 'I think Irma knows that too. Yes, if you gave yourselves up you would face a long jail sentence. But I would be prepared to speak up for you – that may help. You two need to try to persuade the others.'

'Ha!' He slapped his thigh with the gun, then came to his senses. 'Can you imagine trying to persuade Dieter of anything? Or Joachim, come to that?'

'What about Irma? She might have more chance – Dieter's her boyfriend, after all. And she knows I'll be true to my word about speaking up for you.'

'How does she know?'

'Because she's been in a similar position before, Holger. She knows me.'

'*Knows you?* From where?'

Müller drew herself up in her seat – trying to show the authority she wasn't feeling.

'Irma's tried to escape the Republic before.'

'No!'

'Not just tried, she succeeded.'

The young man frowned. 'That doesn't make sense. Why was she back in the Republic then, working in a shitty job in the campsite?'

'The BRD sent her back.'

'I don't believe you. That doesn't happen.'

'It does, I assure you.'

'Why wasn't she in jail? Everyone knows if you're caught trying to escape it's a long stretch in prison – at the very least.'

'That's a good question, Holger. Think about it. *Why wasn't she sent to jail?* Can you think of a reason?'

Müller saw the look of horror slowly make itself clear on his face. Then the penny dropped. 'Surely not?'

Müller nodded. 'I'm afraid so, Holger. Irma works for the Stasi as an unofficial informer. I know that, because I know the

Stasi colonel who arranged it all – her handler. It was a deal to stop her being sent back to the *Jugendwerkhof*.'

The young man continued to shake his head. 'But that means . . . ' He let the thought die in his mouth.

'Exactly, Holger. That means all your plans have been compromised, from the moment Dieter and Irma got together. The Stasi would have known everything.'

'But . . . ' He started to get up from his seat next to Müller. 'I'm going to have to tell Dieter and Joachim.' He prodded her with the gun. 'You'd better come with me.'

'I can and will, certainly, Holger. But is that the best course of action? I could be lying, and you'd make yourself look a fool if you confront Irma in front of the others.' She saw him hesitate. 'It's up to you, of course, but what I'd suggest is you take her to one side in a quiet moment. See if what I've said is true. Ask her about Hamburg. Ask her about the Harz mountains and the Brocken. Ask her what happened to her friend Beate. Ask her who killed Beate's boyfriend, Mathias. She might deny things, but you'll see on her face that I'm telling the truth. Then you use that information to your advantage.' Müller didn't like what she was doing – playing with the young man, much in the way Jäger would. But if it meant she and Tilsner survived this nightmare, it was worth it.

Holger sat down, mulling over what the detective was telling him. 'How?'

Müller knew he'd risen to the bait. Now to reel him in. 'You *threaten* to expose her, but you don't as long as she agrees to do what you want.'

'And what do I want?'

'You want to live, Holger. You don't want to die in some bloodbath when Stasi agents – or even worse, Soviet troops – storm this ship. Yes, you'll be locked up. Probably for quite a long time. But I promise, if you help me now, if you try to put an end to this, I will help you. So you use what I've told you to get Irma to persuade Dieter. She's the only one he might listen to.'

44

It's Dieter's turn for the rota for bridge duty – holding *Major* Müller at gunpoint alongside the Soviet captain. The hours have been ticking by – but this side of the boat we can't see anything other than an unbroken expanse of sea ice.

Dieter gives me a kiss as he takes the policeman with him to begin the handover. I almost shy away. I'm not sure if I even like him any more. My body tells me I do – my head tells me I don't. The policeman obviously senses some of this – I see him smirking at me behind Dieter's back.

Then Holger returns. After he waves *Hauptmann* Tilsner back to his bedroll, he shakes Joachim awake.

'Can you keep an eye on him a moment?' he asks his friend. 'I need to show Irma something.'

It's an odd request, but Joachim shakes himself awake and gets his gun ready.

Holger ushers me out into the gangway.

We move over to the other side of the ship. Here, through the porthole, I can see the sea ice give way in the distance to a snow-covered coastline. The Republic, or the BRD? I've no idea. All I know is, we must be getting close to our destination. All around us, we can hear the repetitive thunderous noise as the vessel ploughs relentlessly through the ice.

'I've got a horrible feeling about this, Irma. It's not going to turn out well.'

Is that all he wants to do? Bleat about our situation? He should have thought about that before he joined this deadly adventure – as should I.

'I don't think they're going to take us to the West,' he continues, 'still less let us get away. It doesn't make any sense.'

'They will – otherwise the two police officers die.'

'And you can say that so callously, can you? I wonder why that is?'

I glare at him. 'What do you mean by that?'

'I mean, what happened to your friends from the *Jugendwerkhof*. Who was it? Oh yes, Beate?'

I look at him in shock. 'What do you know about Beate?'

'Or perhaps I should ask you how Mathias died?'

And then realisation dawns. How could I be so stupid? After all, the notion that *Major* Müller is my friend was ridiculous from the start. She's been feeding him information.

'Do you want me to go on, Irma? I mean, we could talk about why – despite being guilty of *Republikflucht* – you *weren't* sent back to the *Jugendwerkhof*. Do you want to tell me about the deal you made to ensure that didn't happen? About who you had to supply information to.'

That does it. I kick him as hard as I can on the shin, then furiously pummel his stomach until those strong, meaty hands grab hold of mine and he pulls me into a bear hug. 'Calm down,' he whispers in my ear. I'm sure he can feel the wetness of my tears against his cheek. I'm sure he can sense my utter defeat. How I hate myself for what I've become. 'I'm sorry I had to say those things. I swear to you, they will remain a secret between us two. But—'

'But what?'

'But you have to help me. Help us.'

'How?'

'Now I know what you went through before, I'm even more certain that this isn't going to end well. They're trying to trick us. Lull us into a false sense of security. Then they'll strike. Even now, attack helicopters could be on their way to storm the ship. They were probably waiting until it got nearer to the coast. We have to try to persuade Dieter to give up. It's the only way we'll survive. And you're the only person he'll listen to.'

'Ha! You think he'll listen to me? I don't think he will. The man is on a mission. He will see it through to the bitter end, whatever that may be.'

'We know what it will be, Irma. That's why you have to try to convince him.'

'And if I don't, or won't?'

'It's not in my nature to be disloyal. But if you force me to tell him about you, if you won't help us get out of this mess, I won't hesitate to reveal to him what you really are.'

Holger hasn't left me with a choice. It's little more than black-mail – and I thought he was a genuinely nice guy. Looks can be deceptive.

We go together back up to the bridge.

Dieter looks confused and worried.

'What are you two doing up here?' he hisses.

'I'll look after her again for a moment,' says Holger. I see the policewoman throw him a small smile. They're in cahoots, no doubt. 'Irma wants a word with you.'

'Well, she can say what she wants here. We've no secrets between us.'

'In *private*, Dieter,' I insist. 'I don't want the whole world and his wife knowing my business.'

He rolls his eyes, but nods. Before he leaves the detective's side, he makes sure Holger's gun is trained on her instead of his own.

'I hope it's something important,' he says, once I've got him away from the bridge.

'It is. I want to hand myself in. I want us all to hand ourselves in.'

'I thought you were made of stronger stuff, Irma. I didn't take you for a coward.'

I want to tell him it's a bit rich, a construction soldier accusing someone else of cowardice, but I bite my tongue. 'It's not cowardice,' I say. 'It's realism. They are not going to let us get away with this. Look out there,' I urge, pointing through the porthole window. 'What do you see?'

'A frozen sea, and the coast.'

'But do you know if it's the Republic or the BRD?'

'We've been getting closer to the shoreline. But I looked over the captain's shoulder at his radar screen. We're still on course for Lübeck.'

'They won't let us get as far as Lübeck, Dieter, you know that. I'm asking you to give yourself in now. For me, for us. Yes, we'd be apart for some years in prison, but then we'd be released eventually and be together again.' I pull him towards me. Whisper urgently in his ear. 'Please, Dieter. For my sake. For all our sakes.'

He pushes me away. I can see in his eyes he's unmoved. They burn with revolutionary fervour. It's that Che Guevara look I used to find irresistible. Now, it spells danger to me. Danger to all of us.

'I told you before, Irma. You're in it now. In it till the end. But have more faith, please. Everything's worked out so far, hasn't it?'

I swear under my breath. 'I suppose so.'

'Have a little more faith in me then. Everything will turn out fine. Before you know it, we will be celebrating with rum and colas in a Western bar. And none of that Vita Cola shit. The real thing, Irma. That's our goal. No more of the shitty lives we led in the Republic. The real thing is within our grasp.'

45

Müller knew it was the endgame when she saw the helicopter hovering in the distance. Dieter next to her hadn't spotted it yet – but even though it was no more than a dot in the sky, she could tell from the shape it was a *Volkspolizei* Kamov Ka-26, the same model they'd used in their chase of Johannes Traugott through the Thuringian forest to Oberhof. When he and his wife had stolen her twin babies in scarcely credible circumstances at the hospital in Halle-Neustadt – thrusting Müller and her family to the very centre of the missing and murdered babies case she was supposed to be investigating. For that reason, it was an aircraft she'd never forget: she'd been on a desperate hunt for her own abducted hours-old baby son. The thought made her pine for Jannika and Johannes again. Helga too. But she had to hold herself together. It didn't look like they were preparing to storm the icebreaker – at least it wasn't a People's Army attack helicopter – but she knew that could change at any moment.

The question was, would the Republic's authorities allow the vessel to reach the BRD as Dieter expected? Müller scarcely found that credible. Her scepticism was borne out when she saw a well-known building on the horizon – something the icebreaker seemed to be heading towards. The *Teepott* at Warnemünde – next to and below the town's lighthouse – its futuristically curved roof looking like the two wings of a squat beetle about to take flight, rather than the teapot of its nick-name. It might remind some people of the much grander Sydney Opera House, and its sail-like roofs – but Müller knew the Republic's version had been completed several years before Australia's pride and joy.

Dieter still hadn't seen it, hadn't registered what it meant. But – with his gun jammed against her ribs – he looked to be taking a renewed interest at the icebreaker captain's radar screen. Müller prepared herself. Warnemünde meant one thing. Irma, Dieter and their gang had indeed been tricked. This ship wasn't heading to Lübeck – and probably never had been.

It was on a direct course to Rostock.

Slicing through the ice.

Delivering the criminals back into the hands of the DDR authorities.

For Müller, for Tilsner below, this was the most dangerous time.

Suddenly, Dieter realised. 'That's the fucking *Teepott!*' he shouted. '*Ublyudok!*' he shouted towards the captain.

Ublyudok! Bastard! About the only Russian swear word Müller did know. Dieter yanked her towards him, then started backing out of the bridge control room with his gun barrel firmly at her temple. She found herself trembling.

'None of you fuckers move! We're not going back there, I tell you. No way are we going back there!'

Müller half expected him to try to take control of the ship, but he seemed to have other ideas.

He was dragging her, running towards the room where Tilsner was being kept captive by the others. What was he planning to do? Part of her wanted to resist, to refuse to go anywhere, but she'd seen the wildness in his eyes. His gun wasn't for show. She'd no doubt he wouldn't hesitate to use it.

They got back to the room.

'They've tricked us!' he shouted breathlessly, a panicked look on his face.

'*Scheisse!*' responded Joachim. 'Tricked us how?'

'It's not fucking Lübeck. It's bloody Rostock. I can tell by the *Teepott* at Warnemünde. You can see it from the bridge as clear as daylight. They're taking us back to the Republic.'

'Are you sure?' asked Holger. 'Couldn't Lübeck have a similar structure?'

Müller decided to put them out of their misery. 'I can assure you, we saw the *Teepott*.'

'Shut up, police pig!' shouted Dieter, suddenly releasing her from his grip. 'OK, come on, you three – this way. Help me with this.' Müller watched him gesture towards one of the boxes they'd brought all the way by sled, and then on to the icebreaker via the helicopter. For some reason, the Soviets had failed to check the boxes' contents.

'What do we do about them?' asked Joachim, turning towards Müller and Tilsner.

With one hand on the box handle, Dieter used the other to raise his pistol to the firing position. 'They've outlived their usefulness.'

Irma jumped in the way. 'Don't be so fucking stupid. Look – there's a key in the door there. We just lock them in.'

With relief, Müller watched Dieter lower the gun. 'OK,' he said. 'Let's go.'

46

Müller couldn't help herself. She felt relieved. They might be in a locked room, but that was preferable to being in the full glare of the crew with a gun pointing at her head. And the fact that it *was* a locked room meant their inquiry – their case – was, in effect, over. If Irma, Dieter and their gang were planning to go back on the ice to try to reach Lübeck, good luck to them. With the snow clouds having cleared, they wouldn't get there. The police helicopter Müller had seen hovering near the coast would ensure that.

Tilsner seemed to have other ideas. She wondered what he was doing, given his hands were scrabbling down the back of his trousers. He fished something out and threw it towards her.

Instinctively, she caught it – then remembered where it had been, and wished she hadn't. It was one of the spare Makarov magazines he'd taken from the Prora barracks at the start of all this. Clearly any search the Soviets had carried out on her deputy hadn't included his more intimate orifices. He held the other in his hand, and was in the process of loading it into his empty pistol. She got hers from her jacket pocket and – ignoring for a moment where the magazine had spent the last few hours – proceeded to copy him. She didn't have time to ask why, if Tilsner had the magazines secreted away this whole time, he hadn't used them earlier.

'We need to find those fuckers,' he said.

'OK. But first we have to get out of here. Any ideas? If we were in a movie, we'd shoot off the lock. But as we know from our police training, that rarely works in real life.'

She watched him kneel down by the door, and peer into the keyhole.

'Aha! Luckily for us, the stupid fuckers have left the key in the lock.'

He got the butt end of his Makarov, and smashed it against the glass of the door's window. It bounced off. '*Scheisse!* It must be reinforced.'

He scanned round the room. In the corner was some sort of metal box, covered in dirty black grease.

'Ah. As I thought. I suspected this was the engineers' room – and this is their toolbox. And—' he theatrically drew out a huge spanner, then pretended to stagger under its weight '—like most things on ships, it's supersized, with supersize tools. Mind yourself.' He pivoted the giant metal tool behind his back, and launched it into the glass. With a splintering crash, it gave way. Tilsner knocked out the rest of the glass out to avoid cutting himself, then reached for the key, pulled it out and brought it round to their side of the lock.

'You looked like a professional burglar for a moment there,' joked Müller.

'That's nearer the truth than you'll ever know,' he replied, as he turned the key, and they were free.

'Up to the bridge!' shouted Müller. 'We might be able to see what's going on and where they've got to.'

When they reached the bridge, Müller realised something had gone horribly wrong. The captain looked ashen-faced, and was barking orders in Russian to the crew, at the same time as trying to deal with angry instructions over the radio.

Müller knew she would have to test her schoolgirl Russian once more. 'What's the problem?' she asked.

'Those East German criminal yobs have shot one of my men,' she hurriedly translated for Tilsner.

'Ask him where?'

She didn't need to translate, as the captain understood enough German.

'Down on Deck 10.'

'What's there?' asked Müller.

'The generators, the turbines . . . '

Tilsner had got the gist of the Russian. *Turbiny* wasn't so difficult. 'The shitting reactors. They're there too, aren't they?'

'*Reactory! Da, da!*'

Müller, in a panic, briefly glanced out of the bridge's viewing window. They weren't on their way to Rostock. They'd already arrived. She had a sudden horrible premonition of what Dieter was up to.

47

'Have you heard, Comrade Minister?'

'Of course I've heard, Jäger. Heads will roll because of this. It looks like they're trying to take control of the ship's nuclear reactors. I've got to go to an emergency meeting of the State Council any minute now. The Soviets are furious. How did you let this happen, Jäger? How in God's name did you let this happen? What have they got with them? I know you said they'd stolen guns – that's self-evident in that they've shot dead a Soviet crewman. Anything else? And you'd better be honest with me here, Jäger.'

'I'm afraid there are two boxes' worth of high explosives missing from the Prora People's Army arsenal, Comrade Minister.'

'Scheisse! It gets worse, doesn't it? You incompetent idiot. Why didn't we know this before? I've told the powers that be in the Soviet High Command that all they have with them is semi-automatic weapons and pistols. That's bad enough. But at least they were confident that wouldn't be enough to damage the reactors. But *two boxes of high explosives*? That's enough to blow the reactors and the whole fucking ship out of the water. It will be an international incident the like of which the Republic has never known. Never mind that Rostock, our most important port and one of our biggest cities, could be contaminated by what – in effect – will be one great massive nuclear dirty bomb.'

48

The frozen Ostsee
2 January 1979

Müller clattered after Tilsner down the metal stairs, deeper into the bowels of the ship, down and down, missing stairs and crashing against walls in their haste.

Once they were at Deck 10, she frantically looked for the notices in Russian to show them where the reactor room was. All she could see was a door sealed with a giant wheel lock – as though they were in a submarine, rather than a merchant vessel. But the notice on the door in Russian was the giveaway.

WARNING! DO NOT ENTER UNLESS WEARING PROTECTIVE CLOTHING!

Tilsner ignored it and began to turn the wheel.

The door led into a giant chamber, full of hissing steam and the clanking of metal. They crossed the threshold, crouching, guns at the ready, scanning to see if they could get a visual on the construction soldiers. They moved along a metal walkway, with a single guard rail between them and a twenty-metre drop to the bowels of the ship. To their side was a huge metal structure, which Müller could only speculate contained the reactors themselves.

They scrambled onwards, Müller's head lighthousing from side to side, trying to see where Irma, Dieter and the others were.

'*Scheisse!*' she heard Tilsner curse under his breath.

Her eyes were drawn to what he'd found.

The body of a crewman. Was this the man the captain had been talking about, or had Dieter and his gang killed again?

With every passing minute, the chances of Irma facing the death penalty grew exponentially.

Then a shot rang out.

Müller flattened herself to the floor of the gangway. Ahead of her, Tilsner had done the same.

She looked down in the direction the bullet had been fired from. There they were, some twenty metres below, at the other side of the reactor casing. They were gathered round something with wires leading from it.

'Stay right there and don't move!' shouted Dieter. 'This can all end peacefully – but only if you agree to our demands.'

'We're not negotiating!' yelled Tilsner. 'We don't negotiate with criminals.'

Another shot, hitting the steel plate above them, the ringing from the ricochets echoing in Müller's ears.

'Just be quiet, Werner,' she hissed. 'It's not the time for macho bravado. I'll do the talking.' Raising her voice, but keeping her head down, she shouted: 'We're listening! What is it you want?'

'We want safe passage. Otherwise we'll blow everyone – including ourselves – sky high. We've nothing to lose.'

On that last point, Müller knew Dieter was correct. He might have forced the others into this last desperate gamble, but now they'd done it, there really were no alternatives. The Republic, and the Soviets, either gave in to their demands – or they stormed the vessel, at huge risk to the civilian population. The option of persuading them to give themselves up via Irma and Holger had failed. They would know that. The death penalty for all of them was a certainty. By judicial process, or more likely via a carefully aimed Stasi or People's Army bullet.

'Safe passage where?' yelled Müller.

'To Lübeck Bay. To the BRD side of the shipping channel in Lübeck Bay. The captain needs to head that way down the Ostsee anyway, and then out to the North Sea via the Kattegatt strait. It's the best solution for all of us.'

Müller wasn't convinced she would be able to persuade the authorities in the Republic to agree to that. She wasn't even sure *who* in the Republic she should be trying to persuade. This went higher than Jäger. Higher than Reiniger. Higher, perhaps, even than Honecker and Mielke.

She had no doubt the request would go all the way up to the Kremlin.

She had no idea how they would react.

But she would do all in her power to try to convince them that this way was the only way to avoid bloodshed and potentially devastating nuclear contamination of a city – never mind saving her own and Tilsner's lives and those of the Russian crew.

49

Up on the bridge, the captain seemed somewhat relieved when Müller claimed they had the situation under control, and that the armed terrorists were being pinned down by her own officer. It was a partial lie, of course, but if this was going to end without bloodshed – and them all being blown to smithereens – then she needed him on her side. The worst thing would be if Stasi special agents or People's Army special forces stormed the vessel.

Via the ship's radio, she was patched through to an incident room that had been set up in Rostock. She was unsurprised by the voice at the other end of the line: Jäger.

'This is an utter mess, Karin. Berlin is leaning on me. Moscow is leaning on Berlin. We need a solution.'

'I think I may have one, Comrade *Oberst*. The terrorists want safe passage to the West.'

'We can never give them that. We do not negotiate with terrorists, counter-revolutionaries, fascists and criminals. This gang ticks many of those boxes.'

Müller glanced up at the ship's captain. He raised an eyebrow. He might not know much German, but he could hear from the tone of Jäger's voice that things weren't going well.

'I'm not talking about some sort of high-profile spy swap at the Anti-Fascist Protection Barrier or the state border with the BRD, Comrade *Oberst*. This would simply be a pragmatic solution to meet their demands without bringing embarrassment to the Republic, and avoid a potentially cataclysmic event.'

'Don't overplay your hand, Comrade Major. We've taken scientific advice. There is no way they can set off an uncontrolled nuclear reaction by attempting to blow up a ship's nuclear reactor with a bit of dynamite. At best they will blow themselves up, at worst there will be some minor radioactive contamination. We're not talking Hiroshima or Nagasaki here. We're not talking about starting a Third World War.'

Müller gave a heavy sigh. She saw the captain look up to the heavens. He, at least, seemed to be on her side. He probably wanted every East German in sight off his ship. 'With respect, Comrade *Oberst*, you're not here at the sharp end. They've already killed one crew member. They're desperate. Whatever advice the scientists have given you, do you want the ship blown up just to prove a point?'

She could imagine the fury on Jäger's face. She didn't care. Müller knew she had to win this argument. She had to persuade him – but that would only be the start of the battle of wills. He would have to persuade his paymasters in Berlin – as far up as Mielke and his ilk.

'What exactly are you suggesting?'

'I'm suggesting we humour them, to some extent. Meet their demands, to some extent.'

'*How?*'

'The *Arktika*'s scheduled voyage takes it through the Ostsee towards the North Sea anyway. When we get near Lübeck Bay, we allow them out onto the ice. Whatever happens after that, doesn't really matter. That's the end of your major incident.'

'*Berlin and Moscow will never accept letting them go without paying the price for attempted terrorism and murder. Two murders now, let me remind you. Frau Richter and this Soviet crewman.*'

'Well, at least let me allow the captain to leave Rostock. Once we're underway again, I'll be able to convince them that we're meeting their demands.'

'*It'll mean sending what is – in effect – a floating nuclear bomb up the Baltic towards the BRD and Denmark.*'

'I thought you'd been advised there was no way this could result in a full-blown nuclear explosion, whatever happened? Anyway, Comrade *Oberst*, if they do their worst – surely it's better it happens in the middle of the Ostsee than in the middle of Rostock.'

'*Very well, Karin. I will make that case to Berlin. I doubt they will agree . . . but, who knows? You realise you and Tilsner will have to stay on the vessel and see this through to its conclusion, don't you?*'

Müller thought again of her little family back in Berlin. Nevertheless, she knew what Jäger said was correct. She and Tilsner had to stay and see things out.

'Of course I do, Comrade *Oberst*. I take my duties in trying to ensure this situation has a peaceful outcome with the utmost seriousness.'

'It can't just be peaceful, Karin. It has to be lawful, too. That means the killers must face justice one way or another. I need to be completely clear on that point.'

50

As soon as Dieter – his wild eyes madder than ever – ushers us down into the depths of the ship with the explosives, I know this isn't going to turn out well.

'This is madness!' I scream at him.

'Shut up, Irma!' He waves his gun at me, and I've no doubt that if I defy him he won't hesitate to use it. 'I've told you, you're either with us or against us. Which is it to be?' I know then, seeing the viciousness of his reaction, that there is no future for us. The dreams, the hopes of a new life in the West already soured before we've even got there. Although the way it is going, I don't believe we'll ever get there.

'Don't bully her,' says Holger.

'Dieter's right!' yells Joachim. 'I said we should have never brought a girl along. She's been a liability from the start.'

Dieter stands at the top of the stairwell – sharing the weight of the explosives box with Joachim. 'Look,' he says to me more calmly. 'I'm sorry I lost my temper, but we are in a desperate situation. I don't want a death sentence conferred on me by one of the Republic's show trials. I'm sure you don't either. You and Holger stay here if you want. Give yourselves up if you want. But mark my words, that will be the end result. If you come with me, follow my advice, you'll still have a chance of fulfilling your dream and getting to the West.'

I lower my head and give a slight nod. He's right of course. Everything's gone too far now.

It's when we get into the reactor room that things go wrong.

We ignore the warning about protective clothing, even though all of us can understand it. We have done Russian at school. But there's a crewman on guard at the entrance. You'd have thought they'd have armed guards, but he isn't armed. He can see we are, but he still tries to stop us.

That's his mistake.

He stands in the gangway, blocking it.

Dieter raises his gun. The seaman won't get out of the way.

The next thing that happens fills me with horror, with shame. I have killed before – so I am no innocent.

But Dieter simply blows the man's brain out with a single shot. Even Holger and Joachim go white in the face. This isn't what any of us agreed to. The man slumps to the floor, twitching, blood and brain matter pooling about his head. Instinctively, I kneel down, cradle his head, try to help him even though I know it's too late.

Dieter yanks me up.

'Get a move on, Irma. He's dead – leave him.'

We descend a set of ladders. It's difficult for Dieter and Joachim. They have to share out the contents of the explosives box between them before they carefully go down, rung by rung. My apprehension grows. But as soon as I saw the radiation warning sign on that first door – the red fan-like emblem that looks a little like a windmill in a yellow cornfield – then I knew the crux of Dieter's plan.

I hope that plan is to threaten to do something. Not to actually cause an explosion.

He and Joachim work to set the explosives, putting them under the reactor, then running wires and cables to where we are. I worry about how stable everything is. What happens if they go off accidentally? Would I ever get to see Oma again? Would I ever get to see Mutti released from prison – freed from behind the bars I, in effect, helped to build around her.

There's a metallic noise on the gangway above.

Scheisse! It's those fucking police officers again.

They haven't seen us yet, but Dieter raises his gun and fires a warning shot. At least, I hope it was a warning shot.

They start trading shouts.

Another shot.

Dieter sets out his demands. I see one of the officers – *Major* Müller – withdraw to the bridge and radio back to the Republic.

Dieter and Joachim are busying themselves with the explosives. Holger and I wait. He looks as fed up with everything as I feel, sitting on the oily metal floor, hugging his knees tightly into himself, as though he's trying to make a foetal ball.

This is the endgame.

The chances of success are – I think – incredibly slim. I don't even want to contemplate what happens if we fail.

51

Müller waited on the bridge for Jäger's radioed reply – even though she had no idea how long it would take to come through. When the captain passed the microphone to her, indicating he was back on the airwaves, she was surprised when she looked at her watch to see fewer than fifteen minutes had elapsed.

'OK, Karin, you've got your own way, up to a point.'

'That's encouraging, Comrade *Oberst*.'

'Berlin has managed to persuade Moscow to allow the icebreaker to continue on its journey to the Arctic, despite the risks. However, their demands to be taken to Lübeck Bay will only be partially met. We can't allow the ship in its present condition to go into the bay. Lübeck is BRD territory – we can't be seen to have simply shifted a potential nuclear explosion from one of our cities to one of theirs. So they will have to be let out onto the ice within the Republic's waters, but in case they insist on checking on the ship's radar screen, the captain will be given the authority to go as near as possible to BRD territory and let them out on the ice there. But no closer than fifteen kilometres to the coastline.'

'Fifteen kilometres? In this weather? They might not survive a walk that far after what they've been through.'

She heard Jäger guffawing with laughter. '*Why should we care about that? You're a murder detective, not a bloody social worker. Anyway, the conditions might not be as bad. There's a thaw on its way. More snow first, so it may get worse before it gets better. But then a thaw, and rain.*'

'What happens if it thaws before they get off the ice?'

'*Again, that's not our problem. But I don't think you understand. The idea is to let them on to the ice. The only way they're getting off is in a coffin or handcuffs. Because as soon as they are back on the ice, as soon as they are off the ship and the threat has passed, your orders are to arrest them. Or kill them. All of them. And just in case I'm not making myself clear, that includes your little friend Irma. If she succeeds in making it to the West, I will hold you personally responsible. And there will be repercussions. Not just for you. But for your family too.*'

Müller let herself back in to the radiation restricted area – again without protective clothing. She wondered if that decision would haunt her in years to come. Jäger had been the one to raise Nagasaki and Hiroshima, but she knew in Japan – while there had been devastating contemporaneous consequences from the dropping of the bombs – some of the deleterious health effects had only become apparent in the following decades.

Taking no chances in case Dieter was still trigger-happy, she crawled along the gangway until she reached Tilsner. He was still lying flat to the ground, his gun trained on the terrorists below.

'What did he say?' he whispered.

Müller edged forward and brought her mouth close to his ear. 'They will meet the demands, up to a point.'

'And what point is that?'

'The point where they're back on the ice and unable to threaten the ship any more. And they're insisting it has to be in DDR waters, and it must be at least fifteen kilometres from the coast.'

'And then what – we let them get away? Start their new lives as capitalists?'

'No, our orders are to arrest them. All of them. Or to kill them. Jäger was clear about that.'

A shout rang out from below. It was Dieter.

'Once you two have finished whispering sweet nothings to each other, we need to know what the decision is.'

The noise of the ship gave him his answer, the hum and vibrations signifying the propellers had been engaged again. The icebreaker was on the move.

Müller cupped her hands round her mouth and shouted down. 'They've agreed to your demands! You'll be taken to the coast off Lübeck, and then released on to the ice!'

If she'd been Dieter, she'd have been suspicious. Governments – especially communist governments – didn't give in to threats like that. But she was telling him what he wanted to know. There was silence from below, and soon the regular thunder of breaking ice had resumed its relentless rhythm.

The *Arktika* was back doing what it did best.

Carving a passage through the frozen sea.

52

'So, what do we do until then?' whispered Tilsner. 'Do we lie here like lemons, soaking up whatever radiation rays are flying around here? I think I'd rather go back to a safer part of the ship.'

Müller looked down at Irma and her friends. They were sitting in a huddle next to their box of explosives and wires. It was too risky to leave them unobserved. But perhaps she and Tilsner could divide up the time until they reached the drop-off point. The captain had indicated that wouldn't be long – at most, two hours of smashing through the ice – until they were approximately equidistant between Boltenhagen in the Republic, and Grömitz in the BRD. Neither he, nor Moscow or Berlin, were willing for him to travel further into the Bay of Lübeck.

'If you want to stretch your legs for a while, feel free. I can keep watch. Though as far as they're concerned, their demands have been met. There seems little sense in them setting off their explosives. But I don't want them moving from here until it's time for them to disembark.'

Müller and Tilsner did a couple of half-hour shifts on watch, then Müller heard the thunder of the ice cracks slowing, the drone of the engines moderating.

While Tilsner kept guard, she moved to the control room on the bridge.

'I think this is about as far as we should go,' said the captain.

Müller looked out – visibility was next to nothing. An icy fog had descended, making the Ostsee look even less hospitable, if that was possible.

'Are we at the agreed point?' she asked.

'More or less. To the east is DDR territorial waters, or rather sea ice, as you can see.' He lifted a pair of powerful binoculars to his eyes, and then swung his head round from side to side. 'Well, to be honest you can't see very much, but I can't control the weather.' He pointed to the other side. 'That way lies the DDR coast. Here in the middle – where we are – is the shipping channel, although no ships have been passing recently. It's too icy. Today, though, the thaw is due to start. First fog, then snow, then rain. That is, if you can trust the forecast.'

'I thought the instructions were to make sure they were only set free in DDR waters?'

The captain shrugged. 'It's not my job to play judge and jury. I want them and their explosives off my vessel as soon as possible. Their lead man might be a psychiatric case, but he's not stupid. I saw him checking the radar screen before. He will want to see they have half a chance before he agrees to leave.'

Dieter was suspicious when Müller yelled down from the gangway that they had reached their destination.

'I want to be able to see the West German coast before we agree to disembark!' he shouted back, his voice echoing and metallic against the heavy steel plate that encased the reactor room.

'That's not going to be possible,' said Müller. 'It's thick fog out there. Fresh snow's on its way again too. But you can come up and check the radar map. The captain will explain where we are.'

It went quiet for a few moments as Dieter and his cronies considered what she said.

'Fine. But we're bringing the explosives with us. And I warn you, they're primed and charged. If you try to trick us, I'll blow us all sky high.'

They'd had a couple of hours of calm, when the threat looked to have receded. But Müller knew they were fast approaching another critical point. Any failure on her part, and her and Tilsner's lives were at risk. Not just theirs though. The future of more than a hundred Soviet seamen, and the four criminals themselves, depended on Müller and Tilsner bringing this to a peaceful conclusion.

53

The wild look is back in Dieter's eyes, and it scares the hell out of me. He might try to play it cool, but this has escalated into something bigger than any of us imagined when we set off from Sassnitz harbour less than twenty-four hours ago. I'm not sure he's fully in control. Either of himself, or the situation. I can sense Holger feels as I do, though Joachim is still playing the role of faithful lieutenant.

We knew our venture would be risky. We knew it had a good chance of failing. What none of us could predict is that we'd end up at the centre of a potential international nuclear incident.

'Do you think they're trying to trick us?' asks Joachim after *Major* Müller shouts down that we've arrived. He's looking scared now too. The way he bites his lip at the end of his question is a giveaway.

'That's why this little baby is our insurance policy,' says Dieter, lifting his makeshift bomb and cradling it. Then he feigns as though to drop it.

'Don't do that!' I yell. 'This isn't funny.' I see Holger raise his eyes – he's getting as fed up of my boyfriend's antics as I am.

'Relax, Irma. I'm not planning to do anything stupid – unless they do first. This is just a bargaining tool. We need a sled, supplies, warm blankets, new white sheets. They're not going to be dropping us off at Lübeck harbour wall, are they? We'll still have a few kilometres to walk. But then . . . then we'll be free.'

I see Dieter peering at the radar screen, still holding his insurance policy.

'Where's the shipping lane?' he asks in Russian.

'We're in the middle of it. Right here.' The captain motions with his arms backwards and forwards along the length of the ship.

'And we're facing Lübeck at the moment?'

'Yes. But the shortest route to the BRD – to a centre of population – is to head for Grömitz, here.' The captain points out a dark green area on the radar screen. 'It's about fifteen kilometres.'

'*Fifteen kilometres?!* That's ridiculous,' says Dieter. 'We might not even get there before nightfall.'

The captain folds his arms. 'Take it or leave it. I'll give you ten minutes to get off my ship. After that, we're setting sail for the Arctic – with or without you on board.'

'What – you'd rather have us and this on board,' Dieter holds up the explosives, 'than take us a few kilometres nearer the coast?'

The captain shrugs. 'It's not my decision. I take my orders from Moscow.'

'Let me talk to Moscow, then.'

His emotion-choked voice tells me he's losing it. And the captain's implacable expression speaks of someone whose decision will not be altered, whatever the threats.

Holger lays one of his huge hands on Dieter's shoulder. 'Fifteen kilometres is not so far. If we make good progress, even across the ice it might only take three hours or so. Let's go with it.'

For a moment, Dieter looks as though he's going to start arguing. Then he gives a small nod of acceptance.

They use one of the vessel's lifeboats to lower us down to sea level – or rather ice level, because the Ostsee is still frozen solid, apart from the channel cut by this massive floating beast with its beating nuclear heart.

The boat they use is the one nearest the bow of the now stationary ship. Dieter seems to have calmed down, and his mood has changed to one of elation that his plan is apparently working. I'm more worried. Once we're on the ice, and the explosives are off the vessel, what's to stop the captain doing what he did before – cutting a circular channel around us so we are stranded, this time without the opportunity to take two police officers hostage?

I nearly suggest to him that we should take Müller and Tilsner with us. That they, rather than the explosives, can be our insurance policy.

But I think, why? And what would happen if they managed to turn the tables on us, as we had on them? I haven't seen them for a few minutes. They're probably getting ready to be helicoptered back to the Republic, their part in this drama now over.

We clamber in to the boat. My teeth are chattering, partly through fear, partly the renewed exposure to the bitter cold.

There's so much that can go wrong, and in this freezing fog would anyone actually know?

The cables attached to the boat creak and groan as we're lowered to sea level.

Two of the ship's crew are with us to help – although I know it's simply because they want rid of us as soon as possible.

With a crunching sound, the boat settles on the broken ice at the side of the larger vessel. One of the crewmen peers over the side and tests the ice with a long pole.

We watch as fog and mist swirl around. Strands of Dieter's hair that aren't under his hat have turned white as the ice-laden atmosphere freezes them solid. I raise my eyes and can see my red hair is the same – already it's become frosty whiskers.

'It's good,' the crewman says. They fling a rope ladder over the side of the lifeboat; one of them stretches out a hand to help me climb out. With my twisted ankle causing me some pain, it's a struggle, but I swing my legs over and lower myself to the frozen surface of the sea.

As my feet touch the ice, feel its solidity beneath, I realise I am nearly there. According to the captain, this side of the ship is BRD territorial waters. If the sea ice was solid land, we would already be in the West.

If . . .

I watch the others climb out, and help them with the equipment. Then once we're all on the ice, the crewmen fling over the sled which was part of Dieter's list of demands.

It lands near our feet with a thud.

As the others start loading it, I peer up for the last time at the icebreaker, marvelling at its power, its majesty, acknowledging that – yes – there are some things the Communist world does better than the West. But in everyday life in Sellin, and before that at the *Jugendwerkhof*, the brilliance of Soviet icebreaker technology was utterly irrelevant.

It's a world I'm finally leaving behind, and not a moment too soon.

54

While Dieter was distracted negotiating with the captain over distances to the shore, and what supplies the Soviet crew would let them have, Müller and Tilsner were executing a pre-arranged plan.

Irma and the construction soldiers would be lowered from a lifeboat towards the front of the vessel. Further back, on the same side, Müller and Tilsner – armed with their Makarovs and with more spare ammunition donated by the Soviets – clambered down a steel cable ladder.

Müller took it more slowly than her deputy, going second and making sure she didn't look down. She'd suffered from a fear of heights ever since that fateful day at the top of the ski jump in Oberhof as a teenager. But she remembered how she'd conquered it in the same town on top of the Interhotel Panorama when the life of her own newly born baby had been at stake. If she could do it then, she could do it now. In any case, she knew there was no point looking down – the ladder simply disappeared into the fog.

From the relative warmth of the ship, the plunge into sub-zero temperatures was a shock. Clinging on to the ladder and easing herself down, she could feel the ends of her fingers becoming numb with cold. Yet she had to keep a steady pace and try to control her panic. They only had a few minutes before the lifeboat containing Irma and the others was lowered. By then, they needed to have hidden themselves among the broken ice blocks at the side of the giant ship.

'You took your time,' hissed Tilsner, when she got to sea level. Once he'd checked the piece of ice he was perched on wasn't going to topple, he stretched out his arms to help her off the ladder, across a treacherous trench of slush between the ice plates and the vessel. 'There's a good hiding place here,' he whispered.

Whether they needed it in this blanket of fog, Müller wasn't convinced. Nevertheless, she followed his example, crouching behind a huge block of ice which shielded them from the bow of the ship. They turned their heads towards the ice, pulling the hoods of their camouflage jackets in on their faces. The fog itself provided excellent cover. But even if it lifted temporarily, she knew their camouflage suits would blend into the icy whiteness.

'Here they come,' said Tilsner, peeking over the top of the ice mound.

Müller couldn't see anything through the murk. But she could hear the groaning of the cables, and the banging of the lifeboat against the metal sides of the ship, getting closer and closer.

Then, through the curtain of mist, they could see shadowy figures being helped out of the boat, onto the ice. For a few moments, they waited as Dieter and Irma's gang readied their sled.

Soon the hum of the icebreaker's engines increased in intensity.

Müller realised with horror the vessel was already moving again – all around her the sound of thunderous cracks, like a thousand bones being broken one by one.

'Quick!' Tilsner's whisper was urgent. He dragged her away from the vessel, and the most perilous part of the ice sheet. Five metres, ten, then he shoved her down in the snow, lying flat alongside her.

Once her heartbeat slowed, Müller risked raising her head. The ghoul-like figures of Irma's group had moved away in a panic with their sled to reach a safer part of the ice. They seemed to be ready now to start their journey – the journey they hoped and believed would see them free in the West in a matter of hours.

It would be a perilous one – for the fugitives, and for Müller and Tilsner.

One fall through the ice would kill.

One bullet from Dieter's gun could pierce her heart.

And one false move with the explosives the gang still carried could send them plummeting to their deaths in the icy Baltic.

Was this pursuit of justice really worth it? Wouldn't it have been better to refuse Jäger's orders? To have demanded to be airlifted from the icebreaker, resigned her position, be reunited with her family and then slowly – somehow – to have rebuilt her life. And why couldn't the border troops have done this final job? Why was it being left to two detectives from the *Volkspolizei*? She knew the answers. If anything went wrong, if this became an international incident, the blame could be directed at two rogue officers following suspects into the BRD's territorial waters. The

Republic could claim it wasn't an official operation or an official decision.

It was too late to turn back. The icebreaker had gone. And in this foggy weather, there would be no helicopter airlift – not until it cleared, anyway.

They'd solved the crime. Now they had to bring the perpetrators to justice. Müller's training and pride demanded it. But, if she had any choice in the matter, this would end without bloodshed.

Unfortunately, she wasn't sure the choice would be hers to make.

She pulled her Makarov from her shoulder holster. Gestured to Tilsner to do the same.

The hunt was about to begin.

55

I panic as the icebreaker pulls away and the ice beneath us starts to shake and crack.

'Quick, everyone!' shouts Dieter. He's pulling the sled off to the side, helped by Joachim. I try to run after them, but my bad ankle gives way.

'Hurry up, Irma!' he shouts, as though yelling at me will somehow make my leg better. He seems more concerned with his precious cargo of explosives and food than he is with me. Holger is more caring. He helps me to my feet and allows me to lean against him as we hobble away to where the ice is safer.

'Don't worry,' he says. 'I'll make sure you're safe.'

I look down at his giant hands and I know I want them to protect me. To help me. To hold me.

The others have waited for us on a safer piece of the ice, but Dieter hardly spares me a glance. He seems to be staring at his feet. Then I see why.

The ice is melting. A thaw is on its way.

'There's no need to panic,' says Holger, seeing the expressions of horror on Dieter and Joachim's faces. 'We just have to pick our way carefully to the shore.' He seems to be taking over from

Dieter, his voice authoritative. 'And I think it's too dangerous to keep dragging that heavy sled. We should abandon it. It's slowing us down, and if we encounter a patch of thinner ice, it might cause it to collapse around us.'

'No!' shouts Dieter, that manic look in his eyes.

'Why not?' asks Holger. 'The explosives have served their purpose. We need to abandon it before we get to the BRD coastline anyway, otherwise *they'll* be arresting us, never mind the Republic's *Grenztruppen*.'

Dieter appears to be about to argue, when suddenly a shout rings out from behind us through the fog.

'Drop your weapons and hold your hands in the air!' It's *Major* Müller. *Scheisse!* 'You're all under arrest for the murders of Monika Richter and a Soviet seaman. Not to mention the attempted terrorism charges.'

Holger drops his gun. I don't have one any more. We raise our hands above our heads.

Dieter and Joachim both raise an arm – but it's their gun hands, holding loaded pistols.

I rush over to Dieter. 'Don't be an idiot.' I try to grapple with his gun arm. He shoves me aside brutally. Then he fires towards the direction of the shout. Joachim copies him, like the faithful lapdog he is. I try to climb on Dieter's back, but Holger pulls me away.

'This way!' he yells, running off and dragging me with him. 'Get your hands above your head. Leave the idiots to it. We've got to save ourselves.'

I turn my head, see the flash from their pistols as Dieter and Joachim fire once more, as though they're outlaws making their last stand. And I suppose they are.

Then I hear two more shots – this time from away to the side. I glance round again. Dieter and Joachim are both slumping in slow motion to the floor, like two trees felled by the same axe.

I try to loosen Holger's grip. 'We've got to go back and help them!'

'No, Irma,' he orders. 'We need to get off the ice. Now.'

I peer into his eyes and look again at his meaty hands. And then I realise. It wasn't Dieter who saved me, pulling me from the icy water under the remains of the pier in Sellin. A flashback of those hands pulling me out is burned on my brain. It was Holger.

He saved me then.

He wants to save me again – this time from myself.

And I realise I'm going to let him.

56

When the first shots rang out, Müller threw herself to the ice. Tilsner had done the same. That was when she noticed the snow on top was damper than before. *Scheisse*. It was beginning to melt. She didn't have time to compute in her head what that meant, except that it was bad news.

She was just about to shout a second warning to Dieter's gang, when two of them fired again. The bullet thudded into the ice a few metres from them. There would be no second warning now.

She raised her head briefly above the ice block they were sheltering behind, got Dieter's head in her sights, and squeezed the Makarov's trigger.

His head was thrown back by the impact, then his body slowly crumpled.

Alongside him, Müller could see his friend collapse almost in a stereo effect. Tilsner must have fired at the same time.

Both were trained police marksmen.

Both had hit their targets.

When she was sure that Dieter and Joachim were lifeless – or at least wouldn't be firing back any time soon, she crept forwards towards their bodies. When she reached them, she felt their pulses.

Nothing.

She looked up, expecting to see Tilsner alongside her. He wasn't there. Instead, he was disappearing into the mist. 'I'll get the others!' he shouted over his shoulder.

'Wait, Werner,' she ordered. But he was already gone.

She rummaged in her pockets for the small camera she carried with her for recording crime scenes. They had completed fifty per cent of Jäger's required target. Müller hadn't wanted it to be this way, but Dieter and Joachim had defied her order to give up their weapons and hold up their hands. They had fired at her and Tilsner, twice.

Before she took the photographs she would need as evidence – in case helicopters from the Republic were unable to recover the bodies – she altered the scene slightly. She'd learnt things from Jäger in their last case. Both of the young men's weapons had dislodged from their hands as they'd fallen.

She put her gloves on, and rearranged the guns back in their hands – how it had been when she and Tilsner fired the fatal shots.

This was a recreation of the truth. Not a perversion of it, as Jäger favoured.

She lifted the camera and clicked the shutter to record the scene.

Whether the Republic would ever publish these photos as a warning to other would-be *Republikflüchtlinge*, she didn't know. Perhaps the authorities would show the proof to the young men's relatives, how they met their deaths as criminals resisting arrest.

Or perhaps everything might get hushed up.

She didn't care. She needed the evidence to protect her job. Her own family.

Should she try to follow in Tilsner's direction? Should she try to track the other two down?

Then she looked down at the melting ice beneath her feet.

57

We know we are in a race against time to get off the ice before it transforms into a raging sea. This might have felt like the Arctic – a Soviet nuclear icebreaker named the *Arktika* had played a central role in our dramatic escape – but this is the Ostsee. Only once in my lifetime has it been frozen like this. I was two or three years old and can barely remember – and as Oma loves to insist, this winter is not – so far – as cold. But now it is returning to its natural state.

Water. Square kilometre after square kilometre of open sea.

And already there is a layer of it on top of the ice, and we are sloshing through slush – hoping to God the ice is still thick enough to hold.

We're concentrating on going as fast as we can, despite my injured leg. The icebreaker has long gone – the option of giving ourselves up and being saved that way has disappeared. Holger would have more chance of saving himself, of reaching the West, if he abandoned me. I can see in his eyes he's not going to do that. Because every time he looks at me, every time he looks with concern at my ankle, I see love there.

Perhaps being in extremes sharpens your senses. Even before he'd fired those two shots I'd seen Dieter for what he was. A hothead who cared more about grand gestures of defiance than taking care of me, his girlfriend. With Holger it's different. We haven't declared our feelings for each other. To all intents and purposes we are just two acquaintances.

But I know he will not leave me out here.

We will die together, or survive together.

And then we see him, camouflaged like us. Gaining on us.

We know that this is it. That we've come so close to reaching freedom, but it will be snatched away.

Holger stops. He's accepted our fate. He holds me close – hugging me.

'Leave me,' I whisper. 'You could still outrun him. It can't be many kilometres further.'

He shakes his head and hugs me tighter. 'I'm not leaving you, Irma.'

Those words, of course, I could have taken at face value. But in that instant, I realise they mean more than that.

He never wants to leave me, and I never want to leave his side.

I want those strong, industrial hands to hold me for the rest of my life – even if that life is short.

The policeman's shouting at us. He's too far away. We can't make out what he's saying. We put our hands above our heads again, assuming that's what he wants before he arrests us and takes us back to the Republic. If any of us survive that long.

But as he takes shape and emerges from the fog, his shouted words take on more clarity.

'Run, run!' he's shouting. He's overtaking us, not stopping to arrest us. I see that he – like us – has a white bedsheet wrapped around him to blend in with the ice that is fast turning to slush. 'Run and save yourselves!' he yells over his shoulder. 'There's not much time left!'

Then I have a horrible thought. Where is his partner?

'What about *Major* Müller?' I shout. He doesn't hear, carries on running. 'What will happen to her? Surely you have to help her?' But he's gone. Either he hasn't heard, or he doesn't care. He's seen his opportunity and – like us – wants to make sure if he gets to dry land, it will be in the West, not the East.

I suddenly realise he's one of us.

A *Republikflüchtling*.

An escaper.

And he's leaving her behind to die.

58

By almost bursting her lungs and running as fast as she could, hoping her pounding legs didn't break through what remained of the ice, Müller realised she had caught them up.

In the gloom ahead, she could make out three figures. One in the mid-distance, two further on. The single figure must be Tilsner – the others Irma and Holger – and Tilsner seemed to be catching them up. Müller renewed her efforts, trying to run faster even though she was already gasping for breath.

She didn't want her deputy to have the sole honour of making their arrest.

Then something odd happened, and she couldn't really believe what she was seeing. The figure she assumed was Tilsner had carried on past the other two – he didn't appear to be making an arrest. And – like them – it looked like he was covered in a white bed sheet as camouflage.

She saw the shock of red hair peeking from the sheet covering one of the nearer pair. Now she knew. It was Irma.

She raised the gun. Brought the shock of red hair into her sights.

'Irma Behrendt!' she cried. 'Stop there and raise your hands! Otherwise I won't hesitate to shoot!'

She thought at that point, Tilsner would turn back. Help her make the arrest. Instead, he'd disappeared into the fog in the direction of the BRD's coastline. What the hell was he up to?

Her focus returned to the girl. Irma had ignored her warning; she'd tucked her hair back under her own bed sheet and she – too – had broken into a run, with – presumably – Holger alongside her.

'This is your last warning, Irma! Don't to this to yourself, to your family! Stop or I'll shoot!'

The girl continued running.

Müller's finger wrapped more tightly around the freezing cold metal of the trigger.

And began to squeeze.

But a millisecond before she pulled the Makarov's trigger, the pair stopped, turned round and held their hands above their heads.

Panting, she drew level with them, still aiming the gun at Irma's body.

'You're both under arrest,' she said. 'We stay here and we'll radio for a helicopter to airlift us back to the Republic.'

She could hardly look Irma in the eye. She knew she was destroying the girl's dreams of a new life – knew she was sending them both back to a jail sentence, or worse. That was if any of them got off the ice.

Then she had a sudden realisation.

She couldn't radio for a rescue helicopter.

Tilsner had the radio in his rucksack on his back – and he was nowhere to be seen. Holger and Irma wouldn't be going to jail – and she wouldn't be getting back to her family in the Hauptstadt. She would never be able to hold or kiss Jannika, Johannes or Helga again. Without a radio, she couldn't even send them a last goodbye message.

They were going to die out here on the ice.

The layer of water now slopping at her feet told her there was no other possible outcome.

59

When I see the panic in her eyes, I know something has gone badly wrong.

She's not making any attempt to arrest us.

Instead her shoulders slump; she falls to the ground amongst the slushy surface. *What the hell's wrong with her?* 'Quick,' I say. 'Get your radio out. Call for help! We haven't got much time. I don't care if you arrest us. We want to live.'

But she's shaking her head. 'He's got the radio.'

Then I realise, she can't help us. She looks at me with tear-soaked eyes.

'Run, Irma – run, both of you – save yourselves. You've still time.'

I try to grab hold of her, to drag her with us, but Holger pulls me away.

'We've got to save her!' I shout.

'I can't carry both of you,' he says. 'She'll have to make her own decisions.'

Finally, I let him drag me away.

Because I realise *Major* Karin Müller – who once saved my life by rescuing me in the Harz mountains – doesn't want to be saved. She is too loyal a servant to the Republic to try and reach dry land by running to the West like us.

Holger is panting, and I'm half-hopping, half-running with him.

Finally, we have almost reached the West. I see the shapes of houses on the shoreline, emerging from the fog.

I take one look back, at the figure sitting on what remains of the ice, her head in her hands.

I cannot understand the choice she has made.

To choose to die, to deny her children a mother, rather than be seen as a traitor to a country that calls itself a Republic, but is in reality little more than a prison of shame.

60

Tilsner was almost bringing his knees up to the horizontal with each stride, frantically trying to reach the shore in time.

This had been planned, of course, ever since they were sent from the Hauptstadt up to the frozen Ostsee coast. He didn't know whether the opportunity would present itself, but he wanted to be ready if it did. When he was marooned on the ice island all those hours ago, before they were picked up by the *Arktika*, he'd thought he might get his chance.

But now, finally, he had.

What was left for him in the Republic? Karin knew about his past at the barn, and what he did – and had forever regretted – as a member of the Hitler Youth. For a time, on this inquiry it had looked like the old relationship was there, but he knew it could never be repaired.

His wife Koletta and the kids had given up on him long ago, thanks to his own philandering.

He'd prepared the ground. Wearing extra layers all the time. Far too many, so that he was always sweating like a pig. Karin had assumed he'd turned to fat, that he was out of condition. He could see the way she looked at him – wondering how she'd ever fancied him. Because he knew, in his heart, that once she had. It was all a ploy – so that when he had to hide the white bed sheet under his clothes, the ultimate camouflage accessory on the ice, it wouldn't look out of the ordinary. He'd simply put on weight. That was all there was to it.

But as he ran, the words of that fucking interferer Irma Behrendt echoed in his head with each stride.

'What about Major Müller? What will happen to her? Surely you have to help her?'

He couldn't. She could only help herself by radioing for help. He knew she would never dream of escaping to the West.

He tried to run faster as the melting ice splashed in a slushy mess round his legs, but that fucking radio in his backpack was weighing him down.

And then it struck him.

The radio.

He slowed to a halt in horror.

Karin couldn't radio for help.

The only radio they had was strapped to his back.

61

Müller had given up. As the cold racked her body, she knew she was shaking as much from the emotion as from the freezing water soaking her knees and boots. She was in a praying position, and she was praying. Not for a miracle. She knew that wasn't going to happen. Just her own little prayers asking God – if he or she existed – to look after her family.

She thought of each of them in turn – picturing their faces, remembering their funny ways. How Johannes had been so thrilled with Jäger's Sandmännchen cosmonaut gift – but how, in the end, that day he and Jannika had sat in the sandpit sharing their Christmas toys. It had been lovely to see. And Helga. That woman had been through so much. Lost her only daughter – Müller's teenage mother – soon after the war, lost her only love in the war, but then – amazingly – granddaughter and mother had been reunited. Müller knew it had brought them both joy. She even spared a thought for her adoptive mother in Oberhof, Rosamund, and her adoptive brother, Roland and sister, Sara. Sara had looked so fulfilled with her new husband when the Berlin side of the family had visited for the wedding that summer.

She thought of her natural father, and the fact that – for all his faults – Jäger had managed to arrange that visit to the Soviet base in the far east, where she'd met him for the first time. How ironic that it would also be the last time.

There was one last thought. Of her former partner, Werner Tilsner, and how he'd changed from a roguish but attractive chancer, into a disillusioned, out-of-shape, middle-aged man. Perhaps she'd been too hard on him. Perhaps her rejection of him because of his Nazi past was what had finally driven him to defect to the West.

She tried to shut her thoughts down, and accept her fate. It was as though she'd been injected with the same drug as Monika Richter at the start of all this.

She took comfort in what had been said about dying from hypothermia. If you had to choose, it was one of the more pleasant ways to go.

She tried to let herself drift off into an ice-induced sleep.

She knew that any further attempts to resist were futile.

Müller knew she'd crossed the line from consciousness to a dreamlike state when a vision of Tilsner started to appear through the mist.

It wasn't the new, spongy, gone-to-seed old-man Tilsner.

This was how he used to be. Slim, trim, powerful. Running quickly across the ice.

Then he was panting by her side.

Pulling off his rucksack.

Forcing her to hold it in her lap to keep it away from the fast-melting ice.

He slapped her across the face.

'Stay awake, Karin. For God's sake. Just fucking stay awake.'

Through the haze of semi-consciousness she saw him setting up the radio.

Heard him frantically trying to get through.

Then she heard another voice she dimly recognised.

Jäger's!

It seemed to jolt her awake, as did what he was saying.

'We can't send out a helicopter. They're all grounded. It's too misty.'

And then Tilsner pulled her own trick, and she almost burst out laughing in delirium.

'Just fucking send one, Jäger. Otherwise my last call on this thing will be to a Western news agency, and Karin and I will tell them everything about what you and I got up to in that small town north of Magdeburg at the end of the Second World War.'

She didn't know if Jäger would respond to the threat.

But it gladdened her heart that Tilsner was here with her – even if it was their final few minutes alive.

She didn't want to die alone.

62

We stagger up the beach, still not quite believing we've done it.

Before we try and find civilisation – to claim our BRD passports and the handful of Deutschmarks the authorities will give us to start our new lives – we turn back and peer in to the mist.

'Do you think she will be all right?' I ask.

'I don't know,' replies Holger. 'When we find a phone box, or a house, we can put in an anonymous call to the police or ambulance. They can help her. Hopefully there's still time.'

It's sensible advice.

I look into his eyes.

'We did it, Holger. We made it. We were the ones who would have given up, but we have been the lucky ones. Poor Joachim. Poor Dieter.'

He must see my eyes glistening because he pulls me into a hug. 'I'm sorry about your boyfriend. My friend.'

But I shake my head. That's not why I'm crying. 'They're not tears of sadness, Holger. They're tears of joy. This is a day I thought I'd never see.'

He looks at me, hesitating. I'm the one who has to initiate things. I put my hand gently round the back of his neck, pull his head towards me, and then we're kissing.

It's a kiss I never want to end.

We make that phone call, as we promised ourselves. We've no idea if it's done any good. The next day, once we've been processed, we head down by train to his uncle's in Munich.

When we're changing trains in Hamburg, I decide to buy a newspaper, just for fun – to see what the news is like when it's not about workers' co-operatives beating their targets yet again, increasing production by some unfeasible percentage, or Honecker meeting with communist leaders from other parts of the world.

I thought I saw a familiar face at Lübeck station, where we caught the first train. This time I see the man again, on the other side of the newspaper kiosk, so he must have been on our train. He's the spitting image of *Major* Müller's former husband, Gottfried – my old Maths teacher at the *Jugendwerkhof*. Different, trendier hairstyle, more *à la mode* spectacles, but otherwise his face is a *doppelgänger* of Herr Müller's. If his ex-wife hadn't told me he'd died, then I might have gone up to him and said hello. But I realise what it is. Guilt at leaving *Major* Müller behind on the ice. I'm transferring that onto this man – seeing things that aren't there. Bringing her former husband back for her, even though – for all I know – she could have become fish food herself.

When we're settled on the train, I get chance to read the paper. It's then that I see the story.

TWO VOPOS SAVED FROM ICE IN DARING RESCUE

Lübeck, 2.1.79
In an unusual joint operation, emergency services from the Bundesrepublik and the DDR have rescued two *Volkspolizei* detectives who had become stranded on fast-melting ice in the Bay of Lübeck.

The officers had been – according to the DDR authorities – engaged in a clandestine operation to arrest a number of 'criminals' attempting to flee across the ice of the frozen Ostsee.

Helicopters from both side of the state border were involved in the rescue.

One of the officers is a 32-year-old woman who was suffering from mild hypothermia. She has been airlifted to Charité Hospital in East Berlin where she is expected to make a full recovery. The other officer, a 48-year-old male, was found in good condition, but was also taken to Charité for precautionary checks.

An East German spokesman declined to comment on reports quoting the Bundesrepublik emergency services which claimed the rescue took place well within West German territorial waters, less than a kilometre from the coast at Grömitz.

The spokesman would not speculate on the fate of the so-called criminals, nor elaborate on what crimes they were suspected of committing.

Reports quoting local residents in Grömitz claimed a young man and woman, thought to be in their early twenties, were seen emerging from the fog on the ice and climbing up the shore to safety.

It's not known if these were the suspects being hunted by the East German police.

Police sources in Lübeck said no DDR refugees matching the description of the young couple had been registered in reception centres. A spokesman said the couple seen by residents were most likely Bundesrepublik citizens who had gone for a walk on the ice.

'We would remind people that venturing out onto the frozen sea or rivers is extremely hazardous at any time, but especially after today's thaw,' the spokesman said. 'Doing so puts yourself and the emergency services at risk.'

63

The fog still hadn't completely cleared when the *Volkspolizei* Kamov emerged out of the gloom. Müller by now knew she was only semi-conscious – the cold freezing her to the core. And the rotors of the helicopter as it hovered above the ice – the pilot judging it too risky to attempt a landing – threw up a violent whirlwind which made her yet colder.

The winchman and Tilsner helped her onto the stretcher, then she was winched aboard. Dimly aware of the pilot shouting – saying he couldn't hold his position for much longer – she saw the winch and stretcher being lowered again.

By the time Tilsner and the winchman were hauled back inside, holding on to the winch at the same time, the pilot was already moving away.

And then Müller knew they were safe. They were both safe. Tilsner had given up his dream of defecting to come back and save her. And she was on her way to the Hauptstadt – for a tearful reunion with Jannika, Johannes and Helga.

Dieter and Joachim hadn't been so lucky, but they'd brought it on themselves.

Irma and Holger? They had almost certainly reached the West to start their new lives. There was no co-operation agreement between the two Germanies to bring them back and put them on trial – they had, literally, walked free. Müller, of course, should have regarded that as a failure.

She didn't.

She was delighted that Irma Behrendt had finally realised her long-held dream.

When Helga brought Jannika and Johannes in to the ward to visit her, she couldn't help breaking into huge, heaving sobs, the tears running down her face.

As she held Johannes, that set him off crying too until Helga had to lift him up to try to calm him. She could see the effort it took her grandmother – she was getting too old, and Johannes too big, to be doing it any more.

Jannika was more inquisitive. 'Mutti crying. Mutti naughty, been bad?'

Müller started laughing through her tears, confusing her daughter even more. Perhaps they would discipline her – after all, she and Tilsner had only completed fifty per cent of the task Jäger had allotted them. But she didn't want to worry Jannika. 'Don't be silly. Sometimes you can cry tears of happiness, that's all Mutti's doing. Mutti's so pleased to see you, and Johannes, and Helga. I thought I would nev—'

'Don't say it, Karin,' warned Helga. 'I wouldn't think of it, if I were you. You're back here in Berlin, you're going to be fine. Let's look to the future.'

The disciplinary hearing was held two weeks later. As they waited outside the hearing room sitting side by side, she was surprised that Tilsner was wearing full uniform too. She looked at his feet. He'd even polished his shoes.

Her deputy patted his stomach. 'Look, firm as a board. Even when I sit down, no rolls of fat. Not bad for an old git pushing fifty. That's all I've been doing, going to the police sports club, keeping fit. Did you prefer the cuddlier version?'

She couldn't help laughing, despite the seriousness of the situation. They could both be kicked out of the force – she had no idea what she'd do if that happened. There would be no hope of getting a job training future police officers if she herself were in disgrace. 'Don't even joke about it,' she warned him. 'Why did you come back to rescue me, anyway? You must have been just metres from the coast.'

He leant down to whisper in her ear. 'Shh! I was. Why did I come back for you? That's obvious, isn't it? You know I can't resist you.'

She mouthed an obscenity at him and pushed him away.

They were lined up, sitting behind a desk, looking self-satisfied, with their well-rounded stomachs. They'd probably stuffed themselves with a meal at a fancy restaurant, the verdict already decided.

Müller tried to defend their actions. Irma and Holger, she insisted, had slipped away while she and Tilsner were pinned down under fire from the other criminals. She argued it was Dieter who'd killed the Soviet seaman. He who constructed the home-made bomb, assisted by Joachim. They were the ones who'd got their just deserts.

Tilsner – too – tried to sing her praises. She'd put her life on the line to defend the Republic. He insisted they should be giving *Major* Müller a medal, rather than going through 'this disciplinary charade'.

There was one important absentee who Müller had expected to be there – even though he wasn't part of the People's Police. Jäger. She thought he might have given evidence against them. Or perhaps, because of what she knew about his past, he might have been prepared to put a good word in. In the back of her mind, though, she knew the reason for his absence. He'd probably had to face the same process as this, except with the Ministry for State Security.

She idly wondered, *what happens to a Stasi officer when he falls from grace?*

Then *Oberst* Reiniger, who'd looked uncomfortable throughout, forever trying to loosen his shirt collar, pronounced the verdict.

The Serious Crimes Department was being disbanded.

Müller and Tilsner were being demoted a rank – she back to *Hauptmann*, him to *Oberleutnant*, with concomitant reductions in salary. They would be reassigned to a murder squad when positions became available, and they would not necessarily be working together in the future. Those new positions could be anywhere in the Republic. It was at the lesser end of the scale Müller had been expecting.

There was one corollary of this that would upset her, though, and there was no point leaving any doubt about it.

'What happens about my police major's accommodation in Strausberger Platz, Comrade *Oberst*?' She wondered if he'd taken pity on her, managed to swing some sort of deal that would allow her to stay in the beautiful apartment overlooking Karl-Marx-Allee.

'I did warn you, Comrade *Hauptmann*.' She gave a start, thinking he was addressing Tilsner at first. Then she remembered – that was her new rank, his old rank. It would take some time to get used to. 'That apartment can only be occupied by someone of the rank of major and above. You are being given three months' notice to quit, with immediate effect.'

64

March 1979
Kleinwalsertal, Austria

I had no idea that mountains could be so beautiful. That air could taste and smell so fresh, so life-affirming. I stop at the top of the run and try to reel off the names of the peaks, glittering like icy stars under the strong March sun. The Walmendingerhorn, the Hoher Ifen, and towering above them all at more than two thousand five hundred metres, the Widderstein. If it could – by magic – be transplanted here, the Brocken would be a little hill of no consequence.

Already, after less than two months on skis, I'm confident on all the runs – better even than Holger. I've got a day off today, while he's working at the Kanzelwand *Bergstation* then meeting me for lunch. On one side of the mountain, the West German Allgäu Alps above Oberstdorf – on the other, the Austrian Vorarlberg. For the moment, that's where we've settled – in Kleinwalsertal, a tiny enclave that's politically part of Austria, but only accessible from the Bundesrepublik.

For us it's the best of both worlds. When we first got to Munich, at first of course it was totally exhilarating. The chance to buy anything you wanted in the shops. No banned records, no banned books. The trouble was, we didn't have enough money to buy lots of the things we wanted, and it started to get a bit overwhelming. The constant drive to make money, to have more material things than your neighbours. It wasn't as bad as it was made out by Karl-Eduard von Schnitzler's rants on *Der schwarze Kanal*, but it was still a bit unsettling despite the joy of finally being free.

However, as soon as we got to Kleinwalsertal, we felt at home. The locals like to take as much of the West Germans' money as possible. In Munich, Holger and I had started to miss the sense of community in the Republic, despite all the shit we'd had to suffer.

Here he comes now, trying to show off his parallel turns. He skids to a halt above me, carving his edges into the snow and showering me with ice. For a second, as the freezing crystals hit my face, I'm back on the Ostsee. I think of Dieter – the first time I think of him in weeks. You might consider me callous, opportunistic, to jump into the bed of a dead man's friend. But I've told you before, you've not experienced all the hell I have. Would you really have done anything different?

Holger sees my face cloud over, and thinks it's because of his skidded stop coming too close.

'Sorry. I rather misjudged that.'

'Ha!' I say, cheering up. 'Race you to the bottom of the lift!'

I set off, facing down the red run, and crouch into a *schuss*. I feel my skis thundering beneath me, the slope rushing by like I'm in a feature film, the exhilaration of risk. Then my legs start wobbling and I know I should have put in a turn. I'm going too fast. I try to turn but my edge catches and I'm tumbling, falling, feeling I'm never going to stop. Thinking how stupid I've been.

But then I hit deeper snow at the side of the piste, and eventually come to a stop. My mouth is full of ice and snow; it's down my ski trousers and back.

'What were you doing, Irma?' shouts Holger as he catches up. 'Are you OK?'

I get my breath back, spit out the snow, and shake myself like a dog after a swim in the sea. 'Sorry. I misjudged the turn.'

'You're mad,' he says. 'Completely bonkers.' He pulls me to my feet, and kisses me full on the lips. He knows all about me now. He understands I was left with no choice but to work for the Stasi – just seeing what Richter was capable of, was evidence of that. I love him, and I don't want him ever to let go.

Our car's parked at the Kanzelwand valley station. Everyone stares as they drive past in their swanky Mercedes and BMWs. It's our bit of the Republic which Holger picked up for next to nothing and then got back on the road. A second-hand Trabi that no one this side of the Wall wanted. The locals love it and always wave as we go by – the mad East Germans in their Trabi. I'm sure most people in our situation would have wanted to forget all about the DDR. But my mother's still there. My grandmother. It helps to remind me of them.

Holger's uncle's kindly lent us his mountain holiday flat for the season while we find our feet in the West. We've got money coming in from Holger's ski lift company work, and my job as a chambermaid and waitress in a three-star hotel. In the DDR, what we're earning would be considered a fortune. Here, the money goes as fast as it comes in.

And being a waitress is a real eye-opener, I can tell you. Yesterday, when the ski groups had finished for the day, and the pupils came in with their ski teachers, I witnessed something that sickened me – and again made me think that perhaps *Der schwarze Kanal* didn't get it all wrong. They come in, drinking round after round of Obstler – a vile-tasting fruit schnapps – singing their songs. It was the antics of one group that really shook me. At the centre of it was a young English youth – maybe an older schoolboy or student on some sort of exchange. It was obvious he didn't speak much – if any – German. He was trying to join in and enjoy things without understanding. The middle-aged German men and their Austrian ski instructor started teaching him this song, as I was delivering their schnapps on a tray, and he sang along. They all thought it was hilarious:

> 'Auf der Heide blüht ein kleines Blümelein
> und das heißt: Erika!'

He had no idea he was singing a Nazi marching song. I could tell a couple of middle-aged women in the party knew – they looked uncomfortable, wouldn't sing along, and then started whispering to him.

But this was the evidence in front of my eyes that not all they told us in the Republic was propaganda. Nazis do live on in the BRD – even as the 1970s draw to a close – and here they were, lustily singing their old tunes. I almost deliberately tipped the tray of schnapps over them. But I knew I couldn't afford to lose my job.

As evening falls, we drive the Trabi down the valley to Oberstdorf – the nearest town in West Germany, and the nearest railway station. I can't contain my excitement. A special visitor is coming, and Holger and I are off to greet her.

To see her again will be wonderful. It's hard to believe it's happening.

I run down the platform when I see her white hair, her leathery face.

'Oma!' I shout. 'Oma!'

I rush to her and hug the life out of her. Then hold her bony shoulders in my hands. 'I couldn't believe they'd let you come. This is a fantastic day.'

I smother her with kisses and can see she looks a little embarrassed, but there's a broad grin on her face. She's as delighted as I am.

'They don't care about us oldies,' she says. 'It's easy enough for us to get permission to come to the West. I think they'd secretly like me to stay – then they won't have to pay my pension any more, never mind the little extra I get for running the campsite.'

'Are you going to stay, Oma? Are you?' I ask excitedly.

She shakes her head. 'No, Irma. My home is in Sellin. On Rügen. But I'm certainly looking forward to this visit. And seeing your new home.'

Holger's drawn alongside us now, and I introduce him. He acts the perfect gentleman and asks if he can take her luggage. Then we realise – she hasn't got any cases with her.

'Where are your bags, Oma?' I ask, thinking she must have had a senior moment and forgotten them at Augsburg, where she changed trains.

'Oh, someone else is bringing them along in a moment.' She has a sly grin on her face. I look over her shoulder.

And then I see her, and I'm running, running, jumping on her, smothering her with kisses as tears stream down my cheeks.

Now I'm older, it's almost like looking in a mirror. The same red hair, the same freckly skin, the same angular nose and features.

'Hello, *Schatzi*,' she says. 'My little *Schatzi*.'

'Mutti,' I sob. Squeezing her tight. 'Mutti, Mutti, Mutti.' That's all I can get out in between my sobs. She doesn't know – and I will never tell her – that her latest stint in jail, just a few weeks short of four years, was down to me. Was a result of my report to *Hauptmann* Steiger. 'I've missed you so much. So, so much.'

'Well, Irma. You don't have to miss me any more. I've been freed.'

'You don't have to go back?'

She shakes her head. 'They bought me out.'

'Who?'

'The West Germans. They paid for my freedom.' I don't ask her how much – it's an open secret that, to raise much-needed hard currency, the Republic sometimes agrees to free dissidents in return for a West German bounty. To many, that would seem like a disgusting trade in humans. Me? I no longer care. I'm just overjoyed to be reunited with my mother, and her next words answer a burning question without me having to ask it. 'I'm here for good, *Schatzi*. I'm a free woman.'

There's more hugging all round, I introduce her to Holger, and he lifts up their heavy bags as though they weigh little more than feathers.

We stroll down the platform, wondering how we'll fit everything in the Trabi. Mutti and I will probably have to sit in the back with one of the cases on our laps. I'm holding her hand, almost skipping with delight.

A winter that started with two near death experiences has ended in freedom – for myself and my mother. The winter of 1978/79 might have been the Republic's 'catastrophe winter' – but for Mutti and me it's something else entirely. It's our Freedom Winter.

It's when we get two thirds of the way down the platform that my blood runs cold.

I see him sitting on a bench, reading a paper, as though he's waiting for a train himself. At Lübeck and in Hamburg I'd managed to convince myself he was just a doppelgänger.

But it's clearly the same man, and it's beyond coincidence that he's here in Oberstdorf – more than eight hundred kilometres further down the line, in the far south of Germany.

I try to ignore him. Try to concentrate on Oma and Mutti.

But as we pass, he drops his newspaper and stares at me, letting me know he's seen me. That he's watching me, and watching Mutti.

'Hello, Irma,' he says.

I ignore him, but Holger looks at me quizzically. 'Who was that? You didn't even reply.'

'Oh, he's just a guest from the hotel,' I lie. 'You know I was telling you about them singing that song? He was one of that group. I don't want anything to do with him.' Holger smiles and rolls his eyes. He obviously believes the lie.

But I know who it was.

Major Karin Müller – his former wife – is back in the Republic, thinking he's dead.

There's only one explanation for him being here, keeping a watch on me and Mutti.

He's been turned. As I was.

He works for them. The Ministry for State Security. The *MfS*. The Stasi.

They're still watching us, and they always will.

I was kidding myself if I thought this was my 'freedom winter'. It's not that at all.

Jäger, Steiger and now Müller. Gottfried Müller, my former teacher. A man I thought was my friend.

But he's like all the rest. Never letting us escape. Never letting us be truly free.

Ensuring that I'll only ever be able to remember these past few months as one thing, and one thing alone.

My 'Stasi Winter'.

Epilogue

April 1979
East Berlin

Müller and Tilsner's new assignments had come through after more than three months in limbo – they'd both find out what they were later today. Reiniger had agreed to extend the lease on Muller's Strausberger Platz apartment until the new job was confirmed, in case Müller was going to be moving from the Hauptstadt. Even Reiniger thought two house moves in the space of a couple of weeks would be unreasonable, despite the fact that Müller's reassignment was a disciplinary measure.

She and Tilsner had gone out drinking together at the bar in Dircksenstraße – the same one they'd been to the night before the start of the graveyard girl case. For old times' sake, Müller had found herself agreeing to Tilsner's suggestion of a bottle of 'blue strangler' – not the weaker, branded version, but the forty per cent crystal vodka.

She knew it had been the real thing because, now – as she tried to force herself awake in Tilsner's bed – the pain throbbed violently inside her skull – like a roadworks gang trying to hammer its way out. This really was a reprise of four years ago. Except that time, she'd been so drunk she wasn't sure how far they'd gone. This time, she'd drunk as much – half a bottle of vodka, matching Tilsner shot for shot. Yet she'd let him take her to bed, and she had clear memories of what had happened between the sheets. Now he was fast asleep, snoring like a steam train.

Müller grabbed her clothes, and rushed to the toilet, out of the corner of her eye noticing something else was different in the bedroom scene. Photos of Tilsner's children were still on the dressing table, but none of his wife, Koletta. She'd moved in with a new man, taking the children with her.

She wasn't sure if she was going to be sick or not. Hanging her head over the toilet bowl, she tried to let the waves of nausea pass. She took a drink from the cold tap, before cupping her hands under the rushing water and splashing her face, attempting to clear her brain.

Müller took a deep breath, sat on the toilet seat, and tried to think of something other than being sick. She remembered the letter she'd picked up when she'd been to Keibelstraße the previous afternoon, when Reiniger had told her that the decision on the new job would be revealed later today.

She grabbed it out of her jacket pocket, and looked at the postmark. It was franked 'Hirschegg, Kleinwalsertal'. She had no idea where that was, other than it must be in Austria, because of the postage stamp.

She tore open the envelope, then waited a few seconds to stop that tearing sound echoing around her pounding head.

Inside was a newspaper cutting and a letter. She looked at the cutting first. It was a report from a BRD newspaper of her and Tilsner's rescue from the ice back in January. She smiled. It would make a nice keepsake to show Jannika and Johannes when they were older: how their mother nearly died out on the ice.

Then she read the letter.

Dear Frau Müller,

(I hope it's OK to call you that — after all, I'm not in the Republic now!)

I wanted to write to you to let you know that Holger and I did safely get to the West. We're together — that might be a surprise to you. But I realised out there on the ice that he cared for me and loved me, whereas Dieter — God rest his soul — cared more for adventure and excitement. I hope you don't think badly of me for that.

Anyway, we're living in his uncle's holiday chalet in Kleinwalsertal, in the Vorarlberg in Austria. It's a beautiful valley, surrounded by the Alps, but cut off from the rest of Austria — so you can only get to it from Germany. It makes it feel very special. The BRD, as you can probably imagine, is a little overwhelming. I was surprised to find that at least some of what we were told in Der schwarze Kanal was correct! It's a world obsessed with money.

But here in the valley things are calmer. Holger's even bought and repaired an old Trabi, so we drive around in that, much to the locals' amusement. He's working on the ski lifts, and I'm chambermaiding and waitressing — so we're getting by quite nicely.

> *On the way from Lübeck, I saw this report in the newspaper.*
> *I thought I would send it to you as a little souvenir of our 'adventure'*
> *just in case it wasn't reported in newspapers in the Republic.*

Müller laid the letter on the sink for a moment, and took a few deep breaths. Reading about Irma's successful escape gladdened her heart, although she was surprised it hadn't been censored. A letter from a successful *Republikflüchtling* was surely something the Stasi would normally intercept and destroy, wasn't it?

When she turned the page, and read on, she realised why. The Stasi wanted her to see this – they wanted her to know they would always win. She felt the nausea rise in her gullet as she read the words.

> *That's the main reason for this letter. To give you my news and*
> *send you the cutting. However, there is one other rather strange*
> *thing I think you deserve to know.*
>
> *When I mentioned your husband when you came to see me in*
> *Sellin, you said he had died. I didn't really think it was my place*
> *to ask you questions about how or when.*
>
> *I have some rather shocking news for you, I'm afraid. Your*
> *husband is very much alive. I have seen him with my own eyes. At*
> *first I thought it was just someone who looked exactly like him, but*
> *then he greeted me by name.*

The news was a sickening jolt to Müller, literally. She stood up, turned, and vomited into the toilet, again and again, until there was nothing left in her stomach. Still she retched – and she knew it wasn't her hangover. It was what she'd learnt.

The Stasi were toying with her – probably with Irma, too. Jäger had taken Müller to the site in the forest where Gottfried had supposedly been executed. Yet here – in black and white – was the proof of their lies, unless Irma herself was lying. And surely the young woman had no reason to?

She calmed herself with more deep breaths, and read on.

I can't explain what he was doing. All I can tell you is that my own mother has just been released from jail, apparently after the BRD paid for her to be freed and sent over the state border. As you can imagine, this was an incredible – joyful – surprise for me. It was tempered somewhat by the thought that Herr Müller was watching us.

Anyway, I'm not sure if this letter will ever reach you. But I thought I should make the attempt to let you know.

I'm not going to let this spoil my happiness in the West. Maybe one day, if things ever change, you might be able to come and visit us. I know you were an excellent skier and ski-jumper as a schoolgirl. I am sure you would love it here.

With warmest regards,

Irma (Behrendt)

Müller continued to breathe deeply, trying to calm herself down. Did it really change anything? Gottfried and she had already decided to split up anyway. And she was well aware of the Stasi's tactics. But it was another piece of her belief in the system this side of the Wall that had been chipped away.

There! She'd said it – if only to herself. *The Wall.* Not the Anti-Fascist Protection Barrier. She'd always felt she was on the right side of it – working with others for a fairer, more equal society, a better future for herself and her twin children.

Now she wasn't so sure.

Out on the ice, she couldn't have decided – as Tilsner obviously had, before changing his mind and coming back to save her – to escape to the West, even though it had been less than a kilometre away. She knew she had to stay to be with the twins and Helga, her family.

But as to what the future held, she had a horrible feeling that Irma and Holger were on the right side of the divide. They had their freedom, even if it was a freedom governed by the rules of capitalism.

For the first time, she felt that she, Jannika, Johannes and Helga might be in the wrong place after all. She would have to do all in her power to make sure their future was as good as it could be, despite the Wall around them.

Glossary

Anti-Fascist Protection Barrier/Rampart	The euphemistic official East German term for the Berlin Wall
Bezirk	District
BRD	Bundesrepublik Deutschland. West Germany
Deutsche Demokratische Republik (DDR)	The German Democratic Republic, or DDR for short, the official name for East Germany
Der schwarze Kanal	*The Black Channel.* Weekly propaganda current affairs show on East German television
Fallschirmjäger	Paratroopers

Hauptmann	Captain
Hauptstadt	Capital city (in this book, East Berlin)
Interhotel	East German chain of luxury hotels
Jugendwerkhof	Severe reform school dedicated to socialist re-education
Keibelstraße	The People's Police headquarters near Alexanderplatz – the East German equivalent of Scotland Yard
Kriminalpolizei	Criminal Police or CID
Kriminaltechniker	Forensic officer
Langlauf	Cross-country skiing
Major	The same rank as in English, but pronounced more like *my-yor*
Ministry for State Security (*MfS*)	The East German secret police, abbreviated to *MfS* from the German initials, and colloquially known as the Stasi – a contraction of the German name

Mutti	Mum, or Mummy
Neues Deutschland	East German Party newspaper
Nord-Ostsee-Kanal	Kiel Canal
Oberleutnant	First Lieutenant
Oberst	Colonel
Oma	Grandma, granny
Ostsee	Baltic Sea
People's Police	The regular East German state police (*Volkspolizei* in German)
Republikflucht	Escape from East Germany
Republikflüchtling/e	Escaper/s from East Germany
Sandmännchen	*Little Sandman.* East German children's TV programme
S-Bahn	Rapid transit railway system
Scheisse	Shit
Seebrücke	Pier
Stasi	Colloquial term for the Ministry for State Security (see above)

Volkspolizei	See People's Police above
Vopo	Short form of *Volkspolizei*, usually referring to uniformed police officers, as opposed to detectives

Author's Note

Firstly, a mention of the real-life weather conditions in the winter of 1978/79. It was indeed a 'catastrophe winter' for East Germany, and conditions on Rügen were particularly severe – with snowdrifts as high as houses as described in the book, and power cuts across the country.

However, I have used some authorial licence with the weather for the sake of the plot, and 'borrowed' some elements from the even more severe winter of 1962/63 (which I still remember from my British childhood – building igloos in our back garden in East Yorkshire which seemed to last for weeks on end without melting). So it was really in '62/63 that the Ostsee or Baltic was frozen to such an extent that escapes were possible across the ice – and several did happen, with people camouflaging themselves with bed sheets, either to walk across the ice, or in one case by using bicycles. A newspaper article by Sven Felix Kellerhof in *Die Welt* in 2017 says there were at least forty successful escapes that winter – but he argues that reports of up to four hundred escapees were exaggerated. There is evidence that the authorities were sufficiently rattled to set up exclusion zones around coastal cities, however.

The Soviet icebreaker *Arktika* as far as I know operated solely in Arctic waters, so again I've stretched the truth there for the sake of the plot. It was, however, built in the Baltic shipyard in what was then Leningrad.

When I wrote the original draft of the novel, the Seebrücke in Sellin featured – as it did in *Stasi Child*. Then one of my East German contacts pointed out that in fact it was demolished earlier in 1978 (you can find photos of the demolition work online). But a short rump of platform remained by the steps which led down to the pier. (It's since been completely rebuilt.)

One other slight stretch of the truth is the New Year's Eve masked ball. There were occasionally masked events, apparently, but they would be more likely to happen in February around Carnival time.

What was very much true, though, was the English youth who spoke little or no German being encouraged to sing along to a Nazi marching song during an après-ski drink in the Kleinwalsertal in Austria in the 1970s. It actually happened a couple of years earlier than described – but that youth was me.

Acknowledgements

Once again, many thanks to my friends and former East German citizens, BBC journalist Oliver Berlau and renowned concert pianist Andreas Boyde, who both kindly agreed to read the draft of this novel and correct its many mistakes. Remaining errors are solely my fault.

I'm also very grateful for the work put in by the team at Zaffre – particularly my editors Margaret Stead and Jennie Rothwell.

Huge thanks as always go to my agent Adam Gauntlett and the rest of the team at Peters, Fraser and Dunlop literary agency.

Lastly, a big thank you to you, the readers – and especially those of you who've contacted me via Twitter or email with kind words and support, or have taken the trouble to write reviews of the series. It's very much appreciated!

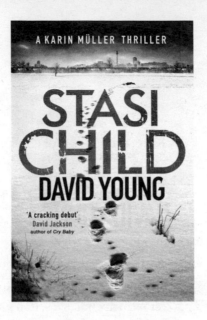

A KARIN MÜLLER THRILLER

STASI CHILD

DAVID YOUNG

'A cracking debut'
David Jackson
author of *Cry Baby*

East Berlin, 1975

When Oberleutnant Karin Müller is called to investigate a teenage girl's body at the foot of the Wall, she imagines she's seen it all before. But when she arrives she realises this is a death like no other. It seems the girl was trying to escape – but from the West.

Müller is a member of the People's Police, but in East Germany her power only stretches so far. The Stasi want her to discover the identity of the girl, but assure her the case is otherwise closed.

The evidence doesn't add up, and it soon becomes clear the crime scene has been staged. But this is not a regime that tolerates a curious mind, and Müller doesn't realise that the trail she's following will lead her dangerously close to home . . .

'Chilling'
Daily Telegraph

AVAILABLE NOW

BESTSELLING AUTHOR OF

STASI WOLF

DAVID YOUNG

'Reminded me of Robert Harris at his best'
Mason Cross, author of *The Samaritan*

East Germany, 1975.

Karin Müller, side-lined from the murder squad in Berlin,
jumps at the chance to be sent south to Halle-Neustadt, where
a pair of infant twins have gone missing.

But Müller soon finds her problems have followed her.
Halle-Neustadt is a new town – the pride of the communist
state – and she and her team are forbidden by the Stasi
from publicising the disappearances, lest they tarnish
the town's flawless image.

Meanwhile, in the eerily nameless streets and tower blocks,
a child snatcher lurks, and the clock is ticking to
rescue the twins alive . . .

'An intricate, absorbing page-turner'
Daily Express

AVAILABLE NOW

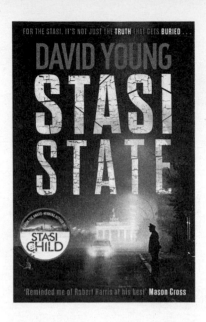

For the Stasi, it's not just the truth that gets buried . . .

The body of a teenage boy is found weighted down in a lake.
Karin Müller, newly appointed Major of the People's Police,
is called to investigate. But her power will only stretch so far,
when every move she makes is under the watchful
eye of the Stasi.

Then, when the son of Müller's team member goes missing,
it quickly becomes clear that there is a terrifying conspiracy
at the heart of this case, one that could fast lead Müller
and her young family into real danger.

Can she navigate this complex political web and find the
missing boy, before it's too late?

'A page turner'
Liz Loves Books

AVAILABLE NOW

A SECRET STATE. A DARK CONSPIRACY. A TERRIBLE CRIME.

DAVID YOUNG
STASI 77

STASI CHILD

Karin Müller of the German Democratic Republic's People's Police is called to a factory in the east of the country. A man has been murdered – bound and trapped as a fire burned nearby, slowly suffocating him. But who is he? Why was he targeted? Could his murderer simply be someone with a grudge against the factory's nationalisation, as Müller's Stasi colleagues insist? Why too is her deputy Werner Tilsner behaving so strangely?

As more victims surface, it becomes clear that there is a cold-blooded killer out there taking their revenge. Soon Müller begins to realise that in order to solve these terrible crimes, she will need to delve into the region's dark past. But are the Stasi really working with her on this case? Or against her?

For those who really run this Republic have secrets they would rather remain uncovered. And they will stop at nothing to keep them that way.

'Reminded me of Robert Harris of his best'
Mason Cross

AVAILABLE NOW

there. I loved the action on the ski slopes and the insight
into the world of ski chalets.'

05334632

Catherine Cooper is a journalist specialising in travel, hotels, and skiing who writes regularly for the *Telegraph* and the *Guardian* among others. She lives near the Pyrenees in the South of France with her husband and two teenage children, and is a keen skier. *The Chalet* is her debut novel.

www.catherinecooperauthor.com
@catherinecooper
@catherinecooperjournalist